T0244896

PENGUIN BOOKS

GΩD'S αSHeS

Before turning her hand to fiction, Marga Ortigas travelled the world for three decades as a journalist, with a career spanning five continents and two of the largest international news networks. She spent much of her time reporting from the frontlines of climate change and seeing first-hand the damages it has wrought on island communities.

A British Council Chevening Scholar, Ortigas earned her MA in literature and criticism from the University of Greenwich. She has authored two other books published by Penguin Random House SEA, *The House on Calle Sombra*, a best-selling family saga published in 2021, and *There Are No Falling Stars in China (and Other Life Lessons from a Recovering Journalist)*, a moving collection of non-fiction essays from her years in the field.

ALSO BY MARGA ORTIGAS

The House on Calle Sombra – A Parable (2021)
*There Are No Falling Stars in China (and Other Life Lessons from a
Recovering Journalist)* (2023)

GΩD'S αSHeS

Apocrypha

Marga Ortigas

PENGUIN BOOKS

An imprint of Penguin Random House

PENGUIN BOOKS

Penguin Books is an imprint of the Penguin Random House group of
companies whose addresses can be found at
global.penguinrandomhouse.com

Published by Penguin Random House SEA Pte Ltd
40 Penjuru Lane, #03-12, Block 2
Singapore 609216

First published in Penguin Books by Penguin Random House SEA 2024

ISBN 9789815144321

Typeset in Garamond by MAP Systems, Bengaluru, India

www.penguin.sg

*For my father, **Tony**,*
who saw the world as an adventure,
and everyone in it as kin

You belong to the place where your dead are.
                    —Island saying

For everyone will be salted by fire . . .
                    —Mark 9:49

The soul is salt, the body is water.
When the water evaporates, the salt remains.
                    —Hazrat Inayat Khan

Ω

The Legend of Tropical Snow

My mother was born the morning the world ended. She cried her first as the dazzling roar of twin suns smashed the ground and doused the clouds in blood. Grandpa said the dawn burst into a blazing rainbow before turning inside out, and the air grew hard as stone. Winter came to the tropics, and the oceans peeled back from the shore. Men were drained of colour as snow fell and the heavens sucked all breath from the Universe. It burned so hot that it scorched the lungs of God. In an instant, He disintegrated to Ash. His sacred embers hurtled to Earth in torrents, covering a chain of fiery islands across what was once the most tranquil sea. A cursed archipelago that our people have always called the Gifts of God—Jolet jen Anij— for we believe this is where He first fashioned paradise.

But since my mother's birth, we were doomed to be thrashed by Nature's Wrath. After the man-made rain of fire and wind of stone, our fresh waters were salted by the tears of the angels, who swore to mourn until humans learned the cost of what they had done.

Expelled from Eden, our vision blurred and now we struggle to return. Ever since that blighted day that my mother was born and God was killed.

—Leilohani Edison Wakamele-Rigold,
environmentalist, addressing Marshallese
children about the US nuclear tests in the
Marshall Islands, 2005

0

WELCOME TO δεU¹S™

Empowerment awaits!

We are so glad you have joined us.

As a NODE, you are now part of a community
dedicated to unlocking your potential.

Our **connection** will **transform** the world,
generating a wave of social development to
enrich us all.

No profiles or verification needed. Your ACTIONS
and USE of this programme will reveal you.

HERE'S HOW IT WORKS:

When you accessed **dεU¹S™**, you became a **Node**,
a **valued** member of our network. To show our
appreciation, a **cryptographic code** unique to
you has been seamlessly installed on your device.
It gauges what you learn from other Nodes, our
videos, and interactive guides about the world
around you.

The more you learn, the **more points you earn.**

Your points are then converted into rewards
of either **Be-Alpha-&-Omega (BαΩ®) tokens or
JUN0® crypto-coins.**

With enough points in your **virtual pouch**, you are **elevated to the next level,** and then the next, until you reach our shared **ultimate goal: Paradise.** A radiant return to Eden, where we can coexist in a just world of peace, equality, and love.

OUR MAIN LEVELS:

1. <u>Expansion</u>:

Explore the beauty, diversity, and complexity of the world around us. **Learn** what makes everything unique, special, and worthwhile.

2. <u>Exhibit Empathy</u>:

The more we appreciate Our World, the better we understand that everyone is kin and everything is shared. This will show in a **Node's behaviour.**

At this higher level, exchanging 50 per cent of your points will get you a **dεU¹S™ ultra nanochip** upgrade. The chip is made with the purest compound mineral known as 'God's Ashes'. Attuned to your elevated energy frequencies, it transposes your thoughts and nodal vibrations into a gain or loss of points. The more points, the more BaΩ® and JUNOs®.

3. <u>Establishing Eternal Elysium</u>:

By this final stage, as an **open** and **thriving** member of our community, you will view everything effortlessly through an **ultra-lux defined dεU¹S™** lens.

Now, as a **Super Node,** you will also receive **the Ultimate ΘMεGα Chip,** which cannot be purchased using digital tokens or crypto-coins. It is designed to drive our quantum network without devices.

With everyone **connected and empowered,** there will truly be **heaven on Earth.**

END NOTE:

What was once unimaginable is here. The time is now.

Thank you for choosing to thrive with **dεU¹S™** and **welcome to the family!**

'You are the salt of the earth . . .'

And this is where **we begin.**

The Celestial Palace Hotel
2023 | Present

Mid-afternoon. A hotel lobby. Sparse. Bright. Reeking of bleach and lemongrass. No hint of the heatwave outside or the rising sea lapping at the coastline across the street. The salt and sweat are kept at bay by thick glass windows and stained, pull-down blinds. The sheer, frayed rollers shade from the harsh afternoon sun without completely obscuring the view.

A slim man in a sharp suit sits alone at a small wooden table draped in white linen. He pats down the front of his shirt, feeling underneath it the carved sandalwood Buddhist beads around his neck. In his coat pocket, an ultra-nano phone. He is earning another thousand in digital $B\alpha\Omega^{®}$ tokens while sipping tea. Chrysanthemum pods, freshly blossomed in hot water, are enthroned in the glass pot before him. Beside the pot, his rimless spectacles lay folded atop the local daily. Printed in a language he currently understands.

The headlines:

- Faster than light—Taiwan's latest microchip
- Another 'miracle' peace treaty credited to 'God' app, signed by warring factions in the Philippines
- So-called neon narcotic worth millions confiscated in Micronesia drug bust
- Chaos in China?: Paramount Leader Zhou Sheng Feng denies ailment. Beijing protesters detained after unrest. More workers thought to be killed in another salt mine explosion.
- Renowned mathematician behind viral app confirmed missing, last seen in Europe

And along the bottom of the front page, next to an ad for Transform—the global energy company—a colour photo of dead, translucent fish washed up on Sabah's eastern shore, Malaysia's poorest state.

The man ignores the paper. His dull eyes burn through the blinds at the melange of pedestrians floating past the hotel's floor-to-ceiling windows like flotsam. They swell towards the market across the street. In bold, striking hues, vendors' stall umbrellas push upward like jellyfish racing for the sky.

He doesn't bother to wonder if any of them are also on the app. He can tell from their bio-waves. He's an elevated node at Level 2.

dɛU^{1}S$^{™}$ is setting people alight around the world. It fine tunes users' cognitive abilities, raising their vibrations and energy frequencies. The popular ultra-tech programme—known as the 'God' app for the way it's transforming lives—is also an easy way for anyone to make money and stay connected. An encrypted digital social network that literally pays rewards. At each stage of 'elevation', nodes get 'dialled up' and receive a new cryptographic code that enables more 'powers'. The man in a suit is at the level where he can spot people's vibrational signatures. And he knows from which end of the spectrum—positive or negative—another node's 'waveform' emanates.

As he sits there sipping tea, the man's patience and calm are getting him closer to unlocking the app's final stage. A discipline he learned following Buddhism. Just one more task and then—liberation.

The man gently puts his teacup back on its saucer.

He taps the special dial on his wrist and shuts his eyes. Nothing.

Blinking, he turns his gaze to scan the lobby. The bellhop by the entrance—not on the app—has removed his left shoe and is picking at a toenail, watching on his mobile what the man in a suit knows to be a cockfight.

To the far right, the receptionist is losing dɛU^{1}S$^{™}$ points while cooing at her screen. She's ignoring the parcels being delivered by a courier from an online marketplace. The messenger is radiant, but the receptionist beams through cyberspace at an unseen beau. Her face appears to be melting from the heat. The air conditioner is on, but—like most things on this island—it defeats itself. It's set at a hot twenty-eight degrees Celsius. Barely five degrees cooler than the streets. The man in a suit wonders why they bother with the air con at all—*oh no*—an uncharitable thought that not only invites bad karma but also costs him some dɛU¹S™ points.

He adjusts himself and sips his tea. His mother always told him the way to keep cool in a hot place is to not have anything cold. It has always served him, his mother's advice. It's why he signed on to dɛU¹S™.

He takes a small stylus from his pocket and uses it to prick his hand.

It bleeds.

He checks his special watch again. Thin and elegant on his wrist.

The numberless dial sparkles softly, pearlescent sand caressed by the sun.

He covers its naked face with his punctured palm and shuts his eyes. Preparing for the sheath of light.

Yes. There it is.

Right on time.

=

1

5.9804° N, 116.0735° E

Kota Kinabalu

2023 | Two months earlier

Anak turned his head towards the murky heavens, pushing his nose and mouth just above the waves—*in*—*out*. In, out. Slow. Steady. He'd learned how to breathe covertly to not be spotted from shore or ship. His life depended on remaining unseen. A few more breaths—in and out—then, back under. The reed-thin fourteen-year-old struggled to keep his balance in the current.

Through the sting of the sea, Anak scanned the fathoms trying to find the other boys. But the sun was low and the only light underwater was the reflection of the bright colourful bulbs hanging above the Filipino Market, just near enough to radiate a soft halo over the sea.

Anak knew that, like him, his friends would be folded somewhere in subaquatic shadows. Looking to breathe. This was the longest they'd had to stay submerged. It was nearly election day, and the police were trying to seem busy by pursuing them.

Afraid of chasmal darkness, Anak rarely looked down—but the tide had other plans.

As he spluttered to right himself, Anak spotted a glimmering pinprick in the distance, unable to tell if it was the evening's first star or an unknown sparkle of a coral. The elders said the reef was once as vibrant as the market, but by the time Anak could dive, the coral had already begun to turn white and many of the fish had gone.

Still holding his breath—*Up? Down?*—Anak laboured to focus. But there it was—calling to him. A shimmering brilliance like that of the tiny pearls he'd seen hawkers show tourists at the market.

Mesmerized by the minuscule glint of pink, he dove deeper.

Slow and steady—he reminded himself. He mustn't swim too fast or get too excited. He learned this from Ondoc, whose people were sea gypsies from Sulu.

Suddenly, a blinding slice of light. Anak had cut himself on the twinkling reef.

He feels a tingle race up his arm as blood oozes from his hand then floats away, suspended in the water like algae. Gelatinous and limpid. Entranced, Anak watches it move away from him . . . glowing. A vibrant, viscous string of red wriggling through the water like captured lightning.

A familiar pain shoots up the back of his neck and radiates through his head. He shuts his eyes, hoping to will it away. When he blinks them open, Anak sees a gossamer web of light spread out across the sea. Like a fisherman's net, but diaphanous and ethereal. It appears to hold everything together, connecting all life—the fish, the reef, the ocean itself—and his blood, threading slowly through the ripples, is mingling with every atom of creation.

Feeling incarnated from the highest of powers, Anak instantly believes he can fly to the moon, dance on the waves, or burrow deep into the seabed and sleep in the thrumming bosom of the Earth. He is no longer afraid of the dark.

Sensing the other boys around him, he confidently casts out a message.

Again, a light in his eye. A brighter one. It spins around, carried by the current.

* * *

'Idiot!'

Night had fallen when Anak awoke drenched, on hard concrete, to the comforting smell of glue and his cheeks being slapped by an agitated Ondoc. Seeing Anak stir, Bitoy swiped back the bag with the open can of glue that Ondoc had used to rouse the prone boy. He shoved his own face into it. If he inhaled deeply enough, the acrid fumes from the industrial strength adhesive overpowered the stench of the sea and the rumbling in his stomach.

Ignoring Bitoy, Ondoc stayed on his knees by the wet Anak. 'Were you trying to kill yourself?'

Anak didn't answer.

'Why did you go deep?' Ondoc snapped. 'You know better than that!'

Anak remembered breathing through water. And seeing things beyond all imagination.

'You could've died,' Tunting said, taking the bag of glue from Bitoy. 'If Ondoc hadn't fished you out'—he took a sniff—'there'd be one less moron to share this with.'

Anak eyed the boys scattered around him, catching their worn, ragged faces just as Jopet switched off the torch.

'This went right by you and you missed it,' Jopet brandished the battered flashlight like a sword. 'We almost lost it, thanks to you.'

Apollo's torch. When it was dropped into the sea, it was a signal to the boys that the police had gone and it was safe to come out of the water.

'Three minutes,' Kuya Apollo hulked over from the shadows of his shack, throwing each of them a rag. 'Impressive. You're turning into right little *syokoys*.'

'But I don't want to be a fish-boy, Kuya—' Bitoy started, as Tunting stashed the glue away.

'Would you rather they put you in a cage?' Apollo barked. 'Or send you back to Sulu—alone—to play hide-and-seek with bandits and live off fish bones and boiled urchin shells?'

Apollo was always tough on them, but Anak knew he meant well. Most of the time.

'No different to here then,' Ondoc expressed, emotionless.

As Apollo and the boys exchanged barbs, Anak remembered the deep gash on his hand from the reef. The sharp pain. The web of light. He felt for the wound—but it was gone. Healed over without a scar. He checked the pocket of his shorts for the twinkling coral he had snapped off before losing consciousness. Maybe he could flog it at the market. It was full of migrant Filipino vendors trying to outdo each other with their wares. Surely someone there would pay for something so sparkly. Enough to get him passage on old *Pak* Gutong's boat. He would finally get back to his parents across the waters.

'What's that?' Jopet asked, seeing a soft glow peek out of Anak's pocket.

Anak tried to cover it by pulling down his shirt.

'I said—what's that?' Jopet's attempt to reach the supine boy was slowed by the numbing effects of the glue.

But Ondoc, the sea gypsy, wasn't as disabled. 'Show me.' He commanded, yanking Anak's hand from his pocket.

Feeling another headache coming, Anak gripped the piece of coral tight and shut his eyes. In the darkness, he was suddenly awash in light.

'Stop playing deaf,' Ondoc admonished, trying to wrestle the item of interest from the younger boy's fist.

'I saw it first!' Jopet, too, tried to lunge for the treasure.

'Oi!' Apollo bellowed but was ignored. He sighed and left them to their foolishness.

Standing unmoved, Tunting barely noticed another boy grab the bag of glue from him.

'What's all the fuss?' Mokong took a hit of adhesive, more interested in getting high than the jumble of boys on top of Anak.

'I said, where did you find that?' Ondoc snarled again. 'Just here? Beneath the boats?'

They were on the docks of Kota Kinabalu. Not in the area where the dive boats or the private yachts were moored but in the section by the market where the fisherfolk and the smugglers tied their vessels. They couldn't really be called ships. They barely even passed as seaworthy.

It's where the unseen boys or 'phantoms'—as they were known— lived. In Sabah's grimiest dockyard, by the shittiest sea craft and Kuya Apollo's hovel. They took turns sleeping on the older man's packed dirt floor. Otherwise, the phantoms kipped on hammocks aboard the fishing boats—if they were lucky to find one where the crew was too drunk to notice.

How long had he lived at the docks? Anak couldn't recall. There were days he remembered little at all. But his goal was always clear: to befriend a ship captain who would let him stow away to another port of call. He just wanted off Sabah. It wasn't his home.

Not that Anak knew where home might be. He only knew he didn't belong where he was. He had vague memories of parents. People who brought him over from another island on a boat. A wooden outrigger barely larger than a canoe. The voyage was dark. And quiet. Other than the unforgettable sound of the boat's motor tearing through the open seas.

Like a fisherman's bountiful catch, there were so many of them from different villages crammed into that outrigger. But no one spoke. It was as if they were collectively holding their breath. Afraid to gasp their last. It got even quieter when the boat's motor was switched off abruptly. Then, there was only the lapping, heaving sea. Until—a pop of rain—like a programmed pellet—turned into incessant rounds fired skilfully by the Night.

All was a blur after that. But Anak remembered how the rainstorm burned and how much cooler was the sea. They were made to jump in, and he hung onto the soft sobbing of a pregnant woman still on the boat who pleaded that she couldn't swim.

She was pushed overboard before the outrigger went back the way it came, without them.

In the turbulent water—with the rain gunning down—Anak clung to his father's back while the man swam for their lives in the roiling darkness. Along with the others from the boat, they were jostled and tossed by waves as rugged as the unpaved roads that wound around Mount Paglu. The boy didn't then realize he might never learn the unmarked, native trails of his craggy homeland. He also didn't know it would be his last chance at a memory of his mother. She was somewhere in the turmoil, but all he remembered was his father wincing with every motion of the tides.

Out of the darkness, the shadow of an island appeared. But instead of swimming towards it, the boat people curved along its empty shoreline towards the other side. There, a huddle of dimly lit shacks shimmered above the water. Elevated by bamboo stilts and posts made of driftwood, the makeshift structures were connected by a precarious network of suspended planks. In the black of night, the floating village appeared like stars fallen from heaven. This haphazard heap was Kampung Pondo, known as the nest of thieves.

The boat people were told they would be safe there. Among others also displaced.

And they were safe, at least for a while. Until election season and the usual police round up of those called 'illegals'.

How was he—*illegal*? Anak wasn't sure what that meant. He was a good boy. He hadn't stolen anything nor killed anyone. But one day, when police boats approached the precarious walkways and hanging ladders of the labyrinthine stilt village, his father told him to hide until they were gone and pushed him into the sea.

In tears, Anak stayed out of view among the bamboo poles and wooden pylons as long as he could.

When he resurfaced, his father was gone. No one could say if and where he was taken or if he'd return.

So, Anak waited. For weeks. Refusing to give up. Slinking soundlessly into the waters whenever police came.

Kuya Apollo—whom everyone knew was the king of the main island dockyard—told him he'd been waiting nearly five years.

By Kuya Apollo's estimate, Anak was going on thirteen or fourteen. His voice had not dropped like the other boys his age, but Kuya said it was probably because he'd been hungry for so long. Which must also be the reason he was shorter and thinner than the rest of the phantoms. And why he was afflicted by such blinding headaches. He could trace them back to when his father pushed him off the planks.

Anak was grateful Kuya Apollo had taken him in, bringing him over from the nest on stilts to Kota Kinabalu on the main island. With the other dockyard boys, Anak learned how to take things from people who didn't need them as much as the phantoms did. A watch here, a wallet there. Sometimes, a mobile phone or two—those always earned them more money.

When they first met, Apollo was ferrying passengers in a motorized rubber dinghy from the nest of thieves—or rather, Kampung Pondo—and Anak understood *Kuya* straightaway, immediately referring to Apollo as 'older brother' in their shared language. They spoke differently to those who were born in Sabah. Just like Kuya, Anak would eventually learn Malay, but by the time he did, he found it easier not to speak. Preferring the silence of the sea to the swell of his thoughts.

Anak didn't recall much of his life before Apollo. Not even his mother's face. There was only one force he recalled pushing him out into the world: his father's fear thrusting him off the nest of thieves toward rough black waters.

Anak felt a headache coming on.

'I said gimme!' Ondoc grabbed the afflicted boy's trembling fist and took the glimmering coral, examining it in the blunted light of an overcast evening.

Anak whimpered.

'I've seen this before,' Ondoc, the eldest of the phantoms, declared. 'They call it *smash* . . . the ashes of God! We can sell it for big money.'

'God's *what?*' Jopet jumped in and tried to grab the rock.

'It's like snow—but from the islands. I saw it on TV at the market,' Ondoc pushed Jopet back. 'The newsman said rich people pay a lot for this.'

That got all the phantoms' attention. And Ondoc did enjoy the spotlight.

'They . . . crush it up and eat it . . . or something,' he said with great authority. 'Smoke it too, I think. And I heard it's better than regular snow—and *shabu!*'

Ondoc held the piece of coral up to the haze of a streetlight.

'Put that down, you idiots!' Apollo rushed back over and swiped the rock. 'Don't touch it—it's too dangerous.' Holding it only with his fingertips, the dockyard king gingerly wrapped the twinkling coral in a rag. 'As if you don't get enough of a high sniffing that glue I know you steal from the boats in repair.'

Kuya Apollo shook his head at the boys and brought their treasure to his shack.

Later that night, when the fisherfolk were tucked away and even the moon had gone to bed, the phantoms decided to reach for the stars. They waited for Kuya to sleep—then they stole into his dreams, searched for the shimmer, and crushed it to dust.

SABAH POLICE DEPARTMENT

CASE FILES

#KK-CP2503-2023

ITEMS 20–21: Newspaper clippings

<u>SINGAPORE CHRONICLE</u> <u>Section D-32, page 52</u>

TOXIC TIDES?

4 April 2023, Kota Kinabalu

An estimated one million fish have washed up dead on Northern Sabah's Mengalum and Gaya islands in the South China Sea. Scientists from the University of Malaysia in Kota Kinabalu are still investigating potential causes. These areas are not usually prone to the algae-caused red tide that can affect Sabah's eastern shores.

The fish appear translucent and luminescent. Some of them are not endemic to the area, raising concerns about changes in global currents. Government officials have asked residents to refrain from going into the water or consuming local seafood until results from a toxicity test are ready and there is more information.

Last month, similar waves of dead fish washed up on Turtle Island and Sandakan in north-eastern Sabah, and in Semporna on the other side of the province facing the Celebes Sea. Initial findings from scientists at the University of Borneo show the fish were exposed to heightened levels of particle and electromagnetic radiation.

* * *

OFFICER'S NOTES: Singapore newspaper. Dated day before death. Story found encircled in victim's hotel room. Unidentified blood stains present.

* * *

25

SABAH DIGEST

Alert: Kota Kinabalu
5 April 2023

Satellite images released by Malaysia's intelligence agency confirm the existence of multiple new landmasses in disputed waters off the western coast of Borneo, fronting Sabah. According to officials, there is evidence to indicate that the man-made islands were built by China to strengthen its claim on areas this far down the South China Sea. Chinese military vessels and installations have been spotted on the artificial 'islands'. Marine experts say the construction of these illegal structures would have caused 'catastrophic damage' to the underwater environment.

* * *

OFFICER'S NOTES: Local story. Also highlighted.

2

5.9804° N, 116.0735° E

Kota Kinabalu

2023 | Present

'You call this ready?'

Raed had not looked at his reflection in nearly five years. Kuya Apollo did not own a mirror, and when going past store fronts, Raed turned away from any glass panes that might show him his face. It was not until the sergeant pressed the knife to his throat in the dockyard restroom, then traced his jaw with the blade, that Raed yielded his gaze to the mirror. He was stained with grease that, in the white light of a single bulb, looked like a bruise. It must have got on his face when he fought Ondoc for the glue earlier that morning.

Instinctively, Raed jerked the policeman's hand off his shoulder. He adjusted the creased shirt he was wearing and angrily wiped away the smudge on his face with a thumb. Then, again, he averted his face from the glass, unwilling to stare down the stranger in his reflection. He couldn't bear the judgment in their eyes.

But, from the brief encounter, Raed noticed his cheeks seemed yellowed and more drawn than he remembered. His tousled, sun-blazed hair was to his collar, and his borrowed clothes hung more awkwardly on his small frame than he imagined. Jopet's button-down shirt was not only wrinkled but too large for him. Mokong's least worn trousers were too roomy and too long. Raed cinched them at his waist with a plastic string he found at the docks. And he hid the ripped, uneven hems by folding them in around his ankles.

'You stupid boy,' the sergeant growled in his ear, keeping the blade against the boy's neck. 'Don't you understand how important this is?'

Anyone else might have gagged at the officer's proximity, but Raed barely flinched at the pungency of overripe mangoes and ylang-ylang mixed with the fat man's sweat. The sergeant always wore the distinct cologne when he aimed to impress.

'I told you to clean up—this is not a regular gig. Are you trying to get me in trouble?'

The sergeant withdrew the knife and slapped the back of the boy's head.

'Wipe your nose, you filthy rat.'

Raed saw red. And induced by the fetid mustiness of the dockyard toilet, he felt the dawning of a headache.

* * *

The first time he recalled being debilitated by blinding pain, Raed was hiding from police—just as Anak had shown him—under one of Kampung Pondo's hanging walkways. He was crouched among the stilts that looked to him like prison bars holding up a nest of vipers.

But the only viper he met there was the sergeant, who dragged him to the precinct after a regular raid on the floating village for petty criminals and illegals.

Raed got out of jail by bargaining with the sergeant and offering to do his bidding. After endless months of earning a pittance pretending to kowtow to the unpleasant Malaysian police officer, he was finally about to meet the big boss *towkay* of the sergeant's towkay. A huge deal for the eighteen-year-old. The other phantoms had never been asked to a meeting. The big boss towkay came all the way from the capital Kuala Lumpur. Any trip that involved an airplane was beyond Raed's imagination.

'Remember,' the sergeant spat saliva onto his hand and patted down Raed's hair, 'just show him on the map, and don't speak unless he asks you a question. Understood?'

Raed nodded. The map. He didn't know how to read a map. He didn't know how to read at all. He never went to school. None in Kota

Kinabalu would take him. He didn't have the right papers. He had no papers at all. The sergeant knew this.

Raed had arrived in KK, without a passport or birth document, from Balabac. A beautiful island just across the waters in the Philippines. It was paradise . . . from what he remembered. He survived a typhoon carrying his elderly mother on his back across the sea. Their outrigger capsized in waves the size of hills. They were fleeing from the men who killed his father. Heading for a new island of riches where his mother, his *inay*, said they could live like kings.

Inay was wrong.

Raed shut his eyes to the light and the pain.

Next thing he knew, the sergeant was gone—as was the dockyard bathroom—and for a blink, he found himself up in the sky, unable to look out a window at the mackerel-coloured sea below.

* * *

When Maki opened his eyes, the headache was gone. So was the nausea. It was the first time in his twenty-odd years that he saw the sea from so far above it. Eighteen storeys to be exact. He didn't know what he expected, but he was surprised to spot the nest of thieves out on the water. It looked so small. From that high, the shacks in the outcasts' village were like prey trapped in a crippling spider's web.

His toes curled in his flip-flops. If not for a huge cut, he wouldn't take these rush jobs from Raed.

He stroked his chin—another nervous habit—and pulled tighter on the plastic string holding up his trousers.

'Is good,' Maki uttered boldly, transfixed by the view out the window. They were the only English words he knew.

Behind him, he heard the client still rummaging through the bedroom. The big, burly man wore an eyepatch and Maki wondered if he was half-blind or just trying to seem tough. He was brown-skinned like a local but only spoke to Maki in English, which didn't surprise the young man as much as the customer's tattoos. He had them down his bulky arms and at the base of his nape. Lines and dots in some sort of pattern. Most people in Sabah were Muslims and it was forbidden to sully the body like that.

Maki didn't know if he himself was born a Muslim, only that he wasn't native to Sabah. Like many of the other phantom boys. And he had always wanted a tattoo—an anchor, like the ones on the ships that docked by Kuya Apollo's hovel.

'Sorry, I don't have any local currency, I paid with crypto . . .' the one-eyed man explained as he combed through the room. 'I'll find something for your trouble . . .'

Maki only understood the hand signal to wait, which he was happy to do in the air-conditioned room. He returned to his image in the window, throwing back his shoulders and running his fingers through his matted hair. Pleased with himself, he winked at his reflection. His clothes—a little tattered—he wore like a custom-tailored suit. No one could say he was underdressed for the space he was in. Carpeted floor, plush wallpaper, and more than one pillow on the massive bed. Maki had been in hotels before, and he wasn't intimidated by this swanky Celestial Palace.

'Just a sec—' the balding slob with the eyepatch requested.

These losers always scrambled to seem like decent people, insisting on tipping so you'd think better of them. It never worked. But you smiled anyway 'cuz the tips didn't hurt. It's not like the towkays paid a decent wage.

'Is good,' Maki smiled his widest. Really, these delivery jobs were a cinch, so quick that most of the time neither Kuya Apollo nor any of the boys noticed he was gone.

With the one-eyed man preoccupied, the phantom teen scanned the room for something to lift. No watch or wallet lying around that he could see. No mobile phone either. He stroked his smooth chin and returned to the window, wondering what it would be like to jump from so high towards the sea. Would he be caught in the colourful wave of umbrellas along the shoreline? An ocean of parasols that shaded vendors and their wares from the scorching sun. Or would he be impaled on one of the weather-beaten coconut trees lining the avenue? Standing shadowless and still in the absence of a breeze.

Maki studied his reflection in the window. Marvelling at his handsome pallor. How did he get—

'—here,' the one-eyed customer had just started to say when there was a soft but unmistakable rattling at the door. Someone was trying to get in. Suddenly, the surly client looked more frightened than anyone Maki knew from the nest of thieves.

* * *

Raed was grateful for the respite from the heat that Maharlika Eatery offered. And for the chance, if even briefly, at a comfortable seat. He tucked his flip-flopped feet behind the legs of the chair, refusing to look at the sergeant and the big boss towkay chain-smoking across from him.

'Would you like a refill?'

The server caught him by surprise. He found such luxuries absurd. Could these towkays do nothing for themselves? Before he could reply to the server, the well-dressed man—nostrils billowing with smoke— nodded and Raed's glass was refilled with the sugary, amber liquid that turned his stomach. Unlike the other phantoms, Raed did not have a sweet tooth.

'Have as much as you want, *anak*,' the big boss towkay instructed, referring to the teen as 'child'. 'All this is on me.' The man lit another cigarette. 'You're about to make me even richer than I already am,' he paused for a drag, 'and stop looking like a fried tilapia. No one's going to hurt you.'

How dare the towkay compare *him* to a tasteless, wide-eyed fish? And he'd heard such promises before—*no one's going to hurt you*—usually right before a pummelling. Raed sat still and tried to breathe in the second-hand smoke.

'Now, tell him where you found the . . . coral,' the sergeant instructed.

The towkay laid open a map on the table, but Raed kept his eyes on the view out the window. In the blinding day, the sea sparkled like a star-filled evening sky.

Damn this towkay, Raed thought. He wasn't terrified—he felt nothing at all. Numb from the glue he inhaled for breakfast. It made everything better, even the turmoil in his gut. And if Kuya Apollo hadn't confiscated his secret stash of smash, then he'd have shown this smarmy towkay just how *not afraid* he was.

Kuya Apollo. He would also not be pleased that Raed was at the Maharlika. A covert spot with an unmarked entrance off the main street. The doorway led up a narrow flight of stairs to a lavishly decorated cavernous room with large picture windows overlooking the shoreline. Along the walls and towards the rear, there were alcoves behind curtains and tables obscured by lacquered Chinese screens.

The eatery was known for its clientele of crooked cops and politicians. 'Where the things they do in the dark are brought to light,' so Raed had heard it once put by Pak Bujang, a middle-aged man with scraggly chin fuzz who sold pearls at the market. They had struck up a . . . working relationship. Pak Bujang kept Raed busy when the sergeant didn't.

Pak Bujang thought the young phantom . . . pretty. And sent him to others, of more means, who felt the same. Raed was adult enough to know he needed cash to get off Sabah. And without papers, he was stuck for choices to eke out a living.

He learned to touch their man parts no matter how ugly and smelly they were and learned not to gag when they were shoved into his mouth. When the men tried to touch between his legs, Raed turned dour—telling them he'd been damaged by rebels in the Philippines. They cut it off—he'd recount in gory detail—and he lost so much blood they thought he would die. After that, Pak Bujang's men were too disgusted to go anywhere near his deformity.

He took their money—gouged their wallets while they slept or showered—and then, he left.

It worked fine until that afternoon at Maharlika.

The big boss towkay received a message on his phone. He showed it to the sergeant, who then produced a small packet from his police cap.

'See, lah? Not everyone is on that silly *God* app,' the towkay laughed. 'No promise of digital riches can ever trump human weakness.'

'Here, boy,' the sergeant handed the packet to Raed. 'No tasting. Celestial, 18-03. The bellboy will let you in at the back and show you how to get to the room without being seen by the security cameras . . .'

Raed rose from the table, ignoring the discomfort he was feeling in his trousers. The effects of the glue were wearing off, and it was as if the wound he told Pak Bujang's men about had reopened. He'd never felt such an odd, indefinable pain but nothing would stop him from proving his value and getting paid. Not even the temptation to use the smash he knew was in the packet from the sergeant.

'. . . and hurry back . . .' the towkay squinted as he took a deep drag, jabbing a finger from his other hand on the map on the table. Ashes from his cigarette fell over the paper sea like toxic rain.

* * *

Maki knew what happened in these hotel rooms—so, when he heard the sound at the door, he grabbed the tip from Mr Eyepatch, shoved it in his pocket, and dashed into the closet without prodding. There was nothing in the shuttered space, which didn't surprise him. No suitcase, no shoes, no jacket. It was like the one-eyed man had travelled empty-handed. But didn't they always when they booked these rooms for their transgressions? It wasn't as if they planned to stay for long.

Curious to know who entered, Maki tried to peer through the louvered closet door. But all he could make out was the new arrival's chin fuzz, which, unlike on many of the locals he knew, was neat and not scraggly. So, he sat down to wait for the one-eyed man and his half-bearded guest to finish their conversation.

Maki's stomach rumbled and he began to feel pangs of hunger.

In the darkened space, he saw a sparkle on his borrowed trousers—*yes!* Coral residue. Just enough for the smallest of highs. Without another thought, Maki bent down and licked the smash. Knowing the hit would soothe the growing tumult in his gut.

'Like I told you on the phone man, I don't know where she is . . .'

In an instant—a flash of light—Maki feels the anxiety in the one-eyed man's heartbeat.

'But I know you do. Please! Just tell me what you want,' and he can grasp the abject fear in the other man's breath.

The men speak in English, but their accents are distinct—and to Maki's surprise, he understands every word.

Hide!—Maki thinks right before the room door opens again. But no one hears him.

Through the shuttered louvers, Maki sees a slim man in a sharp suit enter with certainty, ducking a blow from the half-bearded English speaker who is closest to the door. There's a tussle, and the big man with the eyepatch falls to the floor with a thud.

Maki shuts his eyes and stays in the closet. He feels the effects of the smash beginning to wear out.

In the room, the remaining two men fight like tempests over a weapon. There's a burst of light—and all goes silent. The world stands still.

The shooter in a suit throws a window open and clambers up the sill. He pulls out a long string of beads from under his shirt.

'For the glory of God'—he yells in a flood of languages that Maki suddenly understands—'the time is now!'

Cheeks aglow, beads in hand, he leaps off the sill and takes to the skies.

On the street below, Pak Bujang was cycling to work when a man in a suit slammed into him from above. Scattering pearls like teardrops on the pavement.

By the time Maki stopped tripping and crawled out of the closet, sirens were blaring outside and the hotel room was empty. Except for the dead, one-eyed man on the floor.

The bed was a mess from the fight, and papers were scattered everywhere. It seemed Mr Half-beard—the surviving English speaker—had already scoured the room, and from what Maki could tell, nothing of value was left that he could sell on the street.

He looked at the stiff on the floor. The dead man's skin was raw where he had tattoos, as if they had just been burned off. Resisting the urge to vomit, Maki went through the man's pockets to reclaim the packet of smash he'd just delivered—but it was gone. As was the weapon that was used to kill the guy.

Frustrated, Maki kicked at the one-eyed man, who even in death looked angry, sullen, and stern. His one good eye stared, glazed, at the ceiling.

Out the open window, Maki heard the growing commotion and he knew he had to flee the crime scene. In a last attempt, he removed the dead man's sneakers. A tightly coiled trinket fell out of the left one. Maki tucked it away immediately, feeling a tingle tiptoe surely up his arm.

He bolted for the door, unaware that his blood had dripped on the floor.

* * *

On the streets around Maharlika Eatery, there was mayhem. Traffic was gridlocked. Police were running in one direction and everywhere people were screaming. Raed knew not to stop and look. He went down a back alley that was quieter than the coastal avenue.

When he got near a rundown office block, Raed crouched behind some trash bins to look at the treasure Maki had put in his pocket—a bracelet of polished purple stones, cool and smooth to the touch. He'd never seen anything like it. Not even among the fakes sold in the Filipino Market.

In the middle of the string of stones, there was a gleaming black charm that looked like a coin. Raed ran a finger over the unfamiliar letters etched on its surface.

He didn't plan on telling Apollo about the find. Kuya would have them sell it and share the money with the other boys. And he knew better than to return to the cursed sergeant and the obnoxious towkay.

As the wind began to rustle suffused with heat, Raed sat in the gutter among the trash. Around him, Kota Kinabalu blazed with bewilderment fraught with rage, and market vendors spilled onto the streets like blood. They pooled around Pak Bujang's remains, squashed underneath the glowing translucent corpse of a slim, sharp-suited man wearing an elegant numberless watch. Collecting beads of sandalwood littered along with pearls.

From a nearby mosque, the afternoon call to prayer rose, lifting with it the veil that shrouded Raed and Maki. Like a miracle, they both then thought to find Anak. Maybe Anak, quiet Anak, would know what to do. He was always the smartest of Kuya Apollo's dockyard crew.

Stashing the bracelet as the sky turned the colour of its stones, Raed and Maki disappeared into the urban chaos like phantoms.

* * *

Across the city, in a secluded cove where private yachts could berth, a goateed, middle-aged man in a windbreaker dashed into an unidentified cruiser. It was the only one there and had no visible hull numbers or flags on its masthead.

As he rushed below deck, the goateed man—heart pounding, breathing ragged—signalled to the waiting captain to get underway. They had a long, overnight voyage ahead. The price of needing to stay under the radar.

Once inside, he locked the door to his suite and leaned against a wood-panelled wall with his eyes shut. For the briefest of moments. He knew he'd left unseen, but he had nearly lost his spectacles in the scuffle—which, in a police investigation, would have easily put him at the Celestial.

After a few deep breaths, the goateed man put a palm to his chest, feeling for the items he had gathered in the hotel room. The unknown weapon and a mobile phone. Taking them out of his jacket pocket, he walked across the cabin and put the items down on an opulent desk.

Call Lǎo dà—he commanded in Mandarin without speaking, giving the order mentally over an encrypted network with a neural interface. Then, he went to the liquor cabinet, where he poured himself a Kavalan Symphony No. 1. Neat. In a Baccarat crystal tumbler.

Just as he was about to down the limited-edition whiskey, his employer's soft voice came clear over the line only he could hear. It was piped in directly through a nanochip he wore behind his ear, which was also what translated his thoughts into words and could transmit them to a receiving party.

'Hello Lǎo dà,' he greeted evenly, switching to vocals so he wouldn't have to suppress his thoughts. 'They know . . .' he measured his words very carefully, replaying the scene he had just survived at the Celestial Palace. 'My, uh . . . colleague . . . was killed with a device using a substance like ours . . .'

He returned to the desk with the Kavalan bottle in one hand and his glass in the other. He set them down to pick up the device he was referencing. He studied it closely, but his nanochip interface failed to provide any answers.

The device resembled a small firearm, minus the grip. Rather like a high-tech syringe. A sleek 'gun' barrel that fired something other than bullets—a compact pill filled with fine, lustrous powder.

'Yes, Lǎo dà. God's Ashes. I am almost sure. It was instantaneous,' he explained, cautiously. 'But I believe their formula is off. It caused quite an irregular amplified response.' He recalled how after being 'shot', the man he had met with started to glow then seemed to burn from within. And when he used the weapon on the assailant, the guy jumped to his death—

The goateed man in a windbreaker downed the whiskey in his glass and poured himself another before sharing the worst of it. 'They knew the tagline.' The private catchphrase they planned to use for their yet unlaunched, highly confidential product: *The Time is Now.* The assailant yelled it before jumping out the hotel window. God's Ashes, or smash, was known to make users feel like time had stopped and everything was happening in the present moment. For a second, the goateed man in the windbreaker wondered if the assailant was high—or if his employer might have told someone about the breakthrough compound they expected to flood the market with. But then again, the Lǎo dà would never jeopardize their profit margin like that.

The goateed man poured himself another whiskey, preparing to be peppered with questions. He chose which ones to acknowledge. Hoping to keep the old man from pursuing what he could not answer.

'Yes, Lǎo dà, it was said in Mandarin . . . but the killer didn't seem their usual sort.'

He drank the whiskey and poured another shot. It wasn't the probable replication of their closely guarded product that was pressing on him.

'No, Lǎo dà,' he sounded phlegmatic, despite his apprehension. 'She's in meetings all day. With donors at the temple,' it was almost convincing. 'Yes . . . I have told her to call you . . . as soon as she can.'

And soon, he would need more than Kavalan. He raised the glass to gaze at the soothing amber liquid. The movement pulled up his jacket sleeve and shifted his watch, revealing a small tattoo on his wrist. A linear abstraction of a sparrow formed by flowing curves and strokes. It also resembled the head of a dragon. He didn't know how much longer he could keep to himself that he'd—*lost track*—of the Lǎo dà's daughter. One among many matters he wasn't disclosing to his boss.

The wail of sirens from the opposite cove broke through his fog—piercing the muggy evening like tinnitus. He imagined police and the emergency services crawling over the city. So he had to get out as quickly as he slipped in.

'No Lǎo dà, it was a different colleague. Everything else is settled. The shipment's arranged and the funds will be untraceable,' he shared, methodically. He was about to pour himself another glass of the expensive Taiwanese whiskey but changed his mind, replacing the cap on the bottle instead. 'Yes. I'll be back soon, but I am still in . . . Manila . . .'

He looked out the porthole as the cruiser pulled away from Sabah. He had little choice but to lie about his whereabouts to the Lǎo dà—one of the most powerful men in the world—who also happened to be his father-in-law. Otherwise known in criminal circles as the brutal Lotus Dragon.

3

51.5072° N, 0.1276° W

London

1988

Lu Wei Jing was bent over her desk scribbling furiously on lined paper. Her nose barely an inch above the pen. Scattered around her were components, bits and pieces removed from a Commodore 64 she had fished out of a school bin. The boxy, outdated home computer lay eviscerated on the floor by her feet. She had her back to the door and a beautiful view of the Thames out the window in front of her. But her eyes were fixed on her notes. A thicket of lines and strokes hedged by arcs and angles.

'Uhm . . . hi,' Melody Lin greeted from the half-opened doorway. She didn't want to disturb, but she also didn't plan to stand at the threshold all afternoon.

The scribbler didn't seem to hear her.

'Sorry to interrupt your . . . flow,' Melody tried again, 'but I need to get in—'

Careful not to crease her pressed bone-coloured trousers or snag her pink Polo shirt and the yellow cardigan tied around her shoulders, Melody pushed into the room, taking down the tall stack of books on the ground that impeded her entrance.

Behind her, she dragged an oversized suitcase with a broken wheel.

Dressed head to toe in black, the girl at the desk by the window remained bent over her papers.

Once inside, Melody took in the small space. Still excited but slightly disappointed. There were two single beds, one on either side of the desk fronting the window, and another desk at the opposite wall by the door. Every surface was covered in . . . things. Discarded clothing—all black. Cables and wires. Notebooks—crinkled and used. Half-eaten kebabs. Chocolate. A plate of greasy sausages. Open crisp packets. And half-empty bottles of water.

Melody couldn't believe how lean the girl at the window looked considering the remnants of her diet.

As noiselessly as possible, Melody tried to find a space for her suitcase. She also tried to get a glimpse out the window at the bannered riverside view, peeking inadvertently at Wei Jing's notes.

'The Miracle Equation,' Melody exclaimed at seeing the numbers the other girl was working on. 'Euler's Identity?'

That got the scribbler's attention. She lifted her head just as Melody chuckled: 'Are you trying to better the God Formula?'

In a motion not unlike a skittish dog, the girl at the window turned. 'You're not stupid,' she stated, looking the new arrival up and down.

'I beg your pardon?' Melody didn't try to hide her shock.

'You know Euler's Identity. The "God" equation as you put it. Not many people have even heard of it.' The scribbler had a surprising Cockney accent, sounding to Melody like the gangsters she'd seen in British soaps.

'This is the London School of Economics,' Melody retorted, 'I think it's safe to assume everyone here knows what it is.'

Wei Jing studied her like a feral animal deciding whether the prey was worthy.

'Melody . . . Lin,' the new arrival offered as she scanned the room for a place to sit. 'Which one's mine?'

No response from Wei Jing.

'Look, I get the whole super focused nerd thing, but we're going to have to live together for the next year or so, unless you flunk out. So, you best get used to me. Stare all you want until you tire of it.' Melody stood at attention with her arms outstretched, then she did a twirl. Her long lustrous black hair undulating like in a shampoo advert. Wei Ling scoffed.

'Are you done?' Melody needled.

'You're only here because they won't lump an Oriental with a non-Oriental. They think we're dirty or something . . . great with numbers but bad with people.'

Another unceremonious conclusion from the girl by the window. And the way she said 'whore-ee-yentl' made the word sound even more insulting and obsolete to Melody.

'Yeah,' the girl at the desk continued, 'despite my accent—and the fact I was raised here—they still just see me as a Chink.'

'I'm not a Chink.' Melody instantly replied.

'Really?' Wei Jing appraised the new girl's eyes—not dissimilar to her own—and soft, delicate features. Like beautifully hand-carved ivory. Close enough, but quite unlike Wei Jing's squat round face. 'You could've fooled me.'

'I'm from Taipei—' Melody clarified.

'Ah well, sorry luv, all the same to them.'

'But it's not.'

'Whatever.' Wei Jing dismissed the argument with a wave of her hand.

'For someone obsessed with Euler's Identity, you are not very cordial,' Melody could barely hide the hurt.

'Now that's dumb.' Wei Jing spat out. 'What the feck does Euler's have to do with someone's amiability? And I am not "obsessed". That is so plebeian.' She shook her head and Melody noticed how Wei Jing's shaggy, unkempt hair was as black as the obsidian bracelet her mother gave her to wear for protection before leaving Taiwan.

'Euler's Identity is the most beautiful mathematical equation . . .' Melody expressed, 'it's elegant simplicity—*proof* of God and all that, right? Illustrating the profound connection between the most fundamental of numbers. It's been compared to a Shakespearean sonnet! To appreciate such poetry in math would necessitate a graceful soul.'

'One would think.' Wei Jing smirked.

'You're an ass.'

'And you sound like a bad LSE brochure.'

Silence. A brief impasse. Each one assessing the other.

'What are you doing with it anyway?' Melody, seemingly the softer of the two, wondered.

'I will use this to find a way to *profoundly* connect humanity—' Wei Jing began.

'We got TV and radio for that,' Melody slammed, 'and soon something called the Internet. Governments are already using it. My father says—'

'This will be better than that. And more . . . immediate. There won't be a need for machines. Or governments. I will harness the power of the Earth itself—and humanity will be the conduit.'

Melody tried to hold back a chuckle—'Sure, Lex Luthor'—thinking a comic book superhero's nemesis an appropriate name for her new roommate.

'Just you wait,' Wei Jing advised, unperturbed. 'It will happen.'

'I don't doubt you,' Melody smiled, like an iridescent star of Chinese cinema. Wei Jing shut her eyes and checked herself.

'Good,' she said, coolly, 'neither do I.'

As a light grey blanket descended over the grumbling Thames, Wei Jing turned back to her desk, hoping to refocus, away from the infuriating new arrival.

Melody shoved her suitcase against a wall. On instinct, she touched the bracelet on her wrist. Her mother had it blessed with the power of Mazu, the Sea Goddess and Empress of Heaven, to bring her good fortune on this journey away from home. But so far—Melody glared at her crabby new roommate obstructing the window—the bracelet's powers were failing to impress.

4

X.17XXX° N, 1XX.4XXX° E

Pulau Rahsia

2023 | Present

'Hand me some ice, Luc, I can't take this.'

'Please?' the young, bearded Yazidi doctor teased his wife seated next to him on the motorized boat. Squinting against the blazing sun and the tropical wind whipping in his face, he handed her an ice pack from the cooler in front of him next to the helm. 'Really, Nisha, stop acting like you're not used to the heat, this is cooler than last summer in Kerala.'

'My family might come from there, Luqman'—she pushed up her sunglasses—'but I was raised in Nova Scotia, remember? It's not like a predisposition to Indian summers is genetically transmitted. I know you know that.' She iced her nape and returned her attention to her smart gadget.

Gutong, the boatman, watched the young couple with interest. He had a full load on his small vessel, and they were closest to him on the left. The only foreigners he understood since they spoke to each other in English, despite the darkness of their skin. It wasn't often he had such passengers on this voyage.

Across them, surprisingly silent, was a pale Chinese man dressed unmistakably like a mainlander. Which was how the locals referred to those from communist China.

Like a uniform, mainlanders usually wore brightly coloured Crocs, oversized branded clothing, a large shiny watch—sometimes two, in case the first one failed to adequately grab your attention—and heavily tinted shades. They dripped with obvious wealth, clearly newly earned. Or stolen. *Who could be sure with these rich towkays from China?*

Gutong knew this thought would affect his dᴇU¹S™ points, but he believed the mainlander was up to no good—they never were. Either in Sabah to inspect land they planned to buy in some shady deal—purportedly to build ill-advised golf resorts—or something even shadier. Perhaps looking for a location for their opium farms, their illegal casinos or hiding-in-plain-sight sites for their crooked online operations. He heard that's why they were being kicked out of the Philippines and Cambodia.

Lately, more of these mainlanders were coming to dredge sand from Sabah's beaches. Bringing their own equipment and workers directly from China. They even set up their own mainlanders-only restaurants to feed their people.

With everything their country seemed to have, Gutong couldn't understand why these mainlanders needed to be in other people's countries, and why they wanted other people's sand. *Didn't they have their own?*

Despite knowing he would drop further in dᴇU¹S™ ranking, the Malaysian boatman glared at his oblivious Chinese passenger staring out to sea. He couldn't help it.

Maybe he's a spy—Gutong considered—*sent by the Chinese government to keep tabs on their competition.* These mainlanders weren't the only ones interested in building 'golf resorts' (read: secret military bases) in Malaysia. And they certainly weren't the only ones looking to dig for oil. Or wanting to harness other natural resources to convert into energy. *Next, they might try to steal Sabah's wind!*—Gutong wagered. There must be something of theirs that the Chinese wanted. It's the way those people have always worked. Transactional. And the transaction always inevitably only benefited the Chinese.

In his nearly fifteen years of ferrying people on his small boat from Kota Kinabalu to Sabah's outlying islands, Gutong always came up with backstories for his passengers. It kept him from boredom.

And until he got on dεU¹S™, he didn't have to worry about censoring his thoughts. He was most creative when called in to take these rich foreigners to the fancy resort on the far side of the privately-owned Pulau Rahsia. It only happened when there was a problem with the resort's own boat—and only since he got on dεU¹S™. His cousin, a dedicated dεU¹S™ node, was still teaching him the app's ins and outs, but Gutong was sold a cheap chip upgrade at the Filipino Market. So, unofficially 'fast-tracked', he was already reaping Level 2 crypto-rewards.

On the way to the lush, forested island, Gutong made sure to heed his cousin's—the resort manager's—instructions: At all costs, avoid giving the visitors a view of Kampung Pondo. It meant going the long way around, but the boatman understood. That unsightly nest of thieves would surely frighten the tourists. It scared the locals.

Actually, Gutong thought, *it would be a perfect spot to hide Chinese spies.* Though he doubted the dirty arrogant bastards would want to rough it with the illegals in the cursed stilt village. At that, his false dεU¹S™ nanochip sounded an alarm. His points were rapidly declining, but he didn't realize it.

Gutong felt himself sneer at the visiting mainlander despicably drenched, head to toe, in designer kitsch. He had to mind himself or he might spit at the man, just as he saw these pigs—*ding ding ding*—often do at those around them.

Gutong coughed, a loud gurgling hack in the back of his throat. Then, he expectorated the resulting glob of mucus out to sea. *Ding ding.* The resort manager—the cousin who kindly gave him jobs on the side so he could have extra income—warned him to stop doing that. Apparently, some guests complained, but Gutong was sure no one would hear him above the boat's engine. It revved as if the Earth was being cleaved in two.

The only travellers who turned in his direction were the two *orang kaya* Malaysians at the far end of the boat, who unsurprisingly seemed to have an instinct for picking out poor behaviour. But Gutong knew the hoity-toity city folk were actually looking past him, disdainfully studying their fellow passengers. Their pursed lips were an obvious sign they didn't approve of the dark-skinned English speakers nor the unwelcome mainlander.

At the front of the boat, just beyond the awning, two tanned, *hensem* adventurers were sunning themselves shirtless. They looked like the men Gutong saw on billboards, which they probably were. Likely among those social media 'influencers'. Their mobile phones—the latest models—seemed like extensions of their delicate, manicured hands. They took photos of everything—mostly themselves—pointing and chattering loudly to each other in some European language.

Gutong thought they might be divers, until he saw the skinnier one dump his empty soda can in the water. The idiotic *bodoh* (*ding ding*) didn't even bother to disguise his littering. A diver—with their deep appreciation and devotion to the world's oceans—would never have done that.

Next to the half-naked Europeans, was an understated young man with rimless glasses. He sat still and kept his eyes on the horizon. Gutong knew the kind. Private. Possibly shy or socially awkward. They hoped not to attract attention. Usually, these folks were the richest of the lot. Because he was so silent, Gutong was sure he wasn't one of those financial boys from Hong Kong or Singapore—*maybe Korean?* The boatman studied him more closely. With his clean sneakers, dark coloured T-shirt, and expensive jeans, this guy was definitely not Japanese. He didn't scream mainlander either. The young man had a sophisticated air about him. Educated for sure. And cultured. Possibly Taiwanese? Gutong had seen more of them visiting Sabah, but he still couldn't pick them out for sure.

Before he could pass further judgment on his passengers and completely run out of points, the boat reached its destination. Out of the clear blue waters, a long wooden dock appeared. It was lined with resort staff in matching traditional costumes waiting to welcome guests with fruit drinks and garlands of flowers.

Gutong was used to the exaggerated and phony 'oohs' and 'ahhs' from disembarking visitors. He rolled his eyes. *Ding ding*. It was always such a performance. For everyone involved.

Drinks in hand and fully garlanded, the guests were then ushered to the beach while Gutong started to offload their bags with the waiting porters.

He failed to notice a young boy in ill-fitting, threadbare clothes slink off his boat and slip into the sea. In a well-practised move, the boy hid among the dock posts, where he planned to stay until he could head for the beach and cross into the forest.

The boy had heard that on just the other side of the island, supply boats were moored that did runs to the Philippines.

* * *

As the sun set in gemstone hues over the Royal Pulau Rahsia resort, the hypnotic beat of trance music floated through the beach from Ferran Mateu's state-of-the-art Bluetooth speaker. Bare chested and feet firmly on the sand, the six-foot-tall Catalan model undulated his sarong-clad hips and swayed his slim, toned arms in the air. Lapped by tongues of gold from the light of bamboo torches, he moved like liquid fire.

Not too far away, reclined with legs akimbo on a sun lounger, his equally bronzed companion, Jordi, streamed the dance live on social media, careful to stick to the resort's rules and keep their location vague. One hundred and fifty-seven thousand people were watching across the globe. The digital BαΩ® tokens and JUN0® coins they tipped online were enough to pay for the duo's luxurious holidays over the next few months.

'I hope everything is to your liking,' a young server discreetly queried, expertly placing drinks and a lit votive candle alongside the portable speaker on the small bamboo table by Jordi. 'Dinner will be ready shortly.'

Across the beach, beneath a line of dramatically lit coconut trees, resort staff could be seen grilling the freshest of seafood and mixing cocktails. Elegant chairs and tables had been set by the water, and pillows were scattered on woven mats for those who preferred a more relaxed dining experience.

'Is it true this is the only place you can get alcohol in Sabah?' Jordi asked the server, adjusting his tight white swimsuit before taking a sip of his Mai Tai. His voice was loud enough to be heard by the Malaysian couple on the far side by the pool. They turned to each other, lips pursed, saying nothing. Irritated by the abject ignorance of foreigners.

'No sir,' the server replied with a smile. 'Malaysia not strict, unless you are Muslim.'

'¡Fenomenal!' Jordi exclaimed.

'I heard anything *haram* is allowed on this island,' exhibiting an understanding of Islam, Luc exclaimed to the other guests from the shadows of a poolside cabana. Much to his wife's exasperation. She lifted her gaze from her tablet only long enough to let him know to keep silent—and get her another drink.

'Harrrrram! I've always liked what's forrrbidden,' Ferran's exaggerated 'r' sent a tremor through the veil of trance music. His deep laugh bellowed as he flitted across the sand to pick up his drink, planting a loud, open-mouthed kiss on Jordi before taking a sip of his cocktail.

He splayed himself on a sun lounger, arranging how his salmon-hued sarong fell across his legs.

As he took another sip of his drink, Ferran noticed he was being watched. The quiet, fully dressed *chinito* sitting off to the side alone seemed to be following the condensation from his Mai Tai roll down his chest. Ferran was convinced there was desire behind the clean-cut young man's rimless glasses. No one else would have spotted it, even in daylight. But the model had years of experience in Dubai learning how to read these subtle signals.

'Any of you hear about the hotel jumper in KK?'

The passengers from Gutong's boat turned to the unfamiliar speaker. A North American man who was already on the island when they arrived.

'Crazy, no?' Jordi stated, getting up to stretch and give the sunburned, broad-shouldered guest a better view of him.

'Did you see it?' the North American asked, expectant.

'The jumper?' Jordi batted his eyelashes and rolled his 'r' knowing how that appealed to non-Hispanics. 'No, but I heard the commotion after. The sirens, the people screaming. *Aparentemente*, he landed on some poor *desgraciado* on the street—splat!'

'What? When did that happen?' Luc overheard the conversation on his way back to Nisha with drinks from the bar.

'Yesterday,' Ferran replied, still on his lounger. 'We just arrived at our hotel for the evening . . . before catching the boat here this morning.' He turned to Jordi, who had laid back down as if posing for a magazine cover. 'I think he was partying on smash, eh? Either overdose or he took that . . . that new variant. The waiter told me at breakfast *que* the guy was glowing when he landed. Probably thought he could fly! *Ya sabes. . .*'

'Maybe it was some sort of *hara-kiri*,' the North American suggested, showing off knowledge he had gleaned online.

'You might mean *kamikaze* . . .?' Luc offered, despite his shock. 'And I had no idea that happened.'

'Did you hear about it, *guapo*?' Ferran winked at the shy young man he'd caught watching him. 'They said he was *chinito*, like you . . .'

The man shuffled in his seat, uneasy at being referenced by the shape of his eyes, and worse, categorized as if all people of Chinese descent were the same. 'Uh, no. I just got to Sabah this morning, and I've been off the grid . . .'

Jordi nearly gagged on his drink. 'Off the grid?! *Pero*—why? Wait! Are you that "missing" tech billionaire, Max Bao?! I think there's a reward if I find you . . .'

The man being addressed smiled awkwardly, uncomfortable with the attention.

'They don't all look the same, you know?' the North American declared. 'And from what I read, Max Bao is way older—with some foreign, British type accent. He's so recusing, no one's really sure what he looks like.'

'I think you mean reclusive?' Luc suggested to the tousle-haired American. 'And I like the thought of going "off the grid", that's why *we* came here. To get some space. Sometimes, there's just too much *interconnectivity*.'

'Space!' the Malaysian urbanite said aloud to his own surprise. He was trying to read on a sun lounger but could hear them blathering from the far side of the pool. 'Obviously, any of us here can afford as much *space* as we want.'

This elicited uneasy laughter from the guests gathered on the private island resort.

'Well, you know what's helped me?' The North American pulled his phone out of his shorts pocket. 'These mindfulness tips and guided meditations on Day-Us . . .'

'The man just said he doesn't want to be connected,' the Malaysian muttered to himself as he returned to his book.

'So, for this *off-grid* . . .' Jordi turned everyone's attention back to the guest who had caught his friend's eye. 'Did you become a monk?' he needled, suggestively stroking his cocktail glass. 'Isolated and . . . celibate?'

Ferran kept his gaze locked on the shy young man with a faint, indistinguishable accent. 'This is far from being in a monastery, no . . . ?' Indicating that he was waiting for an introduction.

'Uh—Robbi,' came the soft reply.

'Why are you here . . . Robbi?' Ferran grinned wickedly, taunting the young man by rolling the 'r' on his tongue and exaggerating the pronunciation of his name.

'Last hurrah, I suppose. To slowly break me back into civilization.'

'No better place to do it, sir,' the resort manager approached to redirect the conversation. He felt it wasn't headed down a pleasant path. 'Hope you are enjoying Sabah, Mr X.'

Robbi gave him the slightest of nods.

'Colourful alibi you've chosen, Mr X,' the North American teased.

'You mean *alias*!' the rich Malaysian corrected from his lounger.

The ultra-private Royal Pulau Rahsia resort only accepted payment in cryptocurrency. They required no additional information nor asked questions of their guests. So, visitors remained anonymous when they were on the island. And they needn't interact with others, barring the shared boat ride over. One night a week, there was an exception—a seafood grill was set out for those who wanted to mingle. The only guest who opted out this evening was the Chinese mainlander who arrived with them on Gutong's boat.

As Luc resumed his seat in the cabana, Jordi pulled out a small plastic pouch from his swimsuit. He waved it around in the torchlight.

Its contents sparkled. 'So . . . who wants to make time stop and party like there's no tomorrow?'

'God no,' the North American demurred, 'Not anymore. Not since Day-Us. I don't wanna lose more points. I'm here to clean up. And smash always gives me the hardest of hard-ons—I could go for days.'

'So can Jordi,' Ferran rejoined from his lounger. 'He'll stick it in anything that moves—'

'—or doesn't,' Jordi made a pumping motion with his hips. '*Pues*, no app will tell me what to do . . .'

All the men laughed, except for Robbi who only offered a hint of a smile.

In the shadows of their cabana beyond the pool, Nisha's tablet set her face aglow.

'You're missing everything, Nish,' Luc pleaded.

'Not now, Luc. There's too much going on . . .'

'Like what? We're on vacation.'

'Well, for starters, while those idiots are fooling around, Zhou is rounding up more minorities in China for his "patriot camps". Between that and the mining accidents, we're losing so many workers in Xinjiang it's affecting our ops. Then, that environmentalist was found dead in a hotel in Kota Kinabalu . . .'

'Which environmentalist? Your nemesis? The one-eyed Samoan?'

'He wasn't Samoan,' she corrected, still focused on her tablet.

'They were just talking about a guy who jumped out of a hotel in Kota and landed on someone on the street—'

'That's not him,' Nisha cut her husband off. 'Edi was found *inside* a hotel room. OD-ed on dirty smash, can you believe it? An environmentalist—on smash! Some reports say there was so much in his system, it burned him. And he wasn't even supposed to be in this country.'

'What does that have to do with you?' Luc wondered why she seemed distraught.

'Nothing—and everything.'

Luc tried to hold the space for his wife to expound on her thoughts. As he'd learned in therapy.

'Why the heck was he here, huh? Did he know *I* was here?' Nisha rattled off a string of questions. 'Was he planning to sabotage my plans? How did he know my plans?'

'Not everything in this world is about you, hon,' Luc posited.

'I didn't say it was!' Nisha turned to her husband. 'But come on. I work for the largest energy provider in the world. We're looking to start harnessing a whole new source of power—don't look at me like that. It's safe—*from nature*. And Edi and his damn *greenies* accuse us of ruining the world. For God's sake, we live in it, too. Why would we want to do anything to harm ourselves? Turns out, all this time, Mr Green is shoving corals up his nose! And *we* are the bad guys?!'

Luc was tired of this homily. 'Hmm, why would you do any harm indeed?'

Nisha's eyes burned onyx with anger.

'This is *harming* our marriage . . .' he said in a low voice.

'Excuse me?' She couldn't believe he was making this about them. Couldn't he see how busy she was? She had so much to worry about beyond their relationship.

'Did you suggest this as a second honeymoon because of work?' Luc asked.

'What? No?'

Luc felt the air punched out of his stomach. He felt—defeated.

'I mean—no.' Nisha tried again.

Night had fallen, and unable to face his wife, Luc turned towards the ocean. He could hear the waves, but clouds blanketed the sky, hiding the stars.

On the beach, something gleamed like an oddly-shaped glow stick. There were several such luminous objects washing ashore.

Nisha noticed she'd lost her husband's attention. She gasped when she realized why.

'God,' Luc said through gritted teeth. 'That's it, isn't it? That's why we're here?'

Nisha didn't know what to say. He could always read her like a book.

'Just go,' Luc downed what remained of his drink and left her to join the others.

'Wait . . .' Nisha cried out, instinctively knowing what she had to do. But she also knew her marriage was but a small drop in the larger ocean of things that mattered.

She watched Luc pick up another cocktail at the poolside bar before heading towards the group.

Then, she darted down to comb the beach for dead, glowing fish.

OBITUARY

Leilohani Edison 'Edi' Wakamele-Rigold

6 November 1973 – 5 April 2023

We mourn the loss of noted environmental activist Edison Wakamele-Rigold, who passed away in Sabah, Malaysia at the young age of forty-nine. He was in the region to give a keynote speech at The World Is Us Conference in Singapore.

For more than two decades, Wakamele-Rigold campaigned to clean up nuclear waste and raised awareness about the dangers of global warming. He single-handedly lobbied governments and produced award-winning documentaries to inform of the risks of nuclear energy and drive attention to the plight of countries on the frontline of climate change.

Fondly known as 'One-eyed Edi', Wakamele-Rigold's impressive size and cloudy right eye—the result of a congenital cataract left untreated—made him an easily recognizable presence in international fora, where he openly challenged energy companies, corrupt technocrats, and criminal syndicates destroying the marine biosphere around his native Marshall Islands and depleting it of the coral known as God's Ashes. Particular to the Marshalls, the coral is being used to produce the new drug with the street name: smash, the neon narcotic.

Wakamele-Rigold was born to a family that relocated to an atoll in the Ratak archipelago of the Marshall Islands, which are at risk of disappearing under rising sea levels. His people were displaced from the Ralik Chain by decades of nuclear tests conducted there by the United States.

No information has been released as to cause of death or funeral arrangements.

Wakamele-Rigold's remains will be brought back to the Marshall Islands' capital, Majuro, for burial. He leaves behind no relatives or children, but his work will leave a mark for generations.

—The Green Gazette Staff, Sweden

1

5

Majuro

1999

Edison 'Edi' Wakamele-Rigold did not expect a wave of emotion to swell in his stomach and lurch into his chest at the sight of the Marshalls. But when the propeller plane he was on banked left and dipped over the islands' capital, the razor-thin stretch of green and white that separated the crystal lagoon from the topaz sea was like a shank to his heart. He felt sick. He'd been away nearly fifteen years, and this was not how he envisioned his homecoming.

He stole a glance at the Americans on either side of him. Ramrod straight in their seats. As if they hadn't moved since the plane left Guam. He knew he scared them at take-off when he tried to look out the window. The breadth of his size didn't stoke warm and fuzzy feelings. Nor did the tattoos on his arms and neck. Having only one good eye didn't help matters. Edison knew he came across like an oversized pirate . . . or a mystical oracle, a cyclops whose cloudy right eye made it seem he had the power of spiritual sight. Which was why he hid it behind an eyepatch. At the expense of his already compromised depth of vision.

Edison just wanted a glimpse of Guam during their stopover. It had been years since he was on the US territory in the western Pacific, a lifetime since he served there with the navy. For a while, Edison believed that's when things first went wrong for him—but maybe, it was actually the last time things weren't bad.

The plane banked again and Edi got a quick view out the window—the ocean had never looked so big. It seemed to be squeezing the islands from all sides.

'Please fasten your seat belts,' the pilot called in the melodic timbre of Marshallese English.

Edison balled his hands into fists and braced himself for landing.

When the airplane door opened, an unexpected but familiar crest of heat crashed into the cabin, promptly vaporizing his liberty. Edi was back in the land of his birth—or rather, what remained of the land of his birth—and subsumed in its impotence.

He struggled down the stairs from the plane and on the short walk to the small airport terminal. Shuffling his feet. Confronted everywhere by reminders of how much he'd changed. And how low he'd sunk. The sun was hostile. The weathered coconut trees censured and cajoled. Around the tarmac, chickens clucked, contemptuous and disapproving. The narrow wall meant to hold back the sea looked derisively disappointed. Home was no longer paradise. Time had ravaged the beautiful Pacific atoll like a nightmare his sleep. Edi had had the same night terror since he was eight, when his grandpa first told him the story of his mother's birth.

Edison's *mama*, Ahulani, was born when the US set off a nuclear explosion on their atoll. They had been moved to a neighbouring island before the blast but they still felt it. The Americans had just ended a world war by dropping atomic bombs on their enemy, yet they still seemed unsatisfied. So, out in the Pacific, far away from the mainland, the most powerful country in the world continued testing its most forceful weapon.

Edi's people—the Marshallese—called it 'The Day of Two Suns'. A beautiful tropical morning when a man-made ball of light decimated their environment. They'd lived on the pristine paradise for centuries, only agreeing to move—temporarily—because the Americans told them it was 'for the greater good of mankind'.

And so, they stood aside while the US bombed their home, testing nuke after nuke, for the next ten years. Entire islands were vaporized and turned into craters.

Almost half a century later, they were still suffering the fallout and had not been cleared to go home.

Edi's father, Jameson, died not long after he was born. His grandpa said that every organ inside his *baba* was ravaged by cancer. Jameson had spent his days cleaning up the poison waste from the nuke explosions—leaving Edi in the capital, Majuro, with his grandparents.

Edi's widowed ma could barely work. Her eyes were clouded by cataracts and her limbs were enfeebled by toxic radiation. She didn't live long either. Succumbing to dengue when her son was five.

'Edison! Edison!'

He heard his grandfather's unmistakable voice as soon as he neared immigration. From the arrivals hall just beyond it, the man who raised him waved, spat a betel quid on the ground, then approached to take the papers that needed signing.

Unable to wave back, Edison wished there was a pile of coconut husks large enough to hide him.

'*Iọkwe*, Jimma,' Edison whispered to his grandpa Noa once past immigration.

'Eh?' The older man squinted as he scribbled on the papers. 'Speak up, boy . . . I can barely hear these days. And what is this . . . eye cover?'

'Only said hello, Jimma,' Edison lowered his head deferentially, keeping his hands together in front of him.

'Eh-ya, you greet me like a stranger,' Noa spat out excess saliva from his betel nut chew. 'Come here—'

Edi felt his face burn as the old man reached up to hug him. A combination of the heat and shame. A shade he had not worn in years.

For a heartbeat, he was enveloped in the pungency of betel nut.

Then, his *jimma* pulled away to return the signed documents to the waiting Americans—who undid his humiliating cuffs before walking back through immigration for the next flight out.

As the US agents disappeared around a corner, Edison clasped his wrists, still feeling the handcuffs he'd worn for nearly twenty-four hours, all the way from the mainland.

'Eh, you're home. You don't need to hide your eye here, boy,' Edison's grandpa urged him forward. Edi smiled faintly and bowed his head. Keeping the eyepatch.

'Come on,' his grandfather dropped the matter, leading the way towards the terminal exit. 'Your *bubu* is making your favourite. And there's *bwiro.'*

It was the one thing Edi could not get on the mainland—the fermented breadfruit specialty of his people. The sweetened paste smelled like shit, but it spoke the comforts of home.

Noa offered his grandson a betel quid, but Edi shook his head. After years of fighting addiction, he wasn't about to succumb to another drug.

'You sure? This is old-style. Pure. Not like the one you yung'uns are rolling now with your *extra spice* . . . it's too much for me.'

Edi had no idea what his grandfather was referring to. He had no friends his age left on the islands. No 'young people' who would have been able to keep him up to date or tell him about new things like this 'extra spice'. When he was growing up, quids were packed with tobacco, slaked lime or burned, pulverized coral, and salt. Nothing more was needed.

'Come on, come on,' his grandfather ushered him faster onto the street. 'Mustn't keep Bubu waiting another moment—she always say she been patient for almost fifteen years!'

Edi's chest felt tight. He was being welcomed like a prodigal son, as if he had not sullied their name. Their acceptance made him feel even more ashamed.

488 days sober, Edison Wakamele-Rigold got into the rundown taxi his Jimma Noa flagged down. Embarrassed when the old man paid the seventy-five-cent fare in pennies. Edi should've been the one to cover the cost of such an extravagance. He shouldn't have needed his grandpa to get him at the airport. But it was a condition of his release and deportation. So, at the prime age of twenty-five, he was officially—again—under the old man's care.

'Fuck,' Edison muttered under his breath.

'What was that, boy?' his grandpa cocked an ear in his direction.

'Nuthin, Jimma,' he responded just a little louder than the rattling of the cab, 'nuthin at all.'

* * *

Nestled between the ocean and the lagoon, the small cinder block house in pastel colours had changed little since Edi left. Maybe a new lick of paint on the walls, but the corrugated sheet metal roof had seen better days. The grass was patchy where there were blades, and the soil was still wet from the last storm. From the smell, Edi could tell it wasn't rain but the ocean that flooded the yard.

The front door, as always, was open.

'Edi! Is that Edi? Out here, boy!'

His grandma Lolly called from the back garden. It was the side of the house that faced the ocean. In ten steps, they could go directly from the kitchen to the water. It's where she preferred to prepare their meals.

Between the pandanus and the sea grape trees, there was a grill that Edi had helped Jimma build. Their old canoe was next to it, filled with plants and discarded fishing nets. In the centre of the yard—nearly always—a large, deep pan full of breadfruit sat above a burning wood fire on the ground. Its warm, doughy scent filled the house despite the ocean.

Edi rubbed his wrists, glad his grandma had been spared the sight of him in cuffs.

'Iọkwe, Bubu,' he walked slowly to where she squatted on the grass next to the *dira* pan. In with the blackened fruit, there was an empty wine bottle being heated upside down. Seeing it, Edi knew the treat was almost ready.

'Why is your face like that?' his grandma pointed at him with the stick she was using to turn the fruit. He lowered his eyes as he approached to kiss the top of her head.

'Ah, Edi,' she tutted, 'it's okay,' resuming her stirring of the dira's contents. 'The mainland is not for everyone.'

His grandma smiled at him as she pulled out the hot, empty bottle. She laid it down gently and cracked it to shards with a machete, gesturing for him to join her on the ground.

He took a piece of glass and used it to scrape off the fruit she handed over.

Fuckit—he thought as he skinned the breadfruit for eating. The mainland should've been right for him. Land of opportunity, land of the free. *Fuck-it*. He should've been able to make a go of it. Instead . . . *fuckit!*

'How is Auntie Rita?' his bubu asked about the woman she treated like a daughter. 'Is she bigger? I bet she is bigger with all that super-sized food in the mainland, hehe . . .'

Edi hadn't seen Rita since he was sent to prison. He hadn't seen anyone at all.

Until they moved to the mainland, Rita's family lived next door in Majuro. Edi used to play with her children. When he was thirteen, Edi's grandparents sent him to Rita in Arkansas. She had agreed to take care of him like a son. He was not the only child sent to live in the landlocked state with other Marshallese. It was practically island tradition—seen as the fastest way to improve their lot. Edi remembered his bubu telling him he should meet a nice girl on the mainland so at least he would not have to worry about having jelly babies. Decades had passed since the US tested nukes in the Marshalls, but people were still talking about how the radiation was causing children to be born without bones. There were also children covered in boils. Those were the grape babies. Edi was lucky he was neither. It was only his sight he had trouble with, but he had long learned to live with his wonky eye. He had never known a world of 20/20 vision.

But it was tough for Edi to be away from his grandparents and the sea. Life on the mainland had more constraints than he was used to. And way more rules than he understood. He felt like a visitor—who had to wear shoes and get an ID.

Within months of his move, Edi fell in with a group of other boys from the atolls. They all had the same fears, shared the same story, and spoke the same language. As a sign of strength, they all got tattoos, choosing designs to remind them of home. And just like their elders, the atoll boys in Arkansas learned to chew betel nut. On the mainland, it was easy to go from quids to something harder.

After high school, a bunch of them signed up for the US Navy. They got paid to study, and it was a way to get back to the sea. At the end of the day, all an atoll boy needed to get home were the tides and the stars.

'Lolly!'—his grandpa called out from the house—'I am going now!'

Edi looked at his grandma for an explanation.

'Village meeting,' she told him. 'That American trying to get the Tomb cleaned up is here. It's been leaking and they worry the radiation will kill us all.'

The Tomb. A massive concrete dome more than four times the size of the US Capitol's. Edi had heard about it all his life but never seen it. Growing up, they weren't allowed near it. It was on another atoll north of Majuro, close to where his family originally lived. The Americans—when done with their tests—got the locals to help them bury tons and tons of nuclear waste in one of the bomb craters. Then, they covered it with concrete.

'Why don't you go with him and get reacquainted with everyone?'

Edi didn't know which was worse—staying and possibly lying to his bubu as she subjected him to more questions about the mainland or going with Jimma to face the rest of the village.

He clasped his wrists and rubbed at the phantom cuffs. It felt like ages since he longed for a high.

* * *

Not wanting to further disappoint, Edi accompanied his grandpa to the meeting at the schoolhouse. It was only two kilometres away but took longer than usual to get there because Jimma walked like he was campaigning for mayor. He greeted everyone by name and shook their hands as he passed.

Edi kept his head low but still noticed people back away and whisper at the sight of him. His jimma acted like nothing was amiss.

He didn't hurry nor shy away from the tittering neighbours. Nope, Noa carried on walking with his head high as if he were leading his grandson to an enthronement.

The schoolhouse hadn't changed much since Edi was in the first grade. Extensions were built, but the covered basketball court still had the same cracks on its concrete floor. It seemed to have been repaired over the years, but the fissures had reopened. There was also a top layer of sand. Likely remnants of the last ocean flood.

On the beach beyond, the coconut trees ran horizontal to the shore—like the outstretched fingers of a dying man in a desert, fighting till the end to reach for water.

'Testing . . .'

Edi turned back to the court and caught sight of a tall white man tapping the microphone. It had been set up on a stand at the far end, facing uneven rows of plastic chairs. Jimma took a seat up front while Edi hung back near the exit.

As customary, the village chief began the meeting with a prayer, thanking the Almighty for His blessings. Particularly for giving them the atolls, referring to them in the native language as Jolet jen Anij, the Gifts from God.

Then, the chief introduced the man who had set up the mic—a gangly, rumpled American named Jack. At six-foot-three, he towered over the islanders.

Using a whiteboard, Jack delivered a spirited speech about the dangers of the Dome, which was what the Americans called the Tomb. It was information most of the locals suspected but didn't know for sure. No one ever told them anything in an official capacity. Though every few months, for years, the mainland sent over experts to take medical samples from the islanders. They never explained why nor shared the results. Jack spoke of how his country had turned God's Gifts into God's Ashes and said that it was time to rise up and get the story of the Marshalls 'out there'—so the US would be forced to clean up its mess before it was 'too late'.

Edi wondered what 'too late' might be. He'd already lost both his parents, and Jimma and Bubu had been living with all sorts of radiation-related health issues for years. It's just the way it was for the Marshallese.

'Well . . . that's enough from me,' Jack ended his lecture calling another man forward to address the islanders. He said they would be told about a 'mind-blowing' new 'platform' that would help them spread the word. A thing called the 'Internet'. At that, Jack handed the mic over to a small Chinese man who spoke with a posh English accent. Dressed simply in black, the foreigner explained that he would—efficiently and economically—lay the infrastructure needed to 'connect' the Marshalls to the world. A 'digital web-olution', he called it.

Edi had heard about the Internet on the mainland. The service— the military—had been using it for years, and it was slowly being made available to the public. A few of his fellow inmates were already communicating with their families through electronic mail. He'd have done the same, if the Marshalls were connected and his grandparents had access to a computer.

Before he was deported, Edi spent six long years behind bars in California. He was charged with manslaughter for killing another navy man in Guam. The guy was harassing one of the local girls, and he hit his head on the pavement after Edi struck him in her defence. The sailor was in a coma for months before dying. His family's lawyers insisted Edi planned it all in advance. When they got the criminal charge successfully upgraded to murder, US officials decided to deport him. It's how the mainland dealt with problems it saw as 'not theirs'.

'Edi? Edi?' his grandfather was calling him forward from his stupor. 'Come, boy. Come.'

Jimma Noa was standing with Jack by the whiteboard, while the Internet guy was off to the side, speaking with the mayor.

As Edi approached, the crowd parted like the Red Sea did for Moses in the Bible. And he felt he would have drowned had he not reached for Jack's outstretched hand.

'Is that a stick chart pattern?' Jack grinned, pleased to recognize the traditional navigation tool that was tattooed up the length of Edi's arm. 'I still don't get how y'all know exactly where you are in the ocean just by the swell of the water and the night sky. It's ah-may-zing how ya get from one place to another without technology.'

Jimma Noa beamed. Proud of his ancestors' wisdom.

Edi felt himself exhale. A little. Jack was the only one other than his grandparents who looked at him directly. It was quite the opposite of his experience on the mainland, where people had avoided him or made fun of his appearance. Calling him One-eyed Edi or the Idiot Islander. Many mainlanders made fun of the way he talked and presumed he was stupid or his 'brain' was 'soft' because they thought his people subsisted on tubers and stinky greens. They said this to him all the time. Which only showed how little they knew about their own country.

'Until '78, my island was American too, you know,' Edi would reply to those who mocked him. 'I'm just like you, dude . . . and more of a patriot than you fuckers.'

Then, he would tell them about the nukes, and how much his people had sacrificed for the mainland. He would recount the stories he'd been told as a child and tell them how the bombs they set off in the Marshalls during peacetime were worse than those they dropped on Japan during World War 2. How the poison still afflicted the islands. How his parents suffered, and his neighbours had birth defects from the radiation. He believed it was also why he had the cloudy eye.

But what he said never mattered. Because to the mainlanders, he was no one. Just another large, non-American, brown-skinned man.

Noticing the villagers look away as he passed, Edi realized he'd become 'no one' to his people, too.

Fuckit.

Coming home was like a shank through his heart.

6

51.5072° N, 0.1276° W

London

1989

Cold as steel, the March evening cut through Melody's heavy coat as if it were made of lace. She struggled to keep up with her sure-footed roommate, who—thanks to the higher wisdom of Mazu, the Mother Ancestor and Sea Goddess—turned out to actually be a good fit despite Melody's initial impression. They had become friends enough for her to follow the girl on what seemed a perilous trek across London instead of the expected Friday night of revelry.

Above them, the moon shone a dull jade–white against the graphite sky.

Feeling anything but the usual calm, Melody touched her obsidian bracelet for reassurance as the narrow cobblestone streets they were on turned into narrower alleys. At every corner, it seemed something sinister might jump out at them from the shadows.

'How much further?' she asked her roommate as she pulled her coat on tighter. It was near freezing, but Maggie—which she learned was what Wei Jing was called at university—insisted on walking, saying they needed some 'fresh air'. *Clearly*, Melody thought, *the math genius didn't account for the wind chill factor.*

'Almost there,' came Maggie's concise, per usual, reply.

Melody rolled her eyes and just managed to step over a puddle. 'How do you even know where we are? Much less where we're going?'

'A Londoner always knows.'

'Bollocks!' In the months they'd lived together at the LSE dorm, Melody also learned this—and a few more choice words—from her roomie.

Maggie stopped to light a cigarette. 'You didn't have to come, you know.'

Melody knew that, but the friend Maggie was meeting had piqued her interest. A Catholic girl from Northern Ireland with whom she'd immediately felt a kinship when they were introduced at a riverside book fair. It was like they were in the same boat. Two family-oriented, God-fearing girls—with fragile national identities that larger entities threatened to consume. Where Taiwan had China, Northern Ireland had the UK. As her father intended, she was learning a lot at the LSE.

'Give me that,' Melody took the lighter Maggie was fumbling with and lit her cigarette. It was a challenge lately for her roommate to hold anything with three fingers in plasters. 'Maybe you should wear gloves, you know . . . to stop you getting cut by all those computer bits you play with.'

'Ehhh,' Maggie dismissed the concern with a wave of her bandaged hand. Picking up the pace, she puffed on her cigarette and turned down an even darker alley. It led to a yard of grimy, brick-built tunnels. The place was steeped in an acrid, putrid stench. Overhead, slow trains rumbled east towards the docklands.

'Jesus, Mags—this looks like it's full of squats . . .'

'It is.'

Taking a last drag of her cigarette, Maggie stopped at a small, banged-up wooden door underneath an arch. She pressed an almost invisible buzzer, and after a few moments, the latch was opened.

Without another word, Maggie walked in, moving aside the heavy felt curtain at the entrance. Melody followed a few steps behind. It took a while for her eyes to adjust to the enclosed darkness. When they did, she spotted a narrow stairwell going down at the end of the vestibule. Along the wall, just at eye level, a tiny elephant, barely an inch in size, glowed a soft purple in the black light, a likely reference to why the place was called The Elephant in the Cellar. There was no railing, and only a single bulb illuminated their steep descent. Melody had seen more radiance from a candelabra.

'What the feck, Mags—?' Another phrase Melody had picked up living with Maggie.

'If you're just going to be full of questions tonight, you really should've stayed at the dorm.'

For a moment, Melody reconsidered her decision to go out—until the tantalizing trills of a banjo reached her the closer they got to the bottom of the stairs. It called like the most soothing of breezes warming her chill. Then, it was joined by the sweet notes of a flute and some sort of drum began keeping robust time.

Her heart thrummed with the music, and she wasn't prepared for the cozy cellar that welcomed them at the base of the stairs. She'd never seen a bar venue like it. There was straw and sawdust on the floor, an exposed beam ceiling, and large wooden barrels as tables. People were crammed onto low couches, and cigarette smoke hung heavy in the air. Like a bewitching if pungent mist in an enchanted forest.

'Oi! Over here!'

Melody turned at the lilt she'd come to recognize. There, in a corner alcove lit by a tabletop candle in an empty wine bottle, sat Maggie's friend Orla. The budding artist she met when she dragged Mags to that riverside book fair. The two were old friends. If only for that chance meeting with Orla, Melody was glad she convinced her roommate to accompany her that day to the fair. Because Maggie's friend Orla was just so—*cool*.

In the cellar's dim lighting, Orla's eyes twinkled a vitreous emerald and her auburn hair burned dark and deep. She was holding a glass near empty of a luminous golden whiskey.

'Another one, Pale Face?' Maggie asked, dropping her packet of cigarettes next to the ashtray on the table.

'Subtle as ever, Wei-wei,' Orla teased with familiarity. 'I'm surprised you haven't scared away *this* roommate yet.'

Maggie waved her hand dismissively and walked to the bar without another word.

'Lovely to see you again,' Orla beamed, making room on the bench.

Melody felt her cheeks flush, as they always did when faced
with someone she admired. Which wasn't often. 'Thought I should
experience Saint- . . . Paddy's, is it? . . . at least once while I am here.'
Her way of explaining why she had crashed their Friday night plans.
She desperately wanted to make a good impression.

'Once?' Orla laughed a wonderfully deep *Orla* laugh. 'Trust me,
there won't be no getting away from this Irish holiday . . . even in
London. And tonight should be a corker'—she winked—'there's a full
moon out and that's always a sign o' trouble!'

Again, Melody felt heat race up her body. It had gotten surprisingly
warm in the damp basement. She looked around to see if anyone else
was as hot as her. But most of the women in the crowd still had on
their woolly jumpers or sweaters.

'Melody, aye?' Orla leaned over to be heard above the music.

Melody nodded, suddenly struck dumb by the feel of Orla's breath.
Being around her was like standing in the sun—you knew it was there
even with your eyes shut.

Sooner than Melody would've liked, her roommate returned
carrying two pints of an ebony liquid with a crown of creamy ermine.

'You wanted the full Irish, princess—you start with Guinness.
Then, we move you on to whiskey.'

After setting the pints on the table, Maggie pulled an open beer
bottle from her jacket pocket. She wiped its lip with her sleeve and
took a swig.

'Where's *your* Guinness?' Melody asked.

'She never drinks stout,' Orla replied, 'uncivilized palette.' The Irish
artist winked at Melody, who decided to remove her coat to cool down.

'Scoot.' Maggie waved her bottle, indicating they make room as she
pulled up a stool.

At the opposite end of the venue, jamming musicians—all
women—began another rousing Irish folk anthem. Melody was
amazed by their energy. It set the space ablaze. In the throes of their
improvized rhythms, she could almost see the nostalgia beating out of
Orla's chest—and the pageant of memories flashing across the girl's
gemstone eyes.

Minutes later, the players shifted to a soul-stirring ballad. Led by a solitary flute, wistful in its lamentation. No one spoke, and the room was held in thrall.

Just as the musicians took a break, a woman approached the alcove with a large bowl of chips in one hand and a platter of sausages with soda bread in the other.

'How do you eat all that shite and not get fat?' Orla teased Maggie in a way that revealed it was not the first time she'd asked.

'Asian genes.' Mags replied. Matter of fact.

Melody wondered which side of the family her roommate might've meant. She'd seen photos of Maggie's late mother, and though indeed Asian, she was not what might be called slim. When asked about her, Maggie shut down. Melody got an even worse response when she asked after her roommate's father. There were no photos of him at all in their room.

'Ever wish you were someone else?' Melody pondered aloud.

The women on either side of her looked on quizzically.

'Way to kill the mood, pet,' Orla laughed. 'Was it because nerd-o over here brought up genetics?'

Melody blushed. She should have shut up. But she didn't. 'I just . . . wonder sometimes, you know?' She was transfixed by jade green eyes. 'Like, what if I was born in China instead of Taiwan? Or—or—perhaps in Dublin? And how different would that be to, say, Belfast in Northern Ireland . . .'

Maggie scratched at her crotch with her beer bottle.

'Jee-zus, mate.' Orla chastised, looking away.

'What? It itches.'

Orla laughed again, that wonderful Orla laugh. Sounding to Melody like church bells. Then, the joyous peeling dissipated and she turned momentarily pensive.

'D'you know . . .' Orla eventually answered, 'I never thought about it.'

She reached for Maggie's cigarettes on the table and tapped the bottom of the pack with her palm. 'I was raised to think it is what it is, ye?' *Tap, tap, tap.* 'And praise God for the blessing. Whatever it be.'

She took a stick out of the box, put it between her lips and leaned down to the tabletop candle to light it.

Melody hadn't realized she was watching Orla's every movement as if it were a ballet . . . until Maggie nudged her with the beer bottle.

'Your turn, Taiwan. What do you have to say for yourself?'

Startled, Melody looked from one woman to the other, unable to even recall what she had asked.

'D'you wish you had different parents?' Orla iterated a version of the question.

Melody looked at her for a few moments, seemingly lost in thought. 'I . . . don't think so?'

'You don't think so?' Orla smiled.

'Why would she?' Maggie cut in. 'Daddy's a successful capitalist. Mummy's an angel, by the sound of it. And where *she* was born, even under a dictatorship, women are able to fight for rights just like men. Gasp.'

'Stop teasing the girl, Mags, y'really don't want to be losin' another one.' Orla smiled at Melody. 'The way she drives 'em away, you'd think she doesn't bathe!'

Maggie held up two bandaged fingers and flipped off her friend.

'Rub yourself raw, Magster? Or cut yourself on your wee toys again?'

To Melody's awe, Orla's jabs never seemed to truly upset Maggie.

'Say what you will, Pale Face, but those toys will one day rule the world. I'm just figuring out how to maximize them without sacrificing our humanity—or how to make it so our humanity is maximized by those "toys".'

'Shite . . . here we go again.' Orla held up her empty whiskey glass to a passing woman and asked for a round for the table. 'Trust me,' she said to Melody conspiratorially, 'I've learned that the upcoming Homily According to Mags is best ignored with a double shot of Bushmills.'

Melody couldn't help but chuckle. She'd lived with Maggie long enough to know how passionate she was about her work. It pretty much defined her existence. The genius-level maths scholar rarely left campus, unless coerced by Melody or lured to hang out with Orla.

'You laugh, but this work *is* a religion,' Maggie began as she shovelled multiple chips into her mouth. 'Like wealth'—she gestured towards Melody—'maths—technology—is power. And ultimately, power is God.'

'Well, that sounds bleak . . .' Melody replied, ignoring the dig at her privileged family.

'It's just a fact,' Maggie paused to put another handful of food in her mouth. 'Man is at the mercy of what he worships. So it's best to demystify our deities. Take it from me'—stopping to take a swig of her beer—'my father left us for both power and money.'

'Ah so, that's it—family trauma,' Orla concluded in jest.

'Now that you mention it,' Maggie continued, 'computer circuits are like families . . .'

'Seriously?!' Orla thought she had shifted the conversation only to find she'd actually spurred Maggie on.

'When a component is broken—that means *part*, Pale Face—a circuit can cease to function,' the maths wiz just avoided the deep-fried chip Orla threw in her direction.

'Yes!' Melody chimed in, feeling like she and her roommate were finally on the same page. 'Like I take my strength from my family. We stick together. And if that circuit were broken, none of its "components" would work . . .'

'But that's why you build in parallel,' Maggie interjected, 'so when one node goes down, it doesn't affect the whole *circuit*. It's more efficient.'

'True,' Melody said, nodding distractedly at the server setting down their whiskeys. 'Each has its own path to the power source. And even if the flow of current is divided among parallels, the voltage is constant . . . ultimately, it's all connected.'

'Now imagine what a quantum circuit could do,' Maggie went on, 'with multiplicities and the superposition of states—'

'All right, geeks, enough, so? I have no idea what you're on about and you're boring me to tears now . . .' Orla took a sip of her drink. 'It's St Paddy's—none of that serious shite, like?'

Another jam session was about to begin.

'See now, that'—Orla gestured towards the musicians—'is powerful. Nothing connects us more than—'

In an instant, the world imploded. Orla's thought rang unfinished and Melody's ears reverberated with a deafening silence. A devastating darkness crashed into the cellar from above. Drenching the women's cocoon with poison.

In a heartbeat, the murmurs of the revellers turned into screams. And the crowd in the cellar began to fight to climb up the stairs. They funnelled out of the small doorway, bursting onto the streets like a hunted herd through a fissure.

In the haze of the evening, under a flint-coloured sky, police sirens pierced through the alleys from the high street.

As Maggie stopped to catch her breath in the recessed entrance to an abandoned fish shop, she noticed her two friends running towards her hand in hand. She watched as Orla wiped Melody's tear-stained face and said nothing at the tenderness she saw in their gaze. In her shock from the blast, Melody barely noticed the other girl's touch, and despite it being a habit, she forgot to check for the Mazu bracelet. It was still on her wrist—but again, the protection it brought was unexpected.

'Everyone okay?' Orla asked repeatedly. Living in London, she tried to forget the troubles at home, but she suspected her people might be behind whatever just happened. There were armed groups in this part of the UK fighting the central government for decades. They wanted to be reunited with the independent Irish Republic just across the border. It would not be the first time they'd taken their struggle to the British capital's streets.

Though it was a few hours before official confirmation of a bomb blast at the nearby train station, the ground had shifted, redirecting the tracks the girls were on.

Around the corner, observing the bedlam in the alleyway, a short figure in a dark jacket smoked a distinct-smelling cigarette. Aromatic and slightly sweet. A token of home. Surreptitiously, he took photos of the frightened women. Zooming in on the trio of friends by the boarded-up fish shop.

He stayed as long as they did. Unnoticed by all, bar the waxing jade-white moon.

7

X.17XXX° N, 1XX.4XXX° E

Pulau Rahsia

2023 | Present

The full moon turned the evening into mirrored glass. A silvery sheen danced atop the obsidian sea and the tropical air was sheet metal crisp. The shoreline—soft and diamond-dusted—disappeared into a rainforest dappled in starlight.

In a bamboo thicket that gleamed gold among the hardwood trees, Anak was doubled over in pain. He felt the pull of the moon in his belly. Like the ocean, it roiled and surged. The hunger hurt so much he was bleeding. He didn't know that could happen. And no matter how he tried, he couldn't stop the flow. He even stuffed leaves into the crotch of his shorts to soak up the blood, but there was just so much of it.

Anak had woken up among the trees, not quite sure how he got there or how long he'd been asleep. He walked around and realized he was no longer in Kota Kinabalu. There were no streets, no city, no rundown market, no Kuya Apollo. Just endless forest. But he could hear music thumping in the distance, and he thought to follow the sound. Maybe it would lead to a beach, where he could find a boat bound for the Philippines. If this wasn't already one of its islands.

But the stomach spasms slowed his trek. In distress, Anak sat on the damp ground hoping the pain would pass. Something caught his eye. A small trinket so dark it would have disappeared in the shadows of the forest floor had its glossy surface not given it away. Could it have fallen out of his own pocket? He picked it up and held it to the rising moon. A string of beads so smooth, it shone in the luminous evening. Lustrous and eternal. He fingered one bead and then the next as if in prayer. Convinced that the pain he felt was dissipating.

Struck by another cramp, Anak tightened his grip on the beads. Drawing more blood, this time from his fingernails digging into his palm.

There was a blinding flash of light, and he shut his eyes.

When he reopened them, the air around him buzzed electric, and the same glimmer he saw in the ocean when he first found the coral sparkled through the forest. A glistening web of light began to shimmer among the trees—connecting every living thing.

Immediately, he knows he's in danger. He's been on the island for two days and people are looking for him. He can sense their murderous intent. It is loud. Like a deafening, discordant rhapsody. His killer is near.

Anak knows he must keep moving. He must leave this place as soon as he can.

Around him, the night echoes from within. He hears the snakes slithering on the forest floor and the monkeys clamouring in the trees. From behind the moonlight, the stars call to him and the crickets are marking out an escape path.

It feels like he is on smash. But not enough of a dose to make him invincible. He can't make the swim from the island back to Kota Kinabalu, much less get all the way to the Philippines on his own.

He stuffs the bracelet in his pocket to make a dash for the beach. He will find more coral. He's always more agile in the water.

At the deafening crunch of the leaves in his shorts, he stops. Not wanting to attract his killer's attention.

He goes to remove his padding and is surprised to find he's still bleeding. Unlike the first time, the shimmer doesn't seem to be healing his wound. He looks around him and sees the web of light starting to dissipate.

* * *

On the beach, in a space lit by bamboo torches and strings of bright yellow bulbs, the guests of the Royal Pulau Rahsia resort gathered for another night's adventure in their swimsuits. Not far from where they stood, a sleek forty-two-feet-long boat was docked in the spotlight. It was being loaded with dive gear by hotel staff. Oxygen tanks, fins, inflatable vests, and undersea lighting.

'Well, look who it is,' the North American guest greeted as Luc approached their dive group waiting on the shore. 'Haven't seen you all day! The way you were knockin 'em back last night, I was sure you had a hangover—or that the missus was keeping a close eye . . .'

'My wife's been . . . preoccupied,' Luc replied. 'So, I, uh . . .' he held up his phone, 'decided to "try something new" . . .'

'You joined Day-Us,' the North American stated with a wink.

Luc was visibly surprised to be called out.

'Nah!' the North American laughed, negating any likely assumptions. 'I'm not at the "reading frequencies" stage yet. I just saw you pop up on the app's network. Level 1, right? I'm sort of on Level 2. I found a cheap version of the superchip, offering me a jump to the final level.'

'You caved?!' Jordi teased Luc as he handed his customized dive fins to one of the workers walking past to load the boat.

'I've had the app a while,' Luc clarified, 'but yes, I only just started using it. You were all going on about it last night like it was some miraculous thing—'

'Well, it is—' the North American stated.

'For some—' Jordi cut in, snapping a shot of himself, bare chested, on his mobile. 'I think it's silly.'

'You wouldn't pass the first level, *gordo*!' Ferran retorted, taking his own night-time photo. 'You are not interested in anything but yourself . . .'

'Ouch! *Pero*, can you blame me?' Jordi smirked and struck a pose. The tall, bronzed friends high-fived in gales of laughter.

'See, now that won't get you points,' the North American told Luc.

'I'm still not clear on all that,' Luc stated. 'The app rewards people for being . . . "good"? Right? As in, not mean or selfish—or narcissistic?'

'Makes it sound so simple,' Robbi suddenly spoke, surprising the other divers waiting on the beach. 'It's a little more complex than that . . . from what I understand.'

'And what do you understand, Mr . . . *X*?' the North American turned his attention away from his phone to Robbi, who was zipping up his dive suit.

'Yes, I want to know, too,' Ferran jumped in. 'Isn't that what it does? Reward you for being *good*?'

'You could put it that way I suppose,' Robbi removed his eyeglasses and stashed them in a waterproof case. 'You start at Level 1 learning new things, about people, places—'

'Through videos, texts, and then trying new activities, right?' Luc offered.

'Yes. You open up your world virtually and then, on the physical plane. Once you see past your limitations and biases—in short, your world *expanded*—you move up on the app. You're "elevated". That's when you get the superchip that can supposedly read your "energy". You wear it behind your ear and, basically, it has a neural interface that reads the electrical impulses in your brain. So, if you show *empathy* or do something for someone else, you gain points and advance further . . . and if you don't and think ill of others, your points drop.'

'So, the dɛU¹S app will know if I do charity work because I want to be helpful or only because my job as a doctor required it?' Luc asked.

'Exactly,' Robbi nodded. 'After that, the final level is Elysium. Which goes beyond thought and action to the most cellular of all— our feelings. It speaks to our very natures. Then, there won't be a need for devices. Supposedly, nodes will reach a point when they will be able to communicate without need for words. The mind will be so powerful that the nodes themselves will be a highly integrated network of evolved beings. No Internet. No ill feelings. No war.'

'You left out riches!' the North American jumped in. 'At every stage, you earn points, and the app rewards you with crypto and tokens. It doesn't get any easier than that to make a fortune. You don't have to put any effort into becoming an influencer,' he pointed to the bronzed Spaniards. 'Simple, right?'

'*Bueno*, I keep losing points and falling behind,' Ferran chimed in. 'So, I need to make money other ways too . . .'

'Presumably,' Robbi went on, 'when you reach Elysium, you won't even care about money. None of these social trappings will matter. No hierarchy, no rules, no government. I don't think anyone's reached that level yet. I hear there are barely any nodes at Level 2 . . .'

'No wonder autocratic places like Russia and China are cracking down on the app. Isn't there already a parallel Chinese network—using all their own tech—to attract nodes off dɛU[1]S?' Luc wondered.

'Ufff,' Jordi scoffed. 'It's all about money, eh? People are only on the app to get rich. And all these "peace treaties" that the news says are because of the app, *por favor*. This *Dios* is only bringing peace where money is needed. Each side just wants to be paid. Where we're from, the Basques, the Catalans, and the Castilians have been in conflict for centuries—I doubt that will end just because of some app. See?' The model turned to Robbi, 'Silly.'

'The way you've explained it Mr X, maybe you are the missing tech billionaire?' Ferran shushed his friend and urged Robbi to keep talking.

'He did seem offended when we said it was simple . . .' Jordi taunted.

'Shit'—the North American chimed in—'maybe you are Max Bao. I thought I would recognize him from this old video I once saw, but I gotta admit, it is hard to tell you people apart. Maybe you wanted to disappear so Day-Us would go belly up and you wouldn't need to pay off our points when we got to the top!'

'Talking like that, I'm surprised you have any points at all,' Ferran concluded.

'I am not Max Bao,' Robbi reiterated, calmly. 'But I am in tech. And everything I've told you is public knowledge. dɛU[1]S works as a blockchain, expanding exponentially. Users—the nodes—are "policing" each other through their frequencies. Especially from Level 2, when they get that superchip. So, the network exists with or without the creator. Giving its nodes a sense of self-empowerment that I would argue serves libertarianism . . . the total opposite of the authoritarianism in Bao's native China. At the rate the neural interface is developing, even the alternative app could take those rulers down.' Robbi scanned the blank faces around him. It appeared the others needed further "elevation"—no one seemed to understand a word he'd just said.

'Everybody ready?' the dive master called the group's attention, indicating the gear was all loaded and soon, they could board.

In their focus on the app, the guests failed to notice that under cloak of night, a young boy had scurried onto the boat way ahead of them. He was thin enough to slip beneath a bench on the far end of the deck. Hidden from view by a portable ice chest put in front of it.

'A few things to note before we get on,' the dive master corralled the group on the beach. 'You're going to see some amazing things— and there's beer and champagne on board for when you resurface. You've all had at least fifteen dives, yes?'

Luc raised a hand and shook his head. 'I just want to go snorkelling'—he explained—'maybe see some of the glow fish that's washed up on shore.'

The resort dive master laughed nervously. 'Oh, sir. There's none of that here. Maybe on the other side of the islands, far away. These waters are safe. Not toxic.'

'But I saw some wash ashore the last night—'

'You must be mistaken,' the dive master insisted, 'there is nothing like that here. I'm sorry sir, I would love for you to come along, but—for safety reasons, you will have to stay behind. This is only for certified divers. You understand. Underwater—at night—it's a safety issue. There is a separate trip for snorkelers in the morning. Closer to the beach.'

The dive master then ushered the other guests away from Luc and towards the dock.

'Hey—'

They all turned back to see the Chinese guest—who'd kept to himself since arriving on the island—heading straight for the boat.

'I come,' he stated bluntly. Without a smile or acknowledgment of anyone else. He certainly did not seem an example of the 'new Chinese' whom dεU¹S™ claimed to have transformed.

The mainlander kept looking at his phone and had no dive gear, but nobody dared question him. Powerless, the dive master helped him aboard.

'What the . . . ?' Luc wasn't thrilled.

'Chinks, am I right?' the North American had opted to stay behind.

Despite his displeasure at being bumped off the trip, Luc was not amused by the racist remark. Had he been on dɛU¹S™ Level 2, it would've gained him points.

As the boat left shore and cut further into the evening, the North American checked his phone. He was pleased with his imitation superchip—his dɛU¹S™ points remained the same even after his comment. In the app chart, he spotted the twinkling light he was meant to follow so he could get fast-tracked to the final level. It was on the boat—and moving further away. He still hadn't worked out which of the other guests was emitting the signal—but he wasn't too bothered. He would just wait until the divers returned to shore.

Then, the North American noticed something else on the boat that he hadn't counted on. Another blinking light. Competition. It seemed another node was also in pursuit of the sparkle. *Dammit.*

He should've got on the boat. By the end of the night, he could have been one step closer to Nirvana. Disheartened, he turned to Luc: 'Drink?'

Not ready to return to his room and face his stressed-out wife, Luc agreed.

'Thank Christ the app hasn't banned alcohol.' The North American tucked his phone away as they walked back towards the resort. 'Well, there hasn't been a stage yet that's stopped me wanting it . . .'

'I read the founder was at some bar in London during an Irish republican bombing,' Luc shared, 'so maybe the guy understands that sometimes alcohol is a necessary analgesic . . .'

'Ha!' the North American exclaimed, 'Ain't that the truth.'

One way or another, he was going to get a step closer to Nirvana before the morning. Regardless of whom he had to kill to reach it.

8

Bandar Seri Begawan

2023 | Present

The unmarked luxury cruiser docked at its destination before dawn. By the time its only passenger—the goateed man in a windbreaker—disembarked, faint traces of morning were just beginning to hint at stroking the sky. He didn't plan to stop at the palace as he normally did. There was no time for that. And he was not in the mind for pleasantries. Despite his gratitude to Prince Hashem, his old friend would understand his need to rush home. If 'home' was even still safe for him.

Hashem sent a nondescript Mercedes Benz to pick him up at the secluded Royal Marina and speed him through the Bruneian capital's private roads to the Royal Hangar. Tinted car windows were not permitted in Brunei—even for members of the ruling family—but there was still enough of the night's darkness to shield the goateed guest. There would be no trace of him in the kingdom. No one knew he was there but the prince.

Speak of the devil. There was a slight beep in his ear as the encrypted call came in.

'Well?' The question was asked in French, which was what they always used to communicate. Where they were, both English and Mandarin—their other shared languages—were far better understood by potential eavesdroppers. Not that anyone could even hear their conversation. It was all taking place without any external sounds.

85

Dead end, the goateed man replied mentally in English before continuing in French. *Littéralement.* Literally.

'What do you mean?' Hashem asked.

In his head, the goateed man recounted his conversation with the one-eyed man in Kota Kinabalu. His neural interface transmitted the words to Hashem: *He said he didn't know where she was, and then he was killed.*

'You didn't!' the prince wasn't as surprised as he sounded.

It wasn't me, the goateed guest thought plainly. *But I think it was me they were after . . .*

'What? How?'

He sighed. Hashem was the only person with whom he could let his guard down. They'd known each other so long, he didn't always need to police his thoughts.

Something the killer said before jumping to his death—the goateed man laid bare—*I think they know who I really am.*

'You mean—?'

'Yes. *Them.*' His frustration had him speak aloud. He caught himself and looked at the driver on the other side of the glass divider, who showed no signs of having heard anything. Then, he resumed the inaudible conversation he was having with Hashem. *I think it was a message—to us—or perhaps to my father-in-law. I did wonder if maybe he sent someone to kill me . . . Either way, we have to lay low.*

Hashem wasn't expecting this. He knew how important their— *operations*—were to his friend. They'd been so careful. If they paused, it would be too costly.

'Perhaps you're being paranoid . . .' the prince posited.

No, the goateed man asserted. *For the glory of God . . .*

His thoughts were interrupted by the muffled call to prayer from the Omar Ali Mosque. It wafted into the car in the silence of the pre-dawn city. They must be nearing the palace grounds and approaching the hangar. He looked outside and spotted the bright red and yellow of the city's only Taoist temple. Glinting in the breaking morning like an unsophisticated vagrant among the golden domes of

Bandar's opulent mosques. The man shut his eyes and put his hands to his head before resuming the conversation.

Li-majdillah—he shared with the prince—*for the glory of God. I heard the killer say it before leaping to his death* . . .

'In Arabic?' Hashem was aghast.

Yes. And I think the murder weapon is the same substance we're refining for . . . you know. He used it as a—bullet. They're telling us they somehow have it too—

'The God substance?' The prince recalled his friend telling him in the strictest confidence about a new product their family was planning on distributing.

Yes. Just tweaking the formula, but it shouldn't be long now . . .

A heavy silence hung between them. The connection fraught with shared history and anxieties.

'So, have you told him?' Hashem worried about all the secrets his friend was carrying.

Only about the assailant—and the substance. I wanted to gauge his reaction. But I haven't told him about her. He is already too frail. And this would kill him. I do not want to be the reason he dies . . .

He looked out the window as the car wound through the narrow streets fronting Kampung Ayer. The sky was turning a soft coral and traders were loading their wares on gleaming riverboats to ferry over to the water village. Its precolonial homes on stilts and pastel coloured 'floating' structures looked so pretty in the light of morning. *Pity about the ongoing construction along the riverbank*, he thought to himself. A Chinese company had promised the royals the best entertainment and tourism venue they could build—he only hoped it would not look like the tacky monstrosities in their own country. It would mar an otherwise scar-free city.

'And what of your son?' the prince asked.

Nothing either.

'Have you tried—'

Of course, I have tried. I have tried everything!—the goateed man gritted his teeth to hold back his emotions. It was not like him to get riled up or upset.

He glanced at the bottle of whiskey across from him. Hashem always stocked the bars in his vehicles with guest-appropriate tipples. But he remembered the number of shots he'd had on the cruiser and tamped down any temptation. He took a string of beads from his pocket and calmed himself by moving it through his fingers.

He said he needed 'time', the man sighed. *I didn't mean for it to go so badly with him. He just—took me by surprise, you know?*

'I know,' Hashem agreed. 'Children. They break your heart every time.'

But I didn't think he would just—switch off. I haven't been able to reach him at all. Well, I . . . I have never been able to reach him. But now . . .

'You think they're together?' Hashem proposed. 'Mother and son have always been close.'

I did wonder, but it doesn't seem to be the case. I'm still getting a reading of his bio-field—so, he's likely in the region. But her signal has vanished.

'Think she's dead?'

Silence. Like his heart and his mind just stopped.

And then—

Mon Dieu, Hashem. You never were one to mince words. The goateed man reconsidered the contents of the vehicle's bar.

'I am merely saying what you are thinking, *mon ami.*'

Another heavy silence before the prince got a response.

Don't they say you will feel it—instinctively—should something terrible happen to your other half?

'So they say,' Hashem concurred. 'As you know, I have several "other halves" or three-quarters or, or—or—so I'd rather not be feeling anything from all those fractions! Hahaha . . . '

As indebted as he was to the prince, the man in the car couldn't find the humour. *I don't know where to go from here, my friend.*

'Taipei, no?' Hashem stated the obvious. 'The time is now—to face the music.'

Silence.

'Leave the devices you need evaluated in the usual panel. We will find her, mon ami.'

The car came to a stop and the invisible line between the friends went dead. The man looked out and realized they'd arrived at the Royal Hangar. He put the weapon and murder victim's mobile phone in the car's hidden panel just as his door was opened. Stepping out, he quickly crossed the few feet to ascend his friend's private jet. A special attendant greeted him in expected Hashem fashion. She was a buxom blond with hazel eyes. Wearing a short burgundy dress, she had a thin veil clipped from her cap to her hair.

'Welcome aboard, sir,' the attendant said with the most marked Filipino accent.

The man was unsurprised, certain she must be one of those mixed ethnicity Filipinos so popular among the Brunei royals.

She showed him to his seat and went to get him a refreshment.

As she walked away, he spotted a digital tablet on the table in front of him. The device was not part of the plane.

He picked it up and the screen came on to a video of a small woman with dark, short hair. Sitting on a cot, terrified. She seemed to be shivering. No blanket. No pillow. In a small, windowless room he did not recognize. Behind her, there was a pail he knew—from experience—would contain her excrement. And any other bodily fluids she would expel.

A text in Mandarin began to scroll beneath her image.

'Long time no see, Ayup. You will do as we say, or she will know you betrayed her.'

All along he feared the Chinese state might have taken his wife— instead, it seemed they had his mother.

9

X.XXXXX° N, 1XX.XXXX° E

South China Sea

2023 | Present

The dive boat had gone far enough from shore that the Royal Pulau Rahsia resort seemed like a dying star in the blackness of a distant cosmos. A few metres from where the vessel was anchored, an illuminated buoy bobbed like a miniature sun in the onyx waters—a guide for resurfacing divers. The full moon was high but obscured by an unexpected gauze over the charcoal evening. There was no breeze, and the only sound was the rhythmic lull of the sea against the hull.

In the central cockpit, underneath the starboard bench, Raed had fallen asleep to the rocking of the waves. He was further hidden from view by the portable drinks cooler that had been set in front of the seating. He awoke at a sudden cramp in his stomach. Noticing the quiet, the boy thought to take a look at where the boat had stopped, hoping it was someplace other than Kota Kinabalu. His plan was to slip into the sea and swim to shore.

As he carefully slid on his back towards the aft deck, Raed spotted the Chinese man in the cockpit, sitting portside beneath the flybridge. Just across the cooler behind which he'd been hiding. The man was glued to his mobile. Above him in the upper helm station, the skipper looked out to sea smoking a cigarette. A beer bottle held loosely in his hand. The lights on board seemed to have dimmed, and the three deck hands were napping to the side. Other than the buoy, there was nothing around them but darkness.

Raed's pulse raced. He hadn't considered when he stowed away that the boat would anchor in the middle of the sea.

'*Hei!*' A voice in the void.

The boy turned to see people coming out of the waves. He hurriedly slid back towards his hiding spot, rolling to his side so he could see what happened on deck.

'What a bust!' Jordi proclaimed as he grabbed hold of the boarding ladder in the stern. A newly awakened deck hand rushed to take his scuba vest and help him on to the boat.

'Too murky, sir?' The skipper climbed down from his perch to assist with the dive gear.

'Maybe we should've gone to where those weird glowing things are . . .' Ferran wondered as he climbed out of the water on to the swim platform.

'There are no weird glowing things, sir,' came the dive master's prompt reply. He and Robbi were still in the sea removing their scuba vests. 'That's just some new urban myth. There's usually some bioluminescent squid here—but for some reason, none were out tonight.'

While the deck hands ran around sorting out the wet gear, the skipper grabbed drinks from the cooler and offered them to the divers on deck. Jordi took a beer then sat in the cockpit next to the only dry guest among them.

'¿Qué, *papi chulo,* see anything interesting up here?' Jordi tried to peek at the Chinese man's mobile screen—he didn't flinch. His phone had a privacy film to protect it from rubberneckers.

Thwarted, Jordi turned to the others. 'If I had known this night would be such a bust, I would've brought my goody bag . . .'

With everyone back on board, the boat was readied for its return to the resort. Deck hands scurried to pull in the buoy, put away equipment, and refasten near-empty scuba tanks in the storage area, while the divers unzipped their wetsuits and towelled off, unwinding in the open aft deck.

In the darkness of his hideout, Raed slipped a hand into his pocket to make sure he hadn't lost Maki's beaded bracelet. Anak would think him stupid if he had.

Across the cockpit, the Chinese man's face suddenly lit up. He lifted his gaze from his mobile and stared at the empty bench by the drinks chest. Then, he rose and strode towards it—before turning around and heading for the stern.

Raed lay stock still. Both his hands on his chest. He dropped the bracelet when he heard the man approach and didn't notice that it had slipped out from under the bench. Maki's string of shiny purple stones lay next to the cooler in the hazy moonlight.

From the stern, the Chinese man went onto the outer starboard deck. He looked at his phone and stopped along the safety railing to scan the waters.

'If he came to spot dolphins, he chose the wrong time to do it,' Ferran whispered to Robbi, who stifled a grin. The two divers watched from the swim platform as the silent Chinese guest walked around the boat to the bow, then returned to sit across them at the back.

Irked by the presence, Ferran rose and headed for the drinks cooler. 'What can I get you, Mr X?'

In a heartbeat, Robbi—Mr X—joined the tall European at the chiller.

Unknown to them, just inches away, Raed was beneath the bench struggling with stomach cramps. Afraid he might get discovered, the boy felt the onslaught of another headache.

'You don't seem like a beer man . . .' Ferran bantered over the cooler.

'Good guess,' Robbi replied, self-conscious. Afraid of the sparks he was feeling.

'You blush so easily . . .' Ferran whispered, tracing a finger across Robbi's cheek. 'It's cute . . .'

Robbi pivoted to obscure the gentle touch from prying eyes. But he didn't pull away. With a slight smile, he appraised the chiselled man towering over him. Piercing dark jade eyes, burned chestnut hair, and broad, golden chest. Then, he caught himself—and lowered his gaze.

'It's ok . . .' Ferran intimated as he bent to get a drink from the cooler, covertly grazing Robbi's suited leg in the process.

His skin tingling under the neoprene wetsuit, Robbi stood rigid. In that instant, everything around them disappeared. There was only him—and the sculpted European beside him.

Not knowing what to do, Robbi kept his eyes on the deck. As if the answers he'd long sought were written in the moonlight. In the platinum lunar gloss of the polished planks, Robbi spotted what appeared to be a familiar glint. An unexpected item next to the chiller.

Puzzled, he bent to retrieve the coiled bracelet—just as a crack like thunder ripped open the tender evening.

'Aiiiii!' Jordi leaped behind the heap of life vests. The skipper—shot dead—dropped like an anchor from the upper deck helm into the sea.

A smaller motorized boat pulled up alongside them, loaded with men brandishing machine guns.

Frantic, deck hands raced to get the dive boat moving. *Crack, crack, crack*—each was shot before completing their task.

Agile as praying mantises, armed men hopped aboard to take over. One raised the anchor, while another climbed up to the flybridge to steer the vessel.

The Chinese man by the swim platform was led at gunpoint to the storage area, made to unfasten each scuba tank—potentially explosive—and chuck it into the sea.

In the cockpit, along with the dive master, Ferran had his hands up. Wine spritzer bottles shattered at his feet. Not far, Jordi trembled behind the pile of life vests, and Robbi lay prone on the deck, terrified that his best day in a while might be his last. His head was turned to the side and in the shadows beneath the bench, he was stunned to detect a stowaway. The fear in their eyes united them in silence.

One of the armed men on board called out to the other vessel. There was a loud exchange in a language Robbi didn't understand— then, the smaller craft darted away. Its captain firing his weapon into the air.

Within seconds that seemed eternal, the dive boat's engine roared to life. It swerved sharply to the east, heading further away from Sabah and the Royal Pulau Rahsia resort.

On the aft deck, the frenzied abductors—their faces uncovered—trained their guns at the cowering passengers. Their leader scurried about finishing his cigarette. Gaunt and weather-beaten, he pitched it into the sea when he was done, ordering the hostages to be brought before him. As they were lined up, he walked around each one, appraising them as if buying cattle.

'*Puti!*' he shouted after studying Jordi. White.

'*Puti, din!*'—white, too—he barked when he was by Ferran.

Approaching the dive master, the armed man declared, '*Ay, lokal!*' He then had the Sabah native turn and observed his gait.

Robbi realized the bandits were assessing their identities and how much each of them might be worth.

When he got to the resort's Chinese guest, the armed assessor spat out a wad of saliva, '*Intsik!*' Pointing his weapon, he took the man's mobile and wristwatch.

The bandit stopped at Robbi next and slowly looked him over. Unable to tell where the pale-skinned, clean-cut diver was from. He shone a mobile phone torch in Robbi's face, then again hocked up saliva, '*Intsik, din!*'

Robbi was about to correct him but saw the utter fear in Ferran's eyes. How quickly their moment had turned.

As they stood on deck like unwilling initiates to a cult, another vessel pulled up portside. A multi-hull power boat with even more armed men. They fired a shot in the air.

From what Robbi could tell, the new arrivals were trying to get the dive boat to stop. And for one hopeful moment, he thought that maybe an unmarked coast guard boat had come to save them. All he understood from the heated exchange was 'congressman'—and then, someone on the power boat seemed to call his name.

Had a politician sent a team to rescue him? Robbi wondered. But how would anyone know this soon that they'd been abducted?

Like giant, sinister coconut crabs, armed men from the multi-hull tried to board the dive boat. They were shot at—blindly—by the bandit on the flybridge. It kicked off a heavy firefight. With sharp bursts booming like cannons and New Year's Eve all at once. In the infernal chaos, the boats collided. The dive master was killed, and instinctively, Robbi hit the deck just as Ferran and Jordi were riddled with bullets. Numb from shock, he barely registered when the Chinese man collapsed on top of him, bleeding from a constellation of wounds. Pinned in place, he felt the man's last breath escape—the rawness of it all nearly stopped Robbi's heart.

As the fighting moved towards the bow, he spotted the stowaway. The kid had managed to crawl to the stern unnoticed, using the lid of the portable cooler as a shield. Crouched by the swim platform, the boy's eyes again locked with Robbi's. He was wearing the bracelet that had been by the cooler. Just as Robbi spotted it, the kid pulled his shoulders back and winked, slipping effortlessly into the sea.

Before he could reason otherwise, Robbi went in pursuit of the bracelet. He slid out from under the Chinese man's corpse and crawled over the edge of the stern . . . taking his chances in the open waters.

Under the waves, he swam as far from the boats as he could, trying to keep an eye out—in the expanse—for the stowaway.

He only looked back when he heard the roar of an engine. The dive boat had been freed from the rapidly sinking multi-hull vessel and was being readied to go—manned by the fighters he thought would save them. Instead, the boat zoomed away as the remaining armed men dropped a trail of bodies into the sea.

Alone in the turbulent waters, Robbi crumbled. His silent cry reverberated like phantom knells in the desolate emptiness. He wept until the firmament was punctured and forcefully began to pelt him with rain.

An eternity later, he wearied and lost the will to keep afloat . . . but a scrawny hand pulled his head back out of the water. It was the stowaway, holding on to the chiller lid like a lifebuoy. The familiar purple bracelet still on his wrist.

There was nothing left around them of the duelling vessels. Or the dead who had earlier shared their voyage. The starless night bled into the ink black sea, and they were lost in the hollow vastness of the horizon.

The Myth of the Absent Spring

One winter morning, in the forgotten land of the Brooding Mountains with Countless All-Seeing Eyes, a noble Queendom was attacked by jealous warriors. In her mother's absence, the crown princess was taken prisoner by a warring chieftain determined to make her his bride. She was renowned for her wisdom and her skill in battle, and her abductor told her they would rule the world once they were wed. But the princess had already betrothed herself to the Goddess of Flowers, who searched tirelessly day and night to free her.

Consumed by loss, the goddess forgot to send the Spring, and an impermeable mantle of grief descended from heaven. Dark and dense, it devoured all in its path—the mountain's people and their flourishing fields. Everything alive vanished into the fog, leaving only craggy ravines and dried out rivers—the Earth's deepest veins drained of blood.

When the Cursed Veil of Mourning lifted, all that remained was a forest of stones piled high in columns, erect like spectral sentries on the barren range. Appearing to heaven like pockmarks—monuments to humanity's greed.

Blinded by an eagle when she tried to return, the enchanted Queen arrived too late to save her people's souls . . . and they were trapped forever in hollowed stone towers with haunted eyes that only saw destruction in all directions.

*A native legend told to Ingush refugee children

10

Koror

2023 | Present

It always began with a drop. As if she were staring into an abyss. The vertigo was nearly enough to wake her. Nearly—but it never did. Sleep would not let go until she approached the gorge. A bottomless pit of nothing that she would never forget. As she would never forget the screams of her twin brother when he slipped and fell through the chasm to his death. Or what she presumed it to be. There was no way anyone could know for sure, much less retrieve a body from that colossal canyon.

The vertiginous nightmare always seemed interminable—until, inevitably, she awoke in tears.

Time eased the frequency with which she was plagued with reliving what she thought was the worst day of her life—but she was only twelve then. There was so much more that was awful that lay ahead.

Valya Gorlenkova was born a long way from the ocean. In a rolling field surrounded by peaked mountains. But her dreams held no recollection of their beauty, only the harrowing horror of her war-torn childhood in the Caucuses. A cursed place whose name history has tried to erase and from which her people fled, only to return and again be driven away. They ebbed and flowed like imagined tides over faraway shores.

It was not her tears nor the crowing of the rooster that woke her this morning, but the ringing of the hotel landline on her bedside table.

With her eyes still shut, she put a hand out under the mosquito net to answer the call. No surprise, it was Metik.

'Where are you? The passengers are disembarking!'

'I sent a driver, Metik, do not worry,' she reassured him. The native Palauan rang her constantly with some anxiety or another. So much for his promise to be a silent partner. Other than his citizenship on her business permit, Valya did not need him for much else.

Valya, who took on a name that meant 'the brave one', always did things herself. And she was known for this throughout the islands. But as business improved, she passed on the task of doing airport runs to someone else. There was more at the bed-and-breakfast that needed her attention.

Metik ended the call without a goodbye.

Hot and sweaty, Valya lifted the mosquito net and rolled out of bed. Her single mattress had seen better days, but it was all she needed for her restless nights. That and the creaking ceiling fan. The equatorial heat could be more oppressive than the northern winters of her youth. She quickly padded barefoot across the floor to throw open her wooden balcony doors. She'd shut them the night before in the storm. Her room may have been the simplest in the small dive inn, but it was the only one on the top floor and offered the most dazzling view of the sea. Clear as glass and smooth as silk. Framed perfectly by betel palm trees. From her perch, she could see little damage from the storm. And as the morning sun pushed in, blinding as a blast of ice, Valya told herself this was all she needed. She'd always survived on so much less.

She shut her eyes and raised her face to the bright blue sky. A morning ritual to give thanks for another day. Despite being in her forties, her skin had a youthful glow—which she put down to her tropical life on the tiny island in the middle of the Pacific. It seemed to have spared her from the craggy profile of her people.

Gratitude to the cosmos expressed, Valya ran her calloused fingers through her dark, shoulder-length hair, loosening any tangles that could choke her aura.

Chi released, she went back inside to continue her daily cleansing. From her dresser, she picked up a stick of Palo Santo, lighting it to get rid of any negative energy. The so-called sacred wood had a distinct, transportive fragrance. She enveloped herself in its smoke before setting the stick back down. All the while, she whispered the many names of God.

Then, she struck her Tibetan singing bowl to further clear the day of evil. The bronze bowl's deep clang resounded through every molecule of air, echoing in each cell of her body.

Just as she was about to sit on the floor to meditate, a horde of tourists came into view. Loud, disruptive, oblivious. Rising above them, a tall stick waved a tiny red flag, and a voice in Mandarin blared over a megaphone.

Ugh.

There went her attempt at a peaceful morning. She rose from the grass mat and removed an elastic band from her wrist, tying her hair with it into a loose bun. Then, she exchanged her night shirt for her least stained tee and a fresh pair of linen trousers. Her flip-flops were by the door. She rinsed her face and gargled. She would've brushed her teeth but had run out of toothpaste a few days earlier.

With one more deep breath—and a comforting caress of the sacred beads she wore as a bracelet—Valya opened her door and walked down the three flights of stairs to the open-air lobby.

The Gal/Guy Inn was on the quieter side of Palau. A rustic bed-and-breakfast built to look like a cluster of traditional A-shaped *bai* houses. It sat on stilts—more cosmetic than functional—and had steeply-pitched thatched roofing. It also had a wrap-around patio and a brightly coloured facade that featured drawings and wooden carvings of local legends. Anyone would have thought the inn's name typical for a cheap dive retreat in a modest island country. But they would be wrong. Valya had named it for her homeland, long locked away in her psyche. *Ghalghaï.* She had altered the transliteration to make it easier for English speakers.

There was a private cove that could only be reached through the inn, with fine, iridescent sand and crystalline waters. A highlight for Gal/Guy guests.

Valya was careful to cultivate a subtle clientèle, who liked to scuba dive in small groups and spend the afternoon basking silently in the shimmering rays of a copper sunset. She didn't intend for the inn to be a spot for young adventurers or newly moneyed North Asians.

But the Gal/Guy was not far from Palau's famous Rock Islands and Jellyfish Lake—and lately, with the Internet boom, the inn seemed to have become a popular stop for the increasing tours of Chinese visitors. Every day, more of them came through the lobby to get to the cove. And they never stopped at the inn's beach-facing café for food or drinks.

From the lobby, Valya had a clear view of the Cove Café, which sat to the right of reception. The few in-house guests—just back from a sunrise dive—were nearly done with breakfast. She knew them all on sight. Sometimes, she even learned their names.

But at the table closest to the entrance, there were two men she had not seen before. She noticed them studying her and could almost hear their conversation.

'Hair's too dark . . .'

'They ain't all blondes, y'know?'

Americans—she thought, immediately. You could spot them a mile away. They were never as discreet as they thought. These two screamed military, *obviously GIs*, even in civilian clothing. Like the tourists, more soldiers arrived in Palau by the day. Courtesy of the Pacific island nation's long-standing agreement with its mighty ally. Closer to China but protected by the U-S-of-A.

As she neared the café, Valya pretended not to notice the men. It was a game she played to maintain her peace.

'She don't look like no Russki, bro.'

'Not all Ivans are tall, man . . .'

She was not going to correct them. Only foreigners felt the need to make assumptions. The locals didn't care where anyone was from. As long as they were paid their due, Palauans were happy.

'Check, please?'

She turned at hearing the obscure European accent. She couldn't place it. *A new arrival?* How did this one escape her notice? Valya made a mental note to double check the guest roster. She didn't want another visitor who was hiding from the law. So many came to *disappear* in tiny, isolated Palau. The last one at the Gal/Guy made quite a scene when he was discovered.

'Excuse me?' the older looking American called her attention.

She approached with a perfunctory smile. 'Yes?'

'The uh . . . Wi-Fi . . . doesn't seem to be working?'

'We only have Wi-Fi in the rooms,' she stated, with a twinkle in her sharp green eyes. 'The shared spaces are for guests to make *real* connections . . .'

From the way he looked at her, Valya knew the undercover GI didn't understand what she meant.

'There are better things to do here than be on the Internet . . . yes?' she smiled, indicating the view.

The Americans looked at each other. Neither replied. Without Wi-Fi, they couldn't access their e-wallets to pay for their meal or retrieve the photo they were meant to be verifying. There were troubling allegations about the inn's proprietor, a woman named Volenta something, and they had come to see her up close to confirm their suspicions . . .

But the only suspicion confirmed was Valya's—who thought it an ill-advised move for the two US operatives to have breakfast at their subject's dive resort.

'Enjoy your morning,' she gave them a slight nod as she walked away. Her attention was drawn by a boat far out on the ocean. She could see it just beyond the cove. It wasn't meant to be there, and she presumed it was either a trawler or a dredger. Stealing fish—or sand. Or perhaps, information. Spying on or sabotaging the undersea fibre optic cables that connected the Pacific to the world. Illegal activity no matter how you looked at it. But when their pockets were lined, local officials looked away. Sure, when it came to global warming and rising sea levels, they stood up to the big guys and played the victim card. But like most perps, the 'big guys' threw money at the problem—and like all survivors, the islanders found a way to make the most of a bad situation. They took what they could from anyone who offered—the Chinese, the Taiwanese, the Americans. No matter the politics. A state of affairs by no means exclusive to Palau.

A gong resounded from the check-in desk. An indication that new arrivals from the airport were nearly at the inn. Valya turned back from the beach to head towards reception. She stood by the entrance to welcome the new guests—but everyone who stepped out of the van was on their mobile phone, clearly perplexed at their loss of signal. Valya sighed. The inn was situated in one of the hardest areas in Palau for cellular reception. On purpose.

'What's the Wi-Fi password?'

'I can't be offline for too long . . .'

'But I had data when we landed . . .'

A symphony of concerns about connectivity.

Valya nodded at the employee to again ring the gong. That always got people's attention.

'Welcome to the Gal/Guy,' she bowed, her hands clasped together at her chest. She was met by cursory smiles. Save from a few young women—unabashedly Russian—who were gawking at the view.

'Wow, wow, wow!'

They promptly struck choreographed poses and took photos of each other.

How things had changed in the years since she first arrived in Koror.

'You take BαΩ, right?'

A young man with a trimmed beard broke her reverie.

'Sorry. Cash only. Full board and lodging deposited into the inn's account before arrival . . .' Valya explained, wondering how he got on the airport shuttle if he wasn't a pre-paid guest.

'Ah, I did see that on your site,' the man waved his mobile phone and smiled. 'But I thought since you were online, you'd have digital services . . .'

'Only the website,' Valya checked her annoyance and forced a smile. 'It's part of our . . . *mystique*. Our guests usually want to leave all that technology behind when they come here . . .'

'Of course. Rustic charm,' the bearded man concurred. 'Well, thanks for having us anyway on short notice.' Valya wasn't sure what he meant.

'Luc?' A petite woman with a sharp bob and an even sharper tone demanded his attention. 'Our room?'

'Of course, ma'am,' Valya jumped in, courteously leading *Luc* and his less friendly travel companion to the front desk.

'I bet the crime rate is low here with no cash around . . .' the guest ahead of them laughed, chatting with the receptionist.

Luc's companion sighed impatiently. 'It's all good, Nish'—he put a hand on her shoulder to try and soothe her—'we're in the middle of nowhere, too far for sure for extremists . . . or pirates.'

Valya wondered what had her new guests so anxious.

'There is signal in the rooms though, yes?' Luc kept any fear from his voice.

Valya heard the grating pinging of his mobile. deU¹S™. She would know it's self-righteous chimes anywhere. She learned all about it from Metik because so many of her previous guests were on it too. No matter the nationality, everyone seemed hooked on the nebulous, over-hyped application. Points for personal development. *As if some digital programme could make someone . . . 'better'.* In exchange for money, of course. But Valya knew from experience how terrible people could be. It was inherent. And there wasn't enough wealth in the world to restore a humanity that through the years had so voluntarily been given up.

Valya did not believe in redemption or transformation. Peace was all she ever sought from a spiritual practice.

This Luc seemed to her like a new recruit—he had yet to reach the vapid 'glow state' she'd seen on other users. And the impatient, terse woman with him—whose name Valya surmised was Nisha—was evidently *not* on the God app.

Nisha held up her hand to shush those around her. She was staring at her encrypted phone. The only device that didn't seem to have signal trouble.

'What?' Luc leaned over her shoulder. 'More on the dive boat?'

'Oh God—' the guest at the counter turned back to face them. 'Did you come from Sabah?'

'Sabah?' another guest asked, 'That's where the glowing jumper took a nosedive, right?'

'Did you hear about the bodies?' another new arrival stated. 'It was breaking news before we lost cell service . . .'

Valya did not know what her guests were talking about. A glowing jumper? Bodies? A dive boat? Maybe she should have picked up the latest papers. But she stopped reading them when Chinese 'investors' got involved in their coverage. She also rarely switched on the television. Preferring to get her information from a few, trusted, *direct* sources. Other than that, there was Metik. And he hadn't mentioned any of this. Which was surprising considering he fancied himself a raconteur. But as the proprietor of a dive retreat, she must look into any stories involving divers.

'What's this about a dive boat?' Valya's low voice gave no sign of emotion.

'You have not heard?' one of the young Russian women scanned her feed and found a clip from when she last had a connection. 'Here, look.'

Valya looked, and indeed, a dive boat—a posh one—had disappeared from a resort in Sabah. Also very posh. No trace of anyone aboard. But bodies had just washed up on one of the outer islands, suspected to be members of the boat's crew. They'd been shot. The newsreel ended and another one played automatically. Despite her better instinct, Valya kept watching.

The mobile screen filled with the face of a man she hadn't seen in years—but she'd know him anywhere. Square head, buzz cut, faraway look, cloudy right eye.

Edison. Edi. *Dead?* Dead! Poor Edi.

'Sabah police believe it could have been a drug buy gone wrong, and they suspect Wakamele-Rigold wasn't alone when he died . . .'

The photo of another man filled the screen. Thin, pale, clean-shaven. Valya flinched. It was the most minuscule of movements. She'd never seen the man before—but her veins froze.

'Valya! There you are!' Metik rushed to her side. 'I must speak with you'—he stopped at seeing the new guests—'urgently.'

'Later, Metik,' she seemed distracted. A state Metik had never witnessed her in. 'I must . . . I have . . . more urgent . . .'

And with that, middle-aged Valya, short of stature, seemed to leap towards the stairs, taking two at a time. Once in her attic room three flights up, she locked her door and ripped through the small space like a pent-up cyclone. She dug out a rarely used mobile and switched it on. Then, she went to the metal Buddha figure on her dresser, pressing in both its eyes simultaneously. An inch-wide panel opened on its back. From it, she pulled out a tiny decal. It did feel a little blasphemous—using a sacred statue as a safe—but when you've lived through what she had, you didn't bother with trivial things like religious sensitivities. Valya knew the gods would understand the need to stash certain things away for emergencies. And if this didn't count as an emergency, she didn't know what did.

After making sure her mobile had its VPN and track blocker on, Valya scoured the online news feeds for more information on what the guest had shown her. Then, she pressed the tiny decal from the Buddha behind her ear.

'Call Melody . . .' she ordered the miniature encrypted mechanism, before remembering that she didn't have to verbalize instructions. The decal was a special nano-device she'd only recently received. No larger than a pimple patch. She'd never used it.

'*Fuckit*, Melody . . .' she muttered, distressed.

She took a slip of paper out of the Buddha. It had a code on it that she put into her mobile device. She didn't even know why she bothered. She knew there would be no answer. *Edi.* But she also knew better than to trust what she saw on the news. So, Valya kept trying. To reach both people she had promised to never call—unless imperative. But all she got from either of them was a dead signal.

She punched in another code that she knew by heart. It opened her private JUN0® accounts. All there. Prices had been up and down the past few weeks—but her total number of cyber-coins remained unchanged.

Then, for some reason, Valya felt like she had to do an accounting of her life—as if her time was nearly up. She found a familiar gap along her thatched wall covering and pulled out a small laptop. The roster for the week. She had another of her 'packages' due. She had to make sure this would be the last one for a while. It might be time for her to leave the islands.

Just then, a deep keen could be heard from the beach. Valya ran onto her balcony to see what she could see. She couldn't believe her eyes.

She retrieved her binoculars from the dresser to get a better look.

There, on the shimmering sand of the Gal/Guy cove, lay a pod of bloodied humpback whales thrashing their last.

THE PALAU POST

STORY LAYOUT LIST: Tomorrow's draft for news editors

HEADLINE

Chinese diplomats visit Palau from embassy in the Federated States of Micronesia (FSM).
[INSERT IMAGE]

- Donating millions of dollars' worth of newly-developed reinforced concrete and gravel from Xinjiang to strengthen airport tarmac, which will make it able to take larger charter flights with tourists from China.
[INSERT IMAGE]
- China also wants to help build much needed infrastructure: communications and renewable energy. Exploring contracts for wind and solar farms in waters around Palau.
[INSERT IMAGE]
- Despite official diplomatic relations with Palau, Taiwanese visitor numbers declining . . . they seem to prefer other locations.

BACK PAGE

- Humpbacks wash up on Ngemelachel shores.
[INSERT IMAGE]
Bleeding like they'd been knocked about or bumped into each other violently and repeatedly.
Scientists: No clue why. *Get official statement.*
Unlike fish in Southeast Asia, no sign of glow. Yet.

SUPPLEMENT: REGIONAL ROUND-UP

- Sabah Scandal
  [IMAGE HERE]
  Sabah glow jumper has been identified as a Chinese merchant from Kuala Lumpur. Makes sweaters for Middle East market. Investigators are reconstructing his movements. Believe he was pushed.

  Like the environmentalist, OD-ed on smash. But neither man was a known user. Or seemed known to each other. No mobile phones found on victims.

  One-eyed Edi was burned from within. *Spontaneous combustion?* Police suspect he had company. Female blood stains found on site.

- Coral Rush?
  [NO IMAGE]
  New Report: Smash found in Malaysian waters. Previously, only in Marshall Islands. How many more corals are afflicted with radioactive chemical imbalance? Officials fear it'll be harvested by competing criminal types looking to earn big in some sort of 'Coral Rush'.

  Noticeable differences between the Pacific coral and the South China Sea coral? No data released.

BUSINESS

- PRICES jumped on tech stocks. Speculation of a Taiwan company breakthrough. *Have they crafted holy grail of chips?*

- JUN0 Crypto aims to become greener.

11

London

1989

The abrasive grinding of metal on metal made Melody's hair stand on end, as if razor sharp edges were scoring her skin. She'd been in London a year and still couldn't believe that most British trains ran on diesel. How was her native Taipei—with its network of zippy electric trains—more sophisticated than this reputably progressive European city?

In the twenty minutes since pulling out of London Bridge Station, the diesel-powered Great Southeastern Line to Rye—otherwise known as 'Thumper'—screeched to a halt multiple times. At every sudden jolt and jerk, Melody tightened her grip on Orla. Their clasped hands were hidden from view by her acid-washed denim jacket strewn over their laps.

As had become habit, the two women were seated side by side facing the rear of the train. Melody's choice. She felt that traveling backwards made the short journey seem longer. And she was grateful for any more time with Orla.

It was a cozily overcast summer's day, and in less than two hours—Thumper willing—they would be in the medieval seaside town of Rye. A charmingly small community in England's southeast that they escaped to when they could. Historic architecture, picturesque winding streets, and scenic views. It was like falling through a time hole. An enchanting place where nothing from their current lives could touch them.

The train lurched forward, and again, Melody squeezed Orla's hand.

'S'alright, love,' Orla winked, 'just Thumper's usual diesel jig . . .'

Melody smiled but remained anxious. Since surviving the St Paddy's Day bombing, every little thing made her jump. Even music—long her solace—didn't calm her. Instead, she felt it clouded her focus. Distracting her from the present moment. Maybe if she had been paying more attention to her surroundings that night at the Elephant in the Cellar, she would've noticed something amiss and they would have left the bar before the explosion. She'd replayed that evening over in her mind numerous times, and though there was no way any of them could have known an attack by Northern Irish republicans was imminent, Melody was still convinced she should have *felt* it in the ethers. Her mother raised her to be attuned to her ancestors and the signs of the Universe. Had leaving home affected her *balance* and thus her connection to the spirits? She wanted to put a hand over her protection bracelet for comfort, but she would have to let go of Orla to do so . . . so, she didn't. Trusting that Mazu, the Sea Goddess and Consort of Heaven, would shield her regardless. She was certain Mazu was the only reason they got out alive that night when things could've been so much worse.

As the train thundered slowly through East London, Melody looked out the window to regain her equilibrium. Beneath heavy clouds, a dreary smog hung over the city. All that grey—and Thumper's clangourous chugging—was suffocating. She could barely hear herself think, much less talk to Orla. So, hands clasped, the travel companions sat quietly, side by side. Lulled by the rhythm of the track.

In the six months they'd known each other, Melody felt like she had spilled her entire life into Orla. Finally, her soul felt contained. Seen. Celebrated even. A change from the way she was treated at home. Where she knew her father—the highly regarded Eustace Lin—always wished she were born a boy.

One of Taiwan's most successful entrepreneurs, Melody's father sent her to the LSE as a contingency plan, to give her 'a shot' at success should she take over the family company, which would happen unless she found an appropriate husband. Her father had no choice. And neither did she. Melody was his only child. Destined to inherit his legacy. As such, it was her *duty* to deserve it.

Widely known as Mr Yu—short for Eustace—Melody's father was close to Taiwan's authoritarian regime. His family having come with its rulers' predecessors from China, in exodus after they lost control of the country to the Communists in 1949. This meant that his early businesses got a lot of *official* support when those nationalist Chinese exiles began to rule Taiwan. And when the time came, he was given the government contract to modernize systems and manufacture their computers. So, the family's small electronics firm—Surf Silica LINc—rode what her father called 'the wave of the future' to a multi-million-dollar fortune. Specializing in the microchips that powered digital technology.

Her mother, deemed by her father's associates as an *inoffensive* local woman, spent most of her time in temples. Ornately designed in gold and bold, bright colours, the opulent religious shrines were basically community halls. Like a country club might be in England. Through her temple activities, Melody's mother got to know everyone, but—more importantly for Mr Yu—everyone got to know her. It put the whole family in good stead with the neighbours. Mrs Yu was sweet and unassuming. An understated conversationalist. She may not have been raised speaking Mandarin, but when Taiwan's Chinese Nationalist rulers made it the official language, she learned it quickly. So, Melody was taught English in school, spoke her mother's native Hakka at home, and was fluent enough in Mandarin to not be an embarrassment to her father.

But with Orla—*Orla*—Melody didn't have to speak at all. After finally finding her voice away from family, she realized that the silence she shared with the Irish woman sitting beside her was more potent.

She gazed at the beautiful soul listening to the latest gift sent over by her father from Taiwan—Surf Silica's newest portable music player: the SS2. Orla's thick flowing locks—the colour of roasted chestnuts—bounced along to the beat of a private song. Her burnished emerald eyes sparkled in the carriage's dull lighting. Melody could look into them forever, those eternal eyes which—unlike her father's—saw nothing but the good in her.

This was all she wanted—to be this carefree, happy . . . *stranger.* Melody didn't recognize herself at all. In London, with Orla, it was like she was someone else—but at the same time, she'd never felt more herself.

There was a word for what they were to each other—but neither of them spoke it.

Orla lifted one side of her headphones and winked. 'You sure you don't want a listen?'

Melody shook her head. She didn't need more noise.

Taking their joined hands from beneath the jacket, Orla raised them to her lips and planted the gentlest of kisses on Melody's manicured fingers. The blush immediately rose to Melody's cheeks and just as rapidly disappeared, traveling like the temporary blaze of a million fireflies. She was remembering where things went the last time her fingers were so close to the Irish girl's mouth. The thin, coral-hued lips were a gateway to her core.

'What are ye thinkin?' Orla whispered.

Melody had learned to read Orla's expressions. She was being teased. It embarrassed her that Orla could tell when she thought about their physical . . . *communion.* She had never experienced anything like it. Her family in Taipei would be horrified, despite being Taoists who believed in acceptance and 'going with life's flow'. It went against every conservative social rule they had taught her. Everything she had to be as her father's daughter. Was this why she was . . . *out of sync?*

'Yer da's wee gadget is the *craic*!' Taking off the headphones, Orla's broad grin said it all. 'It hasn't skipped once!'

Previous models of the trendy portable compact disc players were so sensitive to motion that even the slightest bump affected how they read data. Skipping through songs the way diesel trains jerked on the track. But, as always, Melody's father was ahead of the curve. His Surf Silica LINc had found a way to stabilize the delicate disc player and its laser reader. And a perk of being his daughter was getting first dibs on the prototype of any advancements.

'Glad you like it,' Melody beamed. 'I'll let him know his Sonic Strider 2 is a winner. I really didn't think it would pass a British Rail test!'

'Could do with a cooler name though,' Orla remarked, light-heartedly. 'What does Mags think of this?'

'Haven't shown it to her . . . you know how she gets,' Melody confessed.

'Aye, didn't want her taking it apart, yea?'

'Exactly!'

In sync, they burst into laughter. A sound more divine to Melody than the healing bells in Taipei's ancient Bao'an Temple.

Temple. She hadn't gone in a while, but being with Orla was— *transcendent.*

Again, the train ground to a halt. Melody began to wonder if they would ever reach their destination. Not that it mattered. Traveling with Orla was enough.

Sitting on the tracks, it hit her that at some point, the journey would end. They would have to get off the 'train' . . . and what then? Where did this course lead? Would she have to go home? Melody didn't want to think past the present. Past her life in London. She didn't want to think beyond graduation day.

Thumper. She would focus on Thumper. Which had just restarted its painful chugging to Rye. Rye—with Orla. A three-day weekend without Mags. Whom they still hadn't realized they had not fooled.

'D'you think Maggie's been weird lately?' Melody asked.

Orla hadn't even considered it. From the time she first met a teen Wei Jing in an East London squat, the girl had been an odd one. She hardly spoke, only wore black, and kept to herself. But it wasn't a peace-filled silence. And as the immigrant Wei Jing transformed into a more British 'Maggie', her angst reeked off her like the stench of stagnant waters. Orla made it her mission to break through the sullen girl's shell. She knew from experience that sometimes those who most needed a lifeline never asked for it.

'She's . . . been more *sulky* than usual,' Melody expounded. 'I think she feels left out.'

'Well, much as I love her, I don't exactly want a threesome.'

'That is not what I meant,' Melody playfully swatted Orla's knee.

'You might've! In some backwaters of America—'

'Orla!' Melody chuckled, putting her hand over the girl's mouth to stop her speaking. 'I'm serious. I worry about her sometimes. She's . . . quieter and has been glued to the news—Maggie! Plus, she's got really jumpy around other Chinese people. If not for the fact that she *is* Chinese, I would think she's racist!'

Orla chortled, then shrugged. 'Aye, she's just . . . you know. A wounded bird.'

Melody raised her brows. That was never how she'd thought of aloof and detached Maggie.

'Her da abandoning the family really did a number on her . . .' Orla explained. 'At least, she ended up in London. And—you see it—with her smarts, she's going to get very far someday . . .'

'She never speaks of her mom . . .' Melody pondered.

'Ever think that maybe she has no memories of her ma to speak of?'

'Really?'

'Aye,' Orla affirmed. 'That's what I know. Her ma died soon after they moved here. So, she is it. On her own. When we were living in the squat—you know, penniless and hungry—I think she had a crush on me.'

'Stop it,' Melody giggled, 'you think everyone has a crush on you.'

'I was bound to be right sometime. Thank *feck* I was right about you.'

She leaned in for a kiss but was thrown off balance as the train stuttered entering a tunnel. The carriage lights flickered. Once she righted herself, Orla planted a soft one before Melody could demur. Against the tunnel's darkness, the severity of the train's lights made them feel even more exposed. Orla pulled away before any of the other commuters might've seen them.

Across the aisle, towards the opposite end, a man wearing dark glasses and a faux leather jacket was reading a book he had picked up from a thrift shop—Dr Susan Baker's *The Feminine Declaration*. He'd followed the pair onto the carriage from London. Slipping a small camera from behind the manifesto's pages, he snapped a photo of the women, hoping to capture on film how in love they were.

* * *

The rain etched heavy lines of smog down the large glass window. Just beyond the smears on the pane, the churlish Thames churned like sewage. The morning had turned grimy and dank. All streaks and smudges like the blurred lines of an impressionist painting.

Maggie had been sitting in the waiting room of Guys & St Thomas' for nearly an hour. BBC News was on the telly, but she was tired of seeing the images of the massacre in China. The military had mowed down anti-government protesters in Beijing with tanks. Hundreds of people—mostly students—had been killed. It was the first large display of public dissent against the ruling Communists. Breaking news, even in London, going on a week.

Absentmindedly, Maggie flipped through an outdated magazine. Her eyes were on the scene outside. Trains rumbled across the river to Westminster, like despondent light beams trying to cut through a heavy haze. In the paralysing brume, Big Ben marked a plangent 10 a.m. Maggie was certain that by then Orla and Melody must have got to Rye.

'The Chinese government has promoted the interim military commander who led the crackdown on demonstrators in front of the Gate of Heavenly Peace. Calling him the paramount soldier for defusing a "counterrevolutionary riot" . . .'

'It's a massacre no matter how you see it . . .'

'Some of the protest leaders were identified as minority Uyghur students from Xinjiang Province . . .'

'Across China, the army officer is being touted as someone to be emulated and praised . . . for safeguarding the nation's stability against the ravages of "misguided intellectuals" . . .'

'Rising military star . . . Zhou Sheng Feng . . . architect of the brutality . . .'

Maggie had had her fill. 'Could you turn that down please?'

As if there wasn't enough sadness in a hospital—why put the news on in the waiting room? Such savagery. Was that in the Chinese psyche? An undeniable part of their circuitry? Was that in *her* blood? Was she . . . *pre-programmed?* How much do you inherit from your race?

Her week watching the news showed her that the ills of socialism were causing communist governments to fall across Eastern Europe—but why not in China? Were people there so brainwashed and powerless as to be content in their plight as sheep? And what could she do about it from so far away? Did she even want to do something about it? It had nothing to do with her . . . right?

But no matter where she went, people took one look at her and saw her as part of that data tree structure. Just another node in the root dysfunction of her heritage.

'Mr Lu? The doctor will see you now . . .'

'It's Miss.'

'Oh, right. Sorry,' the nurse looked nonplussed despite the apology.

She could be forgiven the misimpression, given Maggie's severe haircut and her lack of breasts or hips. Barely five-foot tall, she often looked like a fifteen-year-old boy. But that's not why she was here.

'Hello again, Wei Jing,' Dr Brown greeted.

'Maggie, please. I prefer it.'

'Yes, yes, of course. Maggie . . .' he stood corrected. 'You weren't named after the old battle-axe Thatcher, were you?'

He looked at her chart and noticed her date and place of birth—long before Thatcher's term. And far away from London.

'Terrible news . . . this business in China. Just terrible . . .'

Maggie said nothing as he waffled on about the Heavenly Gate massacre, all the while riffling through what she presumed were her test results. *Ah, the British*, she thought, *make them uncomfortable and they blather*. He would likely go on and on to fill the silence, unsteadied until she eased his anxiety.

'I was in Beijing once . . .' the nattering doctor offered. 'Looked into your herbal traditions. I wasn't sure how to refer to anyone. Awfully confusing how you all write your surnames first . . .'

Maggie's suspicions were confirmed. He clearly thought they were all connected. To put him out of his misery—and end hers—and if only to stop the talk of China: 'I'm from Limehouse.'

The doctor looked up at her.

'East London?' she continued. Maybe he hadn't heard of the grottiest part of town.

'Ah. Yes. Yes, of course . . .' more blathering. 'So—your test results—you have diabetes. Type 1.'

Right, thought Maggie, *just get stuck in.*

'Let me explain . . .'

'I know what it is.' She shut him down. Her IQ was likely higher than this chap employed by Public Health. She did not need him to explain a disease she had worried about all her life.

'You will need daily injections . . .' he stopped to go through his papers and then his desk. Not finding what he was seeking, he buzzed for the nurse. 'You must change your diet and do some exercise,' he said, 'I'm afraid you may be more sedentary than is good for you . . .'

'Pardon?' The nurse was surprised at the unexpected assessment.

'Sorry, not you, Felicity,' Dr Brown raised a hand in apology, 'I was talking to ah . . .'

'Maggie.'

'Yes, of course. Maggie.' The doctor smiled back at her politely. Pretending he had recalled her name.

'What is it, Doctor?' Felicity seemed impatient.

'My script pad, please—and the latest report on generics. Oh. And my schedule for next week? So difficult to keep track of things these days . . .' he muttered as the nurse left the room.

'Humanity could soon *efficient* itself to extinction.'

'Sorry?' The puzzled doctor reassessed his foreign patient. Her people were known for their precision and meticulous attention to detail, so, he was certain he must've missed something in her statement.

'Not long now. You won't need papers and notepads . . . or even a Felicity,' Maggie tilted her head towards the door. 'The digital revolution has started, and we are on the verge of upending civilization.'

'Ah. How fascinating,' he muttered, as the nurse returned and he quickly filled in the prescription. 'Very *Dr Who* and all that . . .'

'That's science fiction,' Maggie stated. 'But . . . there really are mathematical solutions to the world's problems. Life is one big equation, and soon, we will find a way to control it. Of course, that may also be what kills us.'

Dr Brown looked positively dumbfounded.

'Never mind,' Maggie uttered. She'd done it again. Lost the audience, as her friends often put it. She took the prescription from his hand and left.

The rain had stopped over London and she decided to walk back to the dorm. She needed air. Not that there was anything refreshing about the summer's mugginess. Filth hung in the atmosphere like the spectral dust of ancestors on heirlooms.

Once she got to Waterloo Bridge, instead of going across it for the LSE, Maggie kept on towards Blackfriars, continuing east past Southwark Cathedral and Butler's Wharf. As if pre-programmed, she went north over Tower Bridge, then turned to the dockyards and her mother's last known address. She kept tabs on the woman despite herself.

They'd moved to the UK when Maggie was eight. Her father, an unremarkable civil servant, stayed in Guizhou. One of China's poorest provinces. A stern and disciplined man—as far as Maggie recalled—he studiously rose up the ruling party's ranks, from being their village's dull administrative assistant to its mediocre chief. Somewhere along the line, he left them. Next thing Maggie knew, she and her mother were living in Limehouse. And she never saw her father again. She supposed she should be grateful, but it wasn't easy growing up alone with a broken-hearted alcoholic.

1/4 83-B Leaderbrooke Road E1W. She'd arrived. Through the window, Maggie could see her mother knocking back a can of cheap cider with a stranger. The man had his hand in her shirt. On the table, next to a bottle of pills, were several five-pound notes. Maggie counted a total of thirty quid. Seemed her mother had upped her price. Music was blasting and the BBC was on the telly.

Why the fuck would they not draw the curtain?

Maggie turned away when her mother got on her knees in front of the stranger. She refused to accept this was in her DNA. That she too would be held hostage by such weakness and despondency. She had to find a way to break the family cycle. It was all she thought of at school. How to apply maths to transforming the flow of energy in a circuit.

Diabetes. Her mother had warned her it was in her genes. A legacy of that mediocre man. If cutting herself off from her roots didn't free her from its shackles, then she *had to* find a way to change her wiring.

As she stood in front of her estranged mother's window, it again began to pour. Maggie turned her face to the sky and wondered if the sun was out in Rye. She couldn't understand why her friends still hid their relationship from her. She was no idiot.

People. Sigh. Maggie thought humans the most complex series of mathematical equations. But she was certain that Euler's Identity— the God formula—would help her discover the logic. The harmony underneath Life's chaos. And once deciphered, she would find a way to reconstitute it.

She walked back the way she came, stopping at St Katherine Docks. Against the shadows of its willow trees and repurposed warehouses, the ashen rain quivered like white noise, layering the marina in hurried strokes and textures. Set apart by a canal from the other brick structures, the hulking form of the three-storeyed Dickens Inn called her out of the cold.

Drenched, Maggie clambered up the wooden stairs to the timber-framed pub and went straight for the bar. It was so dim the room seemed lit by candles. The uneven floor felt carpeted by straw, just as it would've been when the place was first converted from a factory. The ceiling's low beams recalled the charms of its eighteenth-century origins, and the multi-paned windows that lined the front wall peered out discreetly onto a flower-draped porch. It was rustic and robust . . . and familiar.

She ordered a pint of Guinness and went up to the second floor, choosing to sit at a balcony table overlooking the docks. How she loved the lifeless marina that contained the gurgling Thames. A few yachts sat idle where cargo ships once berthed, and a lone cyclist crossed a footbridge towards the Tower of London.

She took a sip of her drink and watched its froth rise back up to the top of her pint glass. The slow ebb and flow on a head of stout. It was almost musical. Like the syncopated pulse of East London. As gloomy and morose as she felt.

Then, she thought of the surge and quell in her parents' country, the dynamic of power and weakness in her blood. Her friends, and their chains of heritage . . . the world careening towards its own extermination.

So, on the shadowed balcony of that rebuilt thatched-roof structure, Wei Jing Lu sat alone with her genius. It was midday, but the sky was turned down as if it was evening. And the rain tried to cleanse away the muck. A difficult task in a cursed place that once served as the city's gateway for the world's excesses. She stared quayside at the locks that controlled the river's flow into the marina and began to feel a surge within.

Like everyone else, she was but a node on a universal motherboard—but there had to be a way to change its current. Her mind flipped through all she knew of numbers and sequences and computations. The maths of energy, family, and technology. She pondered over what a renowned scientist once said—that each advancement would be exponential and consume more power, which could then lead to catastrophic instability. But Maggie Lu saw the realm of quantum realities, and she would prove that it was possible to transcend that limitation.

Her pint of stout sat shimmering half-consumed in the half-light, and in the cooling day, her black clothing absorbed what heat there was. A spark, a flame, a flurry of sticks and slashes . . . a swell that urged her to take her pen and start scribbling where she could. The few paper napkins on the table—and the back of her unfolded prescription—were not enough to contain her flow, as Wei Jing Lu rushed to put down what became her manifesto.

Declaration

Transforming Humanity

VIEW:

I attest that it is a verifiable and knowable fact that all human beings are interconnected in a fundamental way. Whether we like it or not. No person can truly be an island. This is rooted in the laws of the Universe and the mathematics that describe it. It is undeniable but not unalterable.

GOAL: (not to make us islands but use our interconnectivity for good)

As a mathematician, a person of knowable constants, I intend to use Euler's Identity, the fixed proof of God's existence, to invert the limitations of 'reality' and change humanity's downward trajectory.

METHOD: $e^{i\pi} + 1 = 0$

With numbers as the basis of all life, the perfect computation that is Euler's Identity will be our gateway to enlightenment. No churches imbued with meaning, no holy books, no lyrical gospels. Just the tangible, reliable figures of the language of maths.

This elegant equation unifies the five constants, in whose simplicity lies the profound revelation of the essence of harmony. The embodiment of the intricate relations governing our world.

DRIVE:

Harnessing the Energy within. We must transform the currents that move our civilizations by learning from our chequered histories and the errors of our institutionalized myths.

If maths can tell us where we are and where we are headed, it can also reveal—beyond deities—how to perform miracles. Not only through mechanical or technological advancements but also in the sphere of human energies. We can transcend the barriers of conventional thinking and embrace the power of mathematical truths to reshape the world we inhabit.

REDEFINING POWER:

The Universe is a closed circuit. The total amount of energy is constant—it is the forms that change. As such, we shall no longer see energy as a limited resource extracted from the Earth but as an abundant force that permeates the very fabric of existence. Our understanding of mathematical principles and their synergy with the physical world shall pave the way for novel systems of energy. I will find a way to harness that power without depleting the Earth.

EMPOWERING COMMUNITIES, EMPOWERING THE WORLD:

Our mission extends beyond mere technological advancements. As we transform humanity's motherboard, we must ensure equitable access to this new energy paradigm. By enabling communities worldwide with knowledge, technological infrastructure, and sustainable practices, we shall bridge the power divide. No longer shall energy be a privilege reserved for the few; it shall become a universal birthright.

CONCLUSION:

In the realm of mathematics, where logic converges with beauty, we find the means to shape a better world. With Euler's Identity as our beacon, we shall transform the energy of humanity.

The time is now to rewrite the code of our existence and thrive.

TO DO:

Create a network wherein everyone is an equal participant and partner. The antithesis to those who weaken a node to service the system. This will unleash a powerful current of potential that will upgrade humanity.

Signed:

Wei Jing Lu
London, England
20 September 1989

12

Runit Island

2001

'I'm your local guide, Edison,' pause for effect, 'thank you for journeying—'

'Dammit . . . wait,' the filmmaker stepped back from his viewfinder to check the recording, 'I think we need to do that again.'

Edison raised a hand over his one good eye to block out the sun. 'What's wrong now?' It was the only way he could see the man behind the camera. Jack, the beanstalk American. Still on a quest to get his country to clean up its nuclear waste in the Marshalls. Since they were introduced by Edi's grandpa Noa at that first village meeting, the two had become fast friends. Colleagues of sorts. More like comrades in arms. Men on a joint mission. Determinedly working together to rid the islands of the irradiated refuse. Their impassioned campaign filled most of Edi's days, especially since he had lost his Jimma Noa earlier in the year. To dysentery, after a storm surge washed the sea and sewage into the source of their drinking water.

But besides the occasional mention in the *Marshalls Weekly*, the men were a long way from being heard by their intended audience. And scanning the blinding horizon from his current elevation, it dawned on Edi how far from anywhere they truly were.

Almost 700 miles from Majuro, they had travelled nearly three days north on a small, rundown ferry to the jaw-shaped Enewetak

129

Atoll—counting unscheduled stops for emergency repairs. They then paid some local fishermen to take them across the ring of coral islands to their final destination. Dodging reefs and sunken wrecks from World War 2, it took them two hours to get to Runit. The narrow, uninhabited island looked like a fish spine wedged between variations of crystal blue waters. On one side, the lapping cobalt ocean, on the other—the turquoise shallows of the world's second largest coastal lagoon.

Without a cloud in the sky nor a tree for shade, Edi stood exposed atop the scorching concrete dome that was the reason for their journey.

Almost as wide as the island, the Dome—aka the Tomb—was nearly 400 feet in diameter. It felt to Edi like standing on a massive light reflector. To make matters worse, all 280 pounds of him were covered, head to toe, in white plastic. A protective polyethylene suit. Under the tropical sun, it was like wearing his own personal sauna.

'Something's interfering with the recording . . .' Jack, the amateur auteur, was fiddling with his camera.

'Is it the Tomb?'

'Uhm . . . Maybe? I dunno—'

'What do you mean you "dunno"? You said this stupid suit was enough of a safety precaution! Now sumthin's messin with your gear?'

They had snuck onto the island to see the Tomb for themselves. A 350-foot crater filled with more than 100,000 cubic yards of nuclear waste. That's thirty Olympic-sized swimming pools of toxic debris and contaminated soil from twelve years' worth of nuke tests, 'disposed' off by being shoved into an unlined hole in the ground and capped with only eighteen inches of concrete. The facts of it blew Edi's mind.

More than twenty years had passed since the—unlined!—Tomb was sealed, but Runit was still entirely off limits due to high radiation levels. So much had been released into the atmosphere—and lingered—it was a wonder more of the Pacific was not blocked off. Halfway in the vast ocean between Australia and Hawaii, these atolls were chosen for testing the most powerful atom bombs because they were deemed sufficiently remote. But how do you stop contamination across open air and water? Edi imagined the hazards from the buried waste already seeping into the porous ground.

From where he stood, Edi thought the enormous Tomb looked like the Earth's navel. A scar left by a traumatic severance. If where life began were toxic and could also spell its end.

'Well, I'm not sure about the radiation . . .' the self-taught Jack was about to explain his non-expert diagnosis of the malfunctioning equipment, but he saw Edi's face go from hot and sweaty to angry at the thought that he knowingly put them at risk. 'I mean—look, I saw some guys come back from here few months ago . . . and they're doing okay, so I figure we'd be fine.'

In the two decades since the waste was 'capped', sea levels had begun to rise. And with storm swells and quakes, the Tomb was showing signs of deterioration. All that toxic shit would surely leak into the ocean. If it hadn't already. Reports said the fallout from the testing in the Marshalls was a hundred times more radioactive than the catastrophic explosion at a nuclear power plant in Chernobyl, but what could the locals do? And for their troubles, the US only offered them a bunch of 'Band-Aids'—money, visa-free residency on the mainland, canned food—and that was meant to be that.

But if plutonium and other radioactive elements were seeping into the mighty Pacific then where would that leave everyone? Surely it would affect marine life and biodiversity? And not just in the Marshalls. Edi knew from childhood that the current travelled west towards the Philippines, then north past south-eastern China, Taiwan, and Japan. It's not like there were borders to the world's largest ocean. And really, only 1 per cent of the toxic waste was even buried. The rest dispersed above ground or was shoved directly into the lagoon.

'Are you kidding me, man?' Edi wiped the sweat trickling into his eyes and was about to march back down to the beach.

'Hang on,' Jack pleaded, nearly done tweaking the equipment. 'We needed to film this, dude. I swear an hour or two here won't kill us. I'm almost sure of it . . .'

'Almost?!' Hot and uncomfortable, Edi couldn't even take in that statement. Had he just put his life on the line to make a video that few people were likely to see? He reminded himself why he was doing this. His jimma, his bubu. How much he wanted to save their homeland. *His* homeland. Hanging out with Jack he learned that God's Gifts—the Marshalls—could be erased from the map in his lifetime and that really scared him. It was bad enough they were already practically invisible to the world. Not many knew where the islands were much less cared what happened to its people. He wanted to change that. Jack let him know that he could at least try. This work, their work, it was important. And it gave him a purpose. He'd never had one before. If anything, this could redefine his legacy. One-eyed Edi would no longer be just the fuck-up loser who was deported from the mainland.

'Man, it might be the tape,' Jack was certain he could sort it. 'Dammit. I thought I'd grabbed a new one . . .'

Seeming unconcerned about toxic poisoning, the boatmen who brought them over had caught a fish in the lagoon and cooked it over an open fire. The locals seemed to be enjoying the morning. They'd just made a week's wage to give the out-of-towners a ride. An infrequent but lucrative sideline. Just because no one was allowed on Runit didn't mean there were no visitors. The island was a magnet for adventurers and scavengers looking for leftover copper wire, steel, or any other material they could sell. The Chinese were buying all sorts of scraps. And every three months, med techs would come from the US to check the islanders around the atoll. Not to check *on* them, to *check them*. For radiation levels. Presumably. Not that they were ever told. The techs tested their food, their stool, their overall sanity. But they never received the results. They were just specimens to be examined.

'Okay, let's try again,' Jack commanded, 'I think it's just a crap tape. I spooled past the kink . . . should be good now.'

Right.

So, again, Edi delivered the closing monologue of their showpiece— this revelatory film, this exposé—they were going to use to wow the world.

'And . . . cut! This'll be great,' Jack was thrilled despite Edi's reticence. 'Trust me, this is exactly what we need to up the drama—not that we need to—and I will have it ready in time for the conference.'

'Are you sure I don't look like a joke?' Edi lifted the plastic hood on his head to flip his eyepatch back down. He didn't want to play up to the stereotype of the ignorant, 'silly' islander.

'You were perfect, man. People will be shocked when they see this—and who better to show them than a local who's living with the consequences?'

Jack-from-the-Mainland—as he was known on the Marshalls—paused the footage on a close-up of the network of long, dark lines that had appeared on the concrete dome. Like ominous cracks on a poisoned egg. Weeds were beginning to sprout like varicose veins. Their roots deepening the fissures on the porous sphere. Edi may not have gone to college but as he always said when he gave a speech about the Tomb, even he knew how dumb it was to bury toxic waste. And not even on hard bedrock but on coral! Coral that had already been damaged from all the testing. It was basically a radioactive coffin with holes in it. A massive marker for the death of civilization. *People could be so stupid.* But Edi's true test was coming up: Did he dare say this to an audience outside the Marshalls? He was meant to present their plight at the approaching Earth Conference in Japan, if Jack found them sponsors in time. He'd been looking on the Internet, but it was slow going. It could take several hours just to load a website. That independent Chinese pro who was handling the islands' connectivity seemed to be sorting everything himself. A much smaller, and likely cheaper, operation than the major providers. And since he seemed unaligned with any governments, there would be no obvious political repercussions for the Marshalls.

Filming done, the intrepid duo descended the Dome to the beach. Jack went to sit by some shrubbery to go over their footage. In front of him lay a teal-coloured tide pool, a watery pit the same size as the Dome. Another memento of atomic testing.

Just feet away, the boat crew were enjoying the last of their lunch. Edi envied their loose t-shirts and shorts. Much cooler than either of the crusaders in their plastic suits. Beneath the polyethylene, the heat sizzled, pinching Edi's skin like a million tiny crabs feasting in the tropical sun. He walked into the water hoping it would cool him. Only later did he worry about possible contamination.

As he stood there trying to breathe, Edi spotted a vessel in the distance like a mirage. It was a large one that he knew wasn't meant to be in these waters. They weren't near any transit passages or international shipping lanes. He thought it might be the Chinese Internet guy finally laying undersea cables so the Marshalls would no longer have to rely on expensive satellites for a connection. But what if it wasn't?

'Jack! Quick—' Edi motioned for him to zoom the vessel into view.

'What the f—?' Jack stood and pointed his lens at the horizon. 'I can't tell man—here, look. Is that a Chinese ship? Maybe Japanese? Their writing looks the same!'

'They're not supposed to be there—and we shouldn't be here!'

'Relax, it's not like they see us . . .'

'Let's get out of here,' Edi didn't want to get trapped on a heap of toxic waste if that ship lingered on the horizon.

'It's okay,' their skipper spoke up, 'they there all the time.'

That got Jack and Edi's attention.

'Sometimes they blow things up and we get fish washing up on our beaches—makes it easier when the catch comes to you!' he joked. 'Once, there was no ship, just a loud explosion—'

'What?!' Jack was surprised the men seemed so unconcerned.

But Edi understood that when people get used to scraps, a wave of dead fish could very well be seen as a gift from heaven. *Jolet jen Anij.*

'Oh, they never come close to shore,' the second boatman remarked. 'They stay out there to do their business—'

'And then they go away . . .' added the last member of their crew.

Done with their meal, the boatmen prepared quids to chew. They took betel leaves out of a small pouch and wrapped them around areca nuts generously sprinkled with a powdered mixture of fire-burned limestone and crushed coral.

'Few weeks later, another ship comes . . .' the skipper again.

Edi wondered what these ships were doing in the Marshalls' internal waters. Were they stealing fish? Mining marine resources?

Through his lens, Jack looked at the ship again. 'You know, maybe they're laying cables to host a data centre? I heard the new mayor was open to it . . .'

'That's nuts! Those use so much energy. It'll just mess up the environment even more,' Edi frowned.

'Well, I guess since it's already damaged, the Marshalls may as well get something out of it in the meantime, right?' Jack lowered his camera. 'It's all about balance, man, we just gotta find a way to tip things in our favour.'

'Last year, there was oil in the lagoon,' the second boatman shared. 'We still don't know how it got there, 'cuz those ships at sea don't come near. Remember that?' he looked to his crew mates.

'What?!' This was the first Edi and Jack had heard of an oil spill. 'Why was that not reported?'

'You know how it is, by the time word got out from Enewetak and someone came to check—it was gone.'

'What do you mean gone?' Edi asked.

'Washed out of the lagoon,' the boatman explained. 'Out to the ocean. But it sure did a number on the reefs . . . eating seafood was really bad for a while . . .'

Sweating profusely in their plastic suits, Jack and Edi watched as the locals carried on rolling their betel chews as if all were right in the world.

'You really think that's doing you some good?' the boatman laughed at their obvious discomfort. 'Just take it off and sit a while. We go when my tummy has settled.' He offered them betel quids as he stretched out on the sand and patted his dome-like stomach.

Edi had no plans of joining them. But Jack ripped off his plastic hood and took a quid. He put it in his mouth and sat down. Unaware that it was made with what was known as special 'spice', the powdered coral from Enewetak's lagoon. It was found to give the quid an extra kick. This porous coral that had long been exposed to radiation.

'Whoa . . . shit,' Jack blinked, looking around him very slowly. As if taking everything in for the first time. He turned to Edi, who was still standing, and smiled. Then, he reached out to the boatmen who were all laughing beside him.

'You okay, man?' Edi knew Jack had chewed betel quid before. But he'd never reacted this way.

Jack laughed—and without saying a word—gestured as if he were *speaking* to Edi.

One of the boat crew held out the last betel quid. Again, Edi refused. He didn't want to risk his sobriety.

Jack took the quid and shoved it in Edi's direction.

'I said no, dude,' Edi roared. 'Don't make me hit you.'

Jack and his new atoll pals just laughed. Seeming to share some secret. Then, he stopped and turned serious.

'You want to see your jimma?'

Edi was surprised by his friend's insensitivity. His jimma had just died—the question was not cool.

'No man, I'm serious . . .' Jack held out his hand.

Edi was so angry he didn't think he could hold it in. His head was pounding from the heat and his breathing had become shallow. His chest felt like it was caving in, squeezing the air out of him. He'd had enough. He ripped off the plastic suit and stretched out his tatted arms to the sky.

'Aaaaaaahhhhh!'

The inked navigational chart of his people rippled on his bicep.

He turned to face the men on the beach. No one spoke, but Jack stood up and put his arms around his friend, giving him a big wet kiss on the cheek.

Edi shoved him back. 'What the fuck, dude?'

You are not alone.

Edi could hear it clear in his head. *You are not alone.* It was Jack's voice—but his friend had sat back down and was spitting out some betel juice.

You are not alone.

'Stop it, Jack.'

It's the truth! Does it scare you?

Edi's cheek tingled where Jack had kissed him and he thought he was going mad from the heat. Yes, that was it. This was heat stroke. And he was hearing voices in his head. Jack's voice.

You are not alone, man. You are not alone . . .

'I said stop it!' Edi put his hands on his head, trying to shut out imagined voices. 'I am alone . . . I have always been alone . . . So stop it!'

Edison kept feeling the warmth of some invisible embrace, but he didn't trust it. He started twisting side to side as if hoping to free himself. Then he dropped to his knees and buried his face in his hands.

'Everyone's gone—Mạmạ, Baba, Jimma—and Bubu is so busy trying not to grieve. I have no one. Maybe that's my role—to end the suffering. To be alone. So no more of our line will have to feel this pain. No child of mine cursed with my lack of vision . . .'

'You are not cursed to be alone, my friend,' Jack spoke the words. Edi was certain he *heard* it. 'You just bear so much sadness that there's no space for joy.'

'Which therapist told you that shit?'

'Oprah.'

The friends burst into laughter. The fishermen, too. Edi's cheek still tingled from Jack's wet, betel juice kiss—and suddenly, he felt a nebulous, tenuous connection among them. He looked at each joyful man on the beach—and was swept by such an affinity that he was certain all five of them were one.

In solidarity, Edi took the remaining nuke-exposed betel quid from one of the boatmen and put it in his mouth. There was a blissful burst of flavour . . . and contentment. All at once, that earlier delicate connection sparkled and transformed into an undeniable web of light . . . shooting out from his limbs, his chest, and his head . . . linking him—and the others on the beach—to every atom of creation.

Shit. So this is what Jack is seeing . . .

For the first time in his life, Edi could see clearly out of both his eyes. And instantly, everything made sense.

There is no pain, no joy, no anger. Just calm and silence—a comforting balance through all timelines. His past and his future live within his present—and everything is happening in the now. He sees Jimma and his mạmạ, and his chest expands. He can breathe. Everything is light. And finally, he understands his people's wisdom about the ocean—how the waters connect them to the world, not set them apart.

Without words, the five of them on the beach understand each other. And sitting alongside the Tomb, they see the atomic explosions that created it. Oh the havoc it is wreaking on the environment! He sees there's also plutonium scattered on the beach like sand. Toxic radiation is everywhere.

They must stop the clock if they're to save the world.

In this moment, Edi realizes the power they all have, and again looks towards the horizon. He sees the vessel in the distance up close, as if he were right in front of it. He knows the flag it flies and can read its identifying marks. The ship waves the banner of the Isle of Man—and on its red hull, it bears the mark: $\Omega\pi L\alpha$. Not Mandarin or Japanese characters, but mathematical symbols.

To his surprise—yet utter acceptance—Edi knows each one. Ω—Omega, for the end of all things. Pi, 'π', the ratio of a circle's circumference to its diameter. The Laplace transform, 'L', a mathematical tool that reveals the hidden rhythms of change over time. And Alpha, 'α', where it all begins. $\Omega\pi L\alpha$ . . . it's not a known equation. But put together, he reads it to mean that the cyclical nature of things can be transformative.

He tries to reach inside the ship to see what it's about—but something in its shell is blocking him.

He looks again at the mark on the hull . . . and realizes it can also be read as Orla . . .

Suddenly, Edi gasps for air. He turns to Jack and the boatmen for reassurance.

They all see what he sees in his timeline . . . God's Ashes, this radioactive waste born of human ambition, will kill him . . . someday, far from home.

Edi spits out the quid and washes his mouth in the ocean.

He vowed then to never touch betel nut again. And this was before the 'spice' flooded the global market as the drug called smash.

He had important work to do—to save the world—and no hallucinogenic substance would distract him. He needed to be strong . . . and make his jimma proud.

13

Siquijor

2023 | Present

Robert Patrick Lin-Chiu was not born where he was from. And that meant he was constantly subjected to a slew of questions on the premise that his name and passport did not match his appearance. Worse, neither did his accented speech. Because of this, he learned not to put people through the same indignity by making assumptions—nor did he take them at face value.

Kai-chung—as he was known to his family—was born in Guam in the early 1990s. His Taiwanese parents were living on the US island to handle family business interests. They nicknamed him Kai for the ocean and chung, as he was the centre of their world. He was their only child, and his mother's unnecessary but induced C-section before a visit home to Taipei made him a US citizen. Blessed for life with the highly desired blue passport. The fulfilment of a dream for many Taiwanese.

But Kai-chung wasn't entitled to his own dreams. That's what his family's aspirations were for. And there was a lot to live up to. Which was why he was sent to boarding school in England when he was nine. Almhurst Hall in East Sussex. Sprawled over forty-five wooded acres just a few hours from London, the highly private preparatory academy was housed in a sixteenth century manor and exclusively for the male progeny of the world's wealthy. Certainly, no secular British school education for the only grandson of Taiwan's most influential mogul. His family wanted the young Kai-chung exposed to a multicultural landscape of privilege. To better build the necessary global connections for someone like him, who came from a place of ambiguous geopolitical status. Engulfed in the shadow of China's heft, any Taiwanese tycoon-in-training needed to get in all the personal networking he could. One needed good friends when a rising superpower on your doorstep constantly threatened your existence.

And so, Almhurst. With the sons of discreet sheiks, reclusive royals, and low-key billionaires. A much broader world than that offered by tiny, tottering Taiwan—which, though emerging, was still reeling from decades of repressive martial law.

It was at Almhurst that Kai-chung became Robbi. An inoffensive, studious lad who nourished himself on world history, geography, and languages. Like his mother, he had a mind for numbers but preferred the arts. Acing his maths while treading the boards. As all Almhurst boys, Robbi also went riding, learned how to sail, and played cricket. He even picked up skills to survive in the English woods. It was a chapter in his life that stayed with him, even more than his years at Hawksbridge University. Not even his postgraduate tenure at MIT could surpass it.

But nothing from his multi-tiered, sophisticated international education prepared him for where he found himself that morning: getting doused with a bucket of sea water and spluttering awake on a white sand beach to a circle of unfamiliar, weathered faces peering down at him. His throat was parched, his eyes stung, and his skin felt clammy and suppressed. He tried to grab hold of his arms and realized he was wearing his dive suit. His fins were gone, and so were his glasses, but he thought he recognized a young boy at his side.

The boy smiled at him then cast a flurry of words at the leather-faced men—who seemed to understand him perfectly.

Smelling of the sun and the sea, the man nearest Robbi lifted his head to give him a drink of water. He let the fluid touch his lips but lacked the energy to swallow. It was warm as piss. A wave of nausea rose in his throat and he thought he might vomit. The boy was staring at him—and an unfathomable scene suddenly flashed through his mind. A starless night. An inky sea. A hail of bodies. There was a storm of blood and an overwhelming fog of fear.

Robbi found it hard to believe it might be a memory. Not even in the seamiest underbellies of his travels had he felt such terror.

Another scene flickered into view: A pristine island. A feast of food. A dancing European. All abruptly punctured by a burst of bullets. Startled, he remembered a wave of corpses crashing with a thud.

Robbi rolled to his side and retched. The sunburned men around him scrambled to get out of the way.

Then, a loud middle-aged woman, holding a bundle of twigs set alight, waved them aside like sand flies. '*Layasa diha! Mga tsismoso* . . .'

She leaned down, circled the burning twigs over him, and offered him a cold bottle of water.

'You drink.'

As the smoke and her shadow engulfed him, Robbi looked up and saw a giant cross gleaming behind her in the sunlight. Astonished, he raised himself on his elbows.

'*Sige na*, drink,' she implored, pushing the plastic water bottle in his face.

The cross was on a modest church with a bell tower. Easily mid-nineteenth century. Made of stone and clay, it was a style Robbi knew was associated with Spain. Where was he?

He took the bottle from the woman and had a sip. The cold water down his throat was both painful and soothing. How long had it been since he last had a drink?

The woman extinguished the twigs and smeared some of its burned end onto her palm. She then lay that hand on his head. Muttering a few words, she traced some sort of symbol on his brow with the ashes.

'Okay. Now you come.'

She urged him to follow her and deluged the crowd of onlookers with a torrent of words.

Next thing Robbi knew, he was being helped to his feet and practically carried to the woman's nearby hut. It was made of wood and dried woven grass. Attached to it was an open-air shed facing the beach, like a covered patio, with a wobbly table and chairs on the bare, uneven ground.

The boy was there too. Stroking his chin, seeming pleased with himself. Then, his shoulders dropped and his expression soured. Turning away, Robbi tried to find anything that would give him a clue as to where he was—but there was little to offer clarity. At the back of the shed, along a large window, there were endless rows of small bottles filled with what looked like pieces of dried herbs. Plastic containers full of twigs and tree bark were scattered everywhere. And against a corner, well-worn, blackened cauldrons in various sizes lay at rest.

He and the boy were shuffled toward the table. Once seated, Robbi took the opportunity to lean in and ask for information. The boy just gaped at him without comprehension and had a look on his face that was practically a scowl. It caught Robbi by surprise. He was certain they had previously understood each other. Hadn't they? He tried again. In Mandarin this time. Wondering if that and not English was the language they had used. But instead of responding, the boy backed away.

Overhearing Robbi, one of the villagers set the crowd abuzz: '*Intsik pala* . . .'

A man from China.

In his dive suit, the locals presumed he was one of the rich boys from the city on a scuba trip. Likely lost and separated from his pack. They were not expecting one of the 'miracles' they'd found at sea to be from the country that had been stealing their fish. This could not be the good omen they thought it was.

Robbi raised his hands to calm the crowd. 'Taiwan . . . Taiwan,' he repeated.

They chuckled at his obvious discomfort.

The woman reappeared from inside the hut, giving both him and the boy a plate. She then brought out a bowl of rice, some boiled vegetables, and two tiny fried fish.

'*Kaon gyud* . . . Eat.'

Robbi watched the boy take a handful of rice and put it on his plate, followed by some veggies. He then picked up a fish and sucked on it. Expertly pulling a multitude of its spines from his mouth. The boy devoured the meal like a feast. Robbi had never eaten with his hands and wasn't sure what to do. Spotting his uncertainty, the woman put a spoon on his plate. He nodded gratefully.

As the two new arrivals ate, it seemed all the neighbours were in attendance—yet more people came to see the strangers brought in with the day's lean catch.

Still disoriented, Robbi tried to piece together what he could to understand how he ended up the highlight at this fishing village—all while also keenly observing his surroundings. He was always a meticulous sort. Just like his mother. And it was their shared drive to understand the world that got him into tech. But where she was very *Western* in her maths orientation, all logic and deductive reason, he was more *intuitive*, focusing on patterns and the relationships between things. Which didn't leave him much bandwidth to deal with his own. Robbi spent so much time in his head—and on his devices—that he didn't feel connected to anything *real*. He longed for a *tangible* experience. That's why he learned to dive. To pause for breath and be at one with nature. Especially after launching JUN0®, the cryptocurrency that went on to outpace the rest. Two years in, his family turned up the pressure for him to join their firm, saying it was time to put his own business—his 'hobby'—aside. It all got too much, and he needed some time free of the chains.

Out of the corner of his eye, Robbi noticed what appeared to be a father and son whispering. The man sent the boy scampering across the yard to another hut. He returned carrying some dry clothing. A large shirt and shorts that he gave to Robbi, and a smaller set of clothes he put before the boy who was still eating. Another villager came forward with flip-flops for each of them.

His mother taught him to always show appreciation for those who did him a kindness. But as he saw it, this went beyond that. The villagers had so little and yet didn't think twice about sharing. He wanted to repay them. As a sign of his gratitude. But he seemed to have lost his watch at sea and had nothing else on him that could serve as a reward. He'd give them some JUN0®—if he had his mobile.

'Internet café?' he suddenly asked, in English. Surely that was universal. *Internet. There must be a place somewhere*, he thought. If he could just get online, he would be able to reach his family in private, without raising an alarm. He wondered if they even realized he'd been in danger. That armed men had taken their boat hostage and spoke his name.

Damn, why would his family know? Robbi chastised himself. He was the one who *disappeared*, who felt the need to 'go offline'. Well, look where that got him.

In the commotion of villagers trying to offer solutions, someone suggested they go to the mayor. Or the police. Robbi understood both words, as they sounded the same in English.

'No. No mayor.' Robbi shook his head. The last thing he wanted was to meet a politician and risk turning this into some sort of scandal or international issue. The boy at the table with him seemed to agree. He went pale at the mention of police. Their eyes met and Robbi implored, hoping the boy would translate for the crowd: 'No police, please. Only . . . go home.'

The woman seemed to understand. She said something to the boy in the local language. And so ensued a loud and lively exchange. Robbi then remembered that his wetsuit had a lined, waterproof pocket he usually kept cash in for emergencies. He rose from the table and pulled down the zipper on his suit. Rooting around his torso, he eventually found what he sought. How his investors would laugh if they realized that the 'King of Crypto' still fell back on fiat money. But one never knew when the power might go out. It was the last kink Robbi hoped to resolve. Digital funds needed a heck-ton of energy for transactions. Imagine how much electricity went into keeping computer blockchains running? More than some countries consumed in a year.

Robbi put the only bill he had on the table. A folded up hundred US dollar note.

The woman immediately slipped it into her skirt.

'*Biyaan sila . . .*' she yelled out to her neighbours, shooing them away. Surely they must have other things to do. They didn't. They stayed put and carried on with their animated chatter.

Surrounded by a swell of strangers, Kai-chung had never felt more alone.

* * *

Tired of all the busybodies, Raed wanted to go into the witch doctor's hut and change out of the clothes he was wearing. His shirt had dried in the heat, but his shorts were still wet. Surprisingly, his skin—coarse where salt had crystallized—was only a little blistered, and his fingers were barely wrinkled despite how long they were in the sea. He didn't know how, but he was certain he could've stayed afloat as long as needed—and kept hold of the man from the boat who nearly drowned. The ungrateful jerk, giving money to the witch doctor instead of to him! Raed couldn't help but glare at that pink-faced merman in the wetsuit sitting opposite him.

After that long, cold night in the water—sometime around dawn—a large, motorized outrigger came upon them. It had been carried out much further than where it dropped anchor, untethered by a strong current. Hauled aboard, Raed was surprised that the unexpected rescuers spoke his language, and they told him they were way past their usual fishing ground. Their boat had also run out of fuel. But waiting on daybreak, they were determined to make their way home.

Carrying the castaways, and using only the wind and their oars, the fishermen eventually arrived at their island the following morning, with barely enough of a catch to feed their families. Like everywhere else on this coast, Chinese ships had been poaching, entering waters far beyond their borders.

The man in the dive suit was unconscious the entire voyage to the island. When asked, Raed couldn't tell the fishermen anything about the diver. He didn't even recall how they both ended up at sea. As the diver slept on the boat among the piddling catch, Raed studied him. He looked rich—even in his sorry state—and harmless. With the face of an angel. Like one of those Korean pop stars Raed had seen on TV. He bet this guy had something to hide. They always did, especially when they seemed so *clean*. Some nasty habit or dark desire. Raed wondered why he bothered to keep the diver alive. *The bracelet!*—he realized he still had it on. Not wanting to attract attention to it, Raed slipped it off his wrist and buried it deep in his pocket. He felt better knowing his precious string of stones was safe. He would sell it as soon as he could. It would be his ticket home . . . and back to family.

When they finally made it to shore, Raed was struck by how everyone spoke like the fishermen. In a language he understood! *What a stroke of luck*, he thought, this must be where he was from.

Raed was told the island was called 'See-kee-hor'. In the central Philippines. His heart raced—he was indeed finally back in his country of birth.

'Siquijor, this. Manila—far,' the woman waved her arms about trying to explain their location to the foreign 'pop star'. Seeing they were done eating, she pointed at the dry clothes they were given and ushered her two guests in the direction of her hut. When Raed stood up, the woman clucked at the bloodstain left on the seat. She covered it with a rag while clearing the table.

On his way inside, Robbi noticed an ice cooler by the doorjamb, and it brought back the memory of a young boy floating in the darkness. The lid of a cooler. A bony hand. His head being pulled back from the water. How had he forgotten that the kid had saved him?

There was only the one room in the hut, so Robbi took the corner opposite Raed to undress.

'Thank you—' he called to the boy who barely turned his way. 'You saved my life, and I am very grateful . . .' He didn't know how to even begin to repay that.

The teen appeared too involved in getting changed to respond.

Before removing his shorts, Raed pulled the bracelet from his pocket and slipped it on. It caught sunlight and he paused to admire its sheen. It radiated in a network of branches.

'Where did you get that?' Robbi called from across the room.

Instinctively, Raed hides his hand behind him.

'I will give you money for it,' Robbi offers. 'I mean, when I have the money . . . I will thank you for saving me . . . and pay you for the bracelet. I promise.'

Raed says nothing. Knowing Robbi means it.

'Can you tell me where you found that?' Robbi asks again. Afraid to move in case the boy bolts out the door. But he thinks he knows the answer.

'My friend gave it to me,' Raed replies. 'For safe keeping. It is his . . . but I will sell it to you . . . for a price . . .' He is certain that neither Maki nor Anak will mind.

Robbi extends a hand to see the bracelet. Raed stays still.

'Please? That's my mother's,' Robbi tells him. 'I would know it anywhere.'

'Your mother was not in Kota . . .'

'Is that where you found it?' Robbi stops to think. 'Kota Kinabalu?' Does his mother have business in Sabah?

'No. She was not there,' Raed repeats with certainty. 'I . . . I . . . cannot feel her.'

Robbi stared at the young teen, completely freaked out. What was happening? How were they communicating—*without words*? And why would the kid think his mother could be 'felt'?

'I will give you the bracelet when you have the money.'

'Then, we need to get to'—Robbi wracked his brain to remember the name of the one place in the Philippines he knew he'd find refuge—'Tamago? Tobacco?'

'Tinago . . . del Sur,' Raed said aloud, as if reading his mind. 'It's further south, across several islands. On the other side of the country.'

'Yes! That's where we need to go. I have a friend there. He will help us. I am sure of it.'

'It's too far. Get the money sent here. I've been looking for my family . . . and I can feel them now . . . so I must be near. I am not leaving.'

And Robbi wouldn't dream of leaving the boy behind. He wasn't letting the bracelet out of his sight. It was custom-made by his mother. She started wearing it a few weeks back, and never took it off. She told him it was the 'pinnacle' of her life's work. Her zenith. It was imperative then that he get to the bottom of this. Imperative that they reach Tinago so he could purchase the bracelet.

'Please, help me,' Robbi pleads with the boy, 'I will give you more money after all this—it will help your family . . .'

Raed ponders the proposal.

'Please'.

Abruptly, Raed's energy shifts. He feels danger. Someone means them harm. The web of light around them buzzes a dark and deadly spark. His gut is prompting him to stay with Robbi until he gets paid—he knows he won't make as much any other way.

Raed puts the bracelet back in his pocket so no one can steal it.

And that severs his connection to Robbi.

But he had it out long enough to unintentionally send a signal.

* * *

A few hours later, just as evening whispered on the horizon, two motorbikes arrived at the woman's hut. It took a while to get the message out and find riders willing to take her guests to the other side of the island. From there, Robbi and Raed were to look for an outrigger to get them across the channel to another island. They would have to repeat the chain of journeys several times on their way to Tinago. Through multiple islands and across waterways. Tinago del Sur was on the eastern coastline of the Philippine archipelago. Tucked into a gulf, protected from the open Pacific. The woman—who Robbi deduced was the village witch doctor—had given them some of her prized potions to hand out along the way, explaining it would open doors when needed.

Once in Tinago, Robbi was confident he could find his friend. Villagers talked and a man like that stood out in any crowd.

The motorbikes had clearly seen better days, and the drivers gave them instructions particular to each one's quirks.

'Balans'—Robbi's driver held his arms out, repeating—'you. Balance.'

As if Robbie wouldn't know how. His whole existence was a balancing act. Between the past and the future. His roots and his wings. Tradition and technology. And he often felt like the fulcrum of his parents' marriage—a shield for their secrets, a repository for their love. Even within himself Robbi struggled—to keep his demons from outweighing his goals. All of life was a balancing act.

Suddenly, in this Philippine island of witchcraft and magic, he found himself balancing what he knew of reality and his sanity. He just survived an outlandish kidnapping attempt, because of a random teen who seemed to have his mother's bracelet . . . and read his mind.

14

25.0330° N, 121.5654° E

Taipei

2023 | Present

Convinced they could read the public pulse, the strategists insisted this would work: on a stark white background, his face—in high-definition—six feet high. Smooth complexion, neat goatee, just a hint of a smile. Rimless glasses. Piercing stare. His expression a mix of sternness and approachability. Reinforced by his receding hairline, which apparently—surveys said—made him seem more trustworthy. Even if, in public, he never smiled. The joke across Taiwan was that he looked like a friendly *heidaoren* or gangster. A triad's so called lǎo dà, the 'elder brother' you'd like on your side. Or at least, the one you would not be too afraid to approach to get on your side.

To the left of his massive portrait, in big, block Chinese characters, the name he came to be known by—then, at the bottom, in English:

Wu Xi 'Wild Willy' Chiu for Mayor

'Well?' his campaign manager beamed at the unfurled banner.

'Right.' The unsmiling goateed candidate hated it.

'I knew you'd love it! It'll be up across the city within the hour.' The campaign manager punched a number on his mobile phone and dashed off into the fray of 'Wild Willy's' political headquarters, which occupied the penthouse of central Taipei's newest skyscraper.

'Taiwan News Today wants you live at 6 p.m.—' a young woman called to him from a distant desk. She had a landline phone tucked between her shoulder and an ear. 'You'll do it, yes?'

'Of course he'll do TNT!' his campaign manager answered, dashing back across the room. 'He'll do any and all media. You got that, people?' The ebullient millennial spun around to address the room filled with volunteers who were being paid. 'Willy will do any and all media!'

'Yes, sir!' the room full of 'volunteers' replied in unison.

Willy was standing to the side trying to seem interested. But there were other things on his mind.

'What do we say when asked if the new chip is almost ready?'

'Sshh! Nothing. Seems they're behind schedule and he's super stressed.'

'Didn't he just get back from a trip?'

'Wasn't a holiday . . . and I don't think whatever meeting he had there went well. He's been kinda—distracted—since he got back.'

They whispered, but Willy knew what they were all talking about. Everyone thought he was snowed under because of his day job. Producing the new superconductor they'd announced was in development. Able to let electricity pass without resistance. It would be the smallest microchip manufactured. The details were highly confidential, but rumours spread they were testing a new, 'game-changing' material. All the tech geeks—and the stock markets—were atwitter. It would mean freedom from silicon. Advancements would no longer be limited by the material's constraints on power consumption and heat dissipation. As it was, silicon microchips couldn't get any smaller or perform additional processes without overheating or malfunctioning. There were already too many transistors on them, so they were near their end life. Soon to be relegated to the past. Humanity was on the precipice of the quantum era—and that required a quantum-capable conductor. Indeed, though still under wraps, their family firm had found the perfect substance. The world would no longer be confined to a binary code of 0s and 1s—or of output being dependent on input. Instead, the future of tech would more appropriately reflect the mind-blowing reality of multiple simultaneous potentialities. This was not some improved version of the derivative, uncreative Metaverse. What was augmented reality when cognition was expanded to go beyond its own consciousness?

But chip production was not what weighed on Willy. He was confident in the new material, which not only conducted electricity without warming or destabilizing circuitry but also transformed energy to create nodal hyperconnectivity. This would enable the most complex processes at instantaneous speeds and revolutionize the flow of information. It would put artificial intelligence to shame and turn its users into quantum, super versions of themselves. Without need for a device or an external battery. Imagine a world where everyone could communicate without risk of being misunderstood? Where connections amplified each other, creating a global network of self-powering bio-conduits. The whole world would become a living, breathing 'supercomputer'. Universal Utopia. Humanity's highest achievement. This would do that. And so, they were calling it the 0MεGα chip. They had an exclusive design that turned their game-changing substance into the most minuscule yet powerful processor possible. All it had to do was touch the user's skin while encased in a protective layer that served as the superconductor. It would make their firm the most important chip company in the world.

What worried Willy was that someone knew this and was taking great measures to get their formula. Including threatening his family.

No one was meant to know that the 'secret' material was a limited substance primarily found in waters around the Marshall Islands. A distinct coral people were calling God's Ashes. It had evolved from being exposed to record levels of nuclear energy. In battling to survive, the coral transformed itself into a powerful conduit. Locals used it as a narcotic—and the firm worked to secure an exclusive license for it from the Marshallese government. Still, they were beating back drug lords who wanted it for their multi-billion-dollar global market.

As a leading tech firm, they were offered the coralline substance in strictest confidence. They started blending it into the nanochips they made for dεU^{1}S$^{™}$ and it improved performance. The goal was to manufacture the 0MεGα chip entirely from God's Ashes.

The black market was being flooded with replica nanochips, all demonstrating problems and proving unstable. They were made from a similarly irradiated substance. Willy suspected a leak in the firm or corporate espionage. He didn't know how else other manufacturers would get wind of their developments. They couldn't afford competitors attempting their own version and beating them to launch. The 0MɛGα chip could control the world. And so, they were treading carefully.

Suddenly, the commotion in the campaign office went muted. Overtaken by a different buzz as people parted for the arrival of his father-in-law. A willowy man in a crisp suit, the elderly entrepreneur—who was still chairman of the family firm—was always flanked by armed guards dressed in black. It was not a subtle look. They also wore dark glasses and carried weapons in holsters around their waist.

'Willy.'

'Baba.'

With the Chairman leading the way, they headed straight into the privacy of Willy's office.

'News?'

The old man took the seat behind the large glass desk, leaving the candidate standing like a lackey delivering a report.

'New campaign posters are here, Baba,' Willy started, respectfully addressing the Chairman as *father*. 'They will be distributed this afternoon. The Xinying temple needs more money for their renovation. People's Alliance is calling for an investigation into the firm's labour practices . . .'

'Yes, yes. Make it go away. You must win at all costs.'

'Of course.'

'Once you are mayor of Taipei, we are a step away from the presidency.' There was nothing the chairman wanted more. He felt he was owed it after everything he did for the exiled Chinese Nationalists. The group lost Beijing to the Communists in the 1940s and fled to Taiwan. They established a government that ruled the island for decades. When democracy set in, the Nationalists grew more reliant on his money to get votes. And he gained business contracts—including from China—in exchange for supporting their policies. As far as the Chairman was concerned, this arrangement was beneficial for all Taiwan.

'I still say you will do better with the Nationalist Party machine behind you.'

'Baba,' Willy said evenly, 'all the surveys show that any ties to China aren't viewed favourably by the public. Especially with the latest clampdown. Zhou comes across like a tyrant bent on disempowering the people. Re-education camps, disappearing minorities, silencing dissent—we can't be associated with any of that.'

'Bah, minorities. Zhou Sheng Feng has been a great leader for China. Look at how powerful it has become. And don't you think he is right? What have those minorities ever done for the country? They all just keep snivelling like those tribal people here on Dragon's Gate—still complaining about the nuclear waste stored on their island . . . don't they realize that helps power Taiwan?'

'Baba—'

The Chairman waved him to silence. Willy took a breath.

'I have followed everything your strategists have said, Baba—and they made it clear that running as an independent is the best choice for us. This way, we are linked neither to the past—nor any talk of a future independent Taiwan. Which as you know, would upset China. Instead, we stand firm on our own . . . within agreeable parameters.'

'And thanks to my money, we can pull it off . . .'

Before he could respond, Willy's encrypted phone vibrated in his pocket and he felt a ring in his ear. His smart watch showed no caller ID. He suspected he knew who it was. But with his father-in-law in the room, he could not answer the call, nor could he step away. That would have been seen as disrespectful, and Willy did not want to anger the Chairman, who would then think that he had something to hide. Which he did—but that was not the point.

So, he discreetly ended the call.

'Tea,' the old man commanded.

One of his security escorts left to get his usual beverage.

'What's for lunch, son?'

Willy then realized the chairman had no intentions of leaving.

'TNT . . .' the old man bellowed. It switched on the screens on the wall across from the desk. All eight of them on the same national news network. He picked up the remote from the table and changed a few of the monitors over to other channels.

A documentary. A cartoon. A musical variety show. World Insight News.

'Muslim minority Uyghurs in Xinjiang are disappearing. Facing persecution from the state, many have gone underground . . . believed to be hiding in tunnels while they wait to escape China. They're abandoning jobs in state-run uranium mines and radioactive salt flats, which, in turn, is jeopardizing global efforts to go green. Affecting the supply of lithium batteries and more domestically, China's pursuit of clean nuclear energy.'

'It is a good thing we found a new source of energy,' Baba said. That was news to Willy. 'See? These minorities are nothing but trouble . . .'

The Chairman was about to mute the monitor when a face familiar to Willy came on-screen.

'The remains of prominent environmentalist Edison Wakamele-Rigold, also known as One-eyed Edi, have gone missing from the morgue before the Sabah government could send them to the Marshalls for burial.'

Willy tried not to seem interested, until the old man muted the screen. 'Wait—' he found himself saying.

'What's it to you?' the Chairman wondered. 'I say, good riddance. Another do-gooder gone.'

Willy made a mental note to look into the missing corpse.

'Speaking of do-gooders—where is your son?'

'Research trip,' Willy had the reply ready.

'Another one?'

'Yes'—Willy expounded on his lie—'he needs to ascertain . . . the viability of a new mining site for his cryptocurrency. They're setting up a new data centre not too far from our warehouse in the Philippines . . .'

'Philippines. Great place for business,' the Chairman smiled. 'You can do anything you want. Including get away with murder.' He laughed. 'Littéralement.'

Willy hid his surprise at the unexpected French remark.

'Your boy needs to get his head out of the clouds and back to reality—who will take over my business when I am gone? You will be busy running the country—someone needs to focus on our other interests . . . until it is his turn as president.'

Characteristically, Willy said nothing. He was just glad the Chairman hadn't asked about his wife.

'Where is my daughter?'

And there it was.

'She is still mad at me about that dinner, isn't she?'

Willy felt a slight relief. He had forgotten that his wife and her father had indeed disagreed a few weeks earlier over something or the other during a family meal. Surely the man would stop pressing him about his wife.

His Baba took Willy's hesitation to answer as confirmation.

'I knew it!' the Chairman laughed. 'And here you are all this time covering for her. Son, she has you by the balls!' More laughter. 'What kind of leader will you be without your manhood? A eunuch. I do not back eunuchs! You were better than this, Willy . . .'

Sure, but many things had happened since he first started working for the Chairman. For one, he fell in love with the man's daughter. They married and had a son. Which only gave Willy something to worry about, particularly in their line of *work*. He risked losing everything if his very real emotions in his fake life ever collided with his buried truths.

His phone rang again. Which couldn't have been a good sign.

Turning his watch on his wrist to hide its face, Willy excused himself from the Chairman.

'Sorry, Baba, the stylist must be here now. I need to join them in the conference room. I'll see you at home.'

'I'll be here when you're done,' Baba leaned back in the chair as his bodyguard returned with his beverage.

Bested, Willy headed for the empty conference room, discreetly answering the call.

'We are waiting,' the voice said coldly in Mandarin.

They're still working on it. Willy replied through his neural interface.

The caller sighed.

I will get it as soon as it is ready.

'It better be ready soon or our next call will be so you can say goodbye.'

Don't you hurt her!—his anger transmitted before he could block it.

The caller laughed. 'Or what? You are in no position to threaten us, Ayup.'

Willy tried to track the call on his ultra-smart watch, but it ended before he could. He readjusted the device on his wrist, making sure it covered his small tattoo of a sparrow, a complex symbol of luck and misfortune in Chinese folklore.

Just as he was about to leave the room, his neural interface buzzed. Only Hashem went by that sequence of tones, so he knew the caller must've been sent by his dear friend.

'You're looking for a bird?' a voice said in French.

Yes. Willy replied without speaking.

'We know where it is. Transport soon.'

How? In exchange for what?

'We will let you know when the cage is open.'

And then the connection ended.

Despite the swing between extreme emotions after the back-to-back calls, Willy was left hopeful that his mother—the bird—would be rescued from detention. He returned to his office an image of composure. The Chairman was still at his desk surfing multiple TV screens.

'You know that bubble tea is bad for your diabetes . . .'

The old man waved him off dismissively. 'You know who they say has diabetes? Zhou. Can you imagine a strongman like that being debilitated by something as ordinary as diabetes? Mark my words, Zhou will fight any notion of frailty. His enemies better watch out . . .'

'Lǎo dà,' one of the Chairman's bodyguards entered with a mobile. 'Beijing.'

'I told you not to call me that in public,' the Chairman roared. His alter ego was widely suspected across Taiwan, but he didn't want it expressly confirmed.

Already missing a finger, the terrified bodyguard put the encrypted device on the table and walked out of the room backwards with his head bowed.

It was not wise to provoke the Lotus Dragon.

15

7.3411° N, 134.4772° E

Koror

2023 | Present

'This is not good for business,' Metik told Valya through gritted teeth. 'People will think we're cursed, especially the Chinese. They're already coming in fewer numbers—'

'I do not see the problem with that.' Valya, unperturbed, kept her eyes on the shore. 'Those day trippers take up space and do not even spend on drinks—we are well rid of them.'

The business partners were standing on the back patio of the Gal/Guy's Cove Café, just feet from the shore where local marine experts were pronouncing more humpbacks dead. It was the third day running that bloodied whales washed in with the tide.

'I don't even wanna know what the *special* guests must be thinking . . .' Metik wiped his brow, worried about the man and woman Palau's head of state asked them to host discreetly at the inn without advance payment. He knew Valya was less than thrilled about the arrangement.

'The couple?' she asked, rhetorically. 'It's what they are most interested in.'

'The whales?' Metik's voice pitched.

'Yes.'

Just then, the couple in question rocked up the shore heading back to the inn. The woman, Nisha, was covered from head to toe. Black tights, sneakers, and a long-sleeved shirt with big, dark glasses and a wide-brimmed hat. Her face was barely identifiable, and she looked like she would've preferred to be anywhere but the beach. The man with her trailed behind, glued to his mobile. They'd spent all afternoon watching Palauan authorities examine the dead whales and organize transport to a lab.

'That's what I've been trying to tell you,' Metik whispered, 'they're not tourists—they're from Transform, the Chinese energy company. They've gone from fossil fuels to renewables and nuclear power . . . who knows what they're after now?'

'I doubt it would be the carcasses of sea mammals,' Valya deadpanned. 'But then again, there are so many uses for blubber.'

Without a sideways glance at her business partner, Valya returned inside, refusing to show her indignation.

The couple from the beach had settled in the lobby as the gong resounded, indicating the airport van was near. Metik dashed to the entrance to meet it. Considering word got out about the whales, he was glad they even got a new guest on the roster. Others had cut short their stay.

'Mate!'

Before Metik could welcome the guest, he was usurped by the man he wrongly suspected worked with Transform: Nisha's husband, Dr Luqman—Luc—Nazari.

'What're the chances!' Luc put his phone away as he rushed over.

'He-he-hey, if it ain't the good doctor!' the new arrival was equally exuberant. Feeling redundant, Metik slinked away, hoping to be of some use at reception.

Valya took a deep breath seeing they would be hosting a North American. There were enough of them lately hanging around the inn. She decided to leave the check-in process to the staff and make herself tea in the back office. Crossing the lobby, she passed Nisha—still wearing her wide-brimmed hat—furiously tapping a tablet. *What a waste of a beautiful day*, thought Valya.

'So, how's *God* treating you?' Teddy, the newly arrived North American, slapped Luc on the back.

'Oh—the app? It's . . . eye-opening.' Luc had not expected to benefit from it as much as he had. Beyond points, dɛU^{1}S^{TM} was making him see the world differently and gain an understanding of life that not even his many years in med school had given him. And he was only on Level 1.

'I tell ya, I learn so much on Day-Us—and I've *made* so much too,' Ted roared with laughter. 'I couldn't afford a trip here otherwise.'

A hotel staff member was leading him to the front desk when Teddy spotted the bar.

'How 'bout you take my passport and sign me in?' he winked at the concierge. 'Just bring me the key later. It's nearly happy hour, so me and your tip will be right over there with my friend here, the good doctor.' Teddy smiled at Luc and handed his travel documents to the concierge. He then marched right up to the bar—which was next to the café fronting the cove—and ordered two shots of tequila and a couple of lagers.

'You good with our usual?' Ted asked, referring to the numerous drinks they downed together just days earlier in Pulau Rahsia. Particularly after the resort's dive boat went missing.

Luc nodded, taking a seat. 'So, uh . . . what's new?' He didn't want to come right out and ask, but he and Nisha left Sabah before Teddy and he wondered if there were any *developments* since their departure. There wasn't much in the news and Nisha never told him anything she heard through work. She mostly acted as if nothing out of the ordinary happened while they were on the private island.

The bartender appeared with their line-up of drinks.

Before speaking, Teddy pushed a shot of tequila at Luc and downed his own, taking a chug of his lager right after. 'You mean the dive boat, yeah?' He didn't notice the barman linger. Every islander and marine enthusiast was interested in the missing vessel. Word spread quick within the diving community that something had happened to a Sabah dive crew, but nothing official had been said. No details or identities disclosed. The resort stayed mum under the guise of protecting its guests' privacy. Even social media could only speculate as to why the accounts of those European influencers were suddenly inactive.

Luc felt his cheeks flush at his lack of investigative subtlety. He took a sip of his beer to hide his discomfort.

'They still hadn't found the boat when I left,' Teddy shared. 'But the staff, obviously concerned, talked about it more than they probably should've. And from what I heard, the boat hasn't appeared moored anywhere or shipwrecked. There's been no ransom demand—so, they think it's probably sunk with all its passengers.'

'Oh. Uhm . . . so the . . . uh . . .' Luc struggled to get the question out.

'Bodies washing up on the other islands? Yeah, they were all shot—but none have been identified.' Again, Teddy replied as if reading Luc's mind.

'Are you—?'

The North American laughed, 'I know what you're thinking—I mean—I don't *know* what you're thinking, but I know you're *wondering* if I'm reading your mind, right? Well, I wish, but I'm not at that level—yet. Dang *hot chip* isn't working like I expected. But it is giving me more points than a regular chip . . . so there's that.'

The hot chip. It's what they started calling the replica microchip Teddy bought on the black market to use with dεU^{1}S™. He did try to earn 'elevation' legitimately, but it was taking him longer than anyone else he knew. So, he decided to 'level the playing field'—as he put it— by taking a shortcut and buying a fast-track solution.

Luc laughed with him, enjoying being able to chat with someone who wasn't constantly looking for a fight. Nisha had been obsessed with work since . . . well, since forever. Which meant she was always cross with him and growing increasingly so. She stopped pretending this trip was a second honeymoon as soon as Luc told her on Pulau Rahsia that he knew she was travelling for work—and that she only brought him along as a decoy. If she had gone on her own, people would've been suspicious of her presence—and her endless questions.

Nisha—Anisha d'Acosta, PhD, ScD—was part of a high-level, clandestine research team for Transform. The world's biggest—and most controversial—energy supplier. Luc didn't know what it was that she as a nuclear physicist and engineer was actually investigating, but with glowing fish and then dead whales, it couldn't have been anything good.

'Did you hear about the whales?' Luc asked Teddy.

'Oh yes . . . Any theories?'

Luc took a slow sip of his pint to organize his thoughts. He'd had a lot of them lately, thanks to the app. 'I think they're responding to a disturbance in the ocean. Maybe an underground explosion? Some sort of unnatural noise? Something could be messing with their sonars, making them bang against each other or against other objects in the water, like boats . . .'

'Boats?'

'Yeah,' Luc went on, 'what if a similar thing was happening in Pulau Rahsia—and that's why there's no trace of the dive boat? What if whales attacked and sank it?'

Teddy just stared at Luc. Unsure how serious he was. Downing the last of his lager, Ted signalled the barman for another round.

'Has your app been—glitchy—lately?' Ted wiped his mouth on his arm.

'I don't think so . . . why?'

'Mine's been showing me some weird shit,' Ted explained. 'Making me do things, I think, that I'm . . . not sure about,' he looked Luc in the eye. 'Thought maybe yours would be doing that too. Would explain this whole whale theory!'

'I was being serious. And what do you mean your app's been *weird*?'

'I don't know how to explain—' Ted stopped speaking when the bartender approached with their drinks. He nodded his thanks, knocked back half his pint, and waited until they were alone again. 'Sometimes, Day-Us brings me to the edge of all these amazing things, you know? And it makes me want to *participate* . . . and then—I don't remember.'

'Sorry, you don't *remember*?' Luc was having trouble following.

'Like a black out or something. There's a chunk of time missing between things I remember. Like, I'm here . . . and then, I'm somewhere else, awake, but I don't know how I got there. I mean, I *know* I am conscious the whole time—but when I try to look back on it, I don't *remember* . . . It's like I was in a trance.'

Luc thought Ted was tripping. Maybe the guy was back on drugs after the dive boat incident. So he just nodded and sipped his beer like he was pondering the possibilities. This was even more bizarre than his own theory about the whales.

'You're a doctor'—Ted was visibly concerned—'what do you think it's about?'

Luc shook his head. 'I don't know, mate—withdrawal?'

The North American was not pleased with the reply.

'I mean, maybe it's a lingering effect from the drugs you did . . . in the past?'

'That's crazy . . .' Ted shook his head and emptied his drink. 'I haven't touched anything in years,' he paused. 'Okay, I had *some* smash before I got to Sabah, but I mean—that just *heightens* everything. It wouldn't erase my memory? Or make me do . . . weird things?'

'What exactly do you mean by *weird?*'

'Like now, see'—Ted looked around to make sure there was no one within earshot—'I'm supposed to be *retrieving* something—something really important that's been stolen. But I don't know what it is . . . and I don't know *how* I know this. It's like something inside is just telling me to follow a signal on the app and take—at all costs—whatever it is I am supposed to retrieve. And then, I forget that's what I'm doing until—bam!—it's there again. Sometimes I think I'm going nuts.'

'Is that why you're here?'

'I don't know,' Ted seemed exasperated. 'I just got this really strong urge yesterday to come to Palau. So, I booked this place—and it had to be *this place*—then, I went straight for the airport. Got there just in time to board a flight that was about to leave. It all worked out perfectly.'

Luc was beginning to wonder if this might be what happened to Nisha's nemesis, the environmentalist. Maybe he and the hotel jumper were on smash, and they were driven mad and to their deaths—a delayed side effect.

'Did you hear anything more in Sabah about that jumper or the environmentalist?' Luc asked, seemingly off tangent.

'Huh? Oh. That's old news now. Why would anyone care about another poor activist? No one cared when the dude was alive . . .'

'Yes, but his death is proving more interesting than his existence . . .' Luc posited, wryly.

'Oh! Here's something'—Ted tried to wave the barman back over—'his body's gone missing . . .'

'What?' Luc wasn't sure he understood.

'The activist. Saw it in the paper on the plane. Just a small blurb. Locals think it was cursed. Who knows. Apparently, he had all these tattoos? Marking him for evil or whatever . . .' Ted paused to let the barman deliver a fresh round of drinks. Then, he turned back to Luc and lowered his voice. 'I'm sure someone stole it from the morgue,' he picked up the next pint and chugged it back. 'Dead guy wasn't local, so I bet the Sabah government's pissed off that someone stomped all over their jurisdiction and took the corpse. Maybe China, maybe the US—heck could be Russia. But less embarrassing if it was an extra-natural *disappearance*.'

'Hmmm,' Luc thought about that for a second. 'Guess that always happens in small countries. The big ones come in and do as they please. When I returned to Iraq after med school, I had to investigate a crime involving a US soldier. The victim—a local woman—was *removed* . . . and without a body, the case was dropped. We had no autopsy and the family was paid off. Maybe that's what happened there.'

Ted lifted a tequila shot to his mouth and downed it. 'I am sorry,' he muttered unexpectedly, setting the empty glass on the bar. 'About . . . you know, the occupation and all that.'

'Sure. Yeah.' Luc stared into his drink. No apology could make up for the destruction of his home country. It's not as if Ted was responsible for any of it. Luc's people, the Yazidis, were always shabbily treated, no matter the occupier. He told himself that being in the minority was better than nothing. Better than being completely rootless. Like tumbleweed. Or cinder blowing in the wind. Luc knew he'd become good at self-deception.

'There you are,' Nisha's voice had a bite to it that was more frequently being exhibited. 'I've been looking for you everywhere.'

'Well, hello there, Mrs Dr Luc.'

She glared at the crass man ignorant of how important she was. Then, she turned back to her husband.

'I need to check on something . . .'

'Should I come along?' He hoped that maybe she would finally want to hear his opinion. He'd been trying to tell her his whale theory all day. He suspected the animals had a lot to do with why they were hopscotching across Asia.

'No. You stay,' she looked at the North American, reappraising his suitability as a companion for her husband. 'Just—don't do anything stupid,' she turned to Luc. 'I don't know what you get up to because of that app . . .'

'Me? Stupid? Never.' Luc smiled at her. Embarrassed at how he was being addressed. He was surprised she even bothered to let him know she was leaving the inn. Since that first night on Pulau Rahsia, Luc was growing convinced it would be better for both of them if they were apart. Maybe Nisha could sense that? He was tired of the push and pull of their relationship. The imbalance of their union. He was tired of being the only one who seemed to care.

* * *

In the Gal/Guy's modest back office, Valya stood at the beverage station with her eyes closed. The sun was disappearing on the horizon, and she rocked herself gently, muttering a chant. Centring herself in the repetition of her *dhikr*, her call to the All-Powerful. The sacred vibrations of her prayer travelled through every cell of her being.

Just before the water boiled, Valya opened her eyes and switched off the kettle on the counter. Like clockwork, she poured a little of its contents into a handmade ceramic bowl and whisked a teaspoon of fine green powder until it was a paste. She then added more hot water. Repeating the process, layer by layer, until the small drinking bowl was filled. Aside from the dhikr, it was preparing the tea that relaxed her. She didn't particularly care for the taste of the matcha.

On the desk, her laptop was open on a news feed from Malaysia. The international news sites were focused on bigger stories, but since hearing of Edi's death, Valya kept a close watch on anything out of Sabah. Thankfully, much of the news online was broadcast in English. What she'd learned so far was perplexing: Edison Wakamele-Rigold died in a Kota Kinabalu hotel. Suspected overdose. Suffered burns that seemed internal. There was blood spatter at the crime scene—female blood. And the latest development, his corpse was missing. As were the remains of a Chinese merchant who seemed to have jumped out of a window at the same hotel.

More confounding still—Edi was meant to be in Singapore for a conference at the time, not in Sabah, Malaysia. There was no record of his arrival in the country.

None of it made sense—and yet, it all sent a clear message to Valya.

'Call Melody . . .' For days, she'd been trying to reach the one person who might be the key to it all, but with no luck. Maybe the blood at the scene was hers? But what would she have been doing there? They were not meant to meet again.

Valya lit a stick of Palo Santo. Seeking comfort in its distinct aroma.

Two things struck her: Either Edi's death and the palaver around it had nothing to do with *the incident*—so she could relax . . . or it had everything to do with it—and she would be next.

Her preoccupation was interrupted by the ringing of the hotel intercom. She was needed at reception.

Valya heard the ruckus before she got there.

'What is going on?' she asked Metik, who was standing at the front desk trying to appease a rowdy horde.

Valya recognized the language immediately. She slunk back, pulling Metik aside and leaving the crowd to Yuyu, the receptionist.

'Why did you call me?'

Metik waved a hand at the gaggle of people as if it were self-explanatory.

Valya said nothing, keeping her face away from the loud disturbance.

'Yuyu needs help,' Metik pointed out the frazzled receptionist. 'They're getting worse, and she can't figure out what they want . . .'

'And I can?' Valya seemed—uneasy. Another state Metik hadn't seen on her.

'Well . . . I thought . . .'

'I am not Russian,' she exhaled through her teeth. 'How many times must I say this?' It was the one thing that always upset her. No matter how much she meditated, chanted, and practised mindfulness, Valya would never take kindly to being thought of as one of those barbarians.

Russians. They killed her family. Simply for not being—nor wanting to be—Russian. Stalinists, Soviets, *new* Russians—by whatever name they went, *they* were the reason Valya was where she was.

'Вот почему женщины должны оставаться дома!'

She prickled at the sexist insult telling women where they 'belonged'. But she wasn't about to let them see it. She didn't want them to see *her*.

'Shut the bar,' she called out to the receptionist. 'When they see it is closed, they will leave . . .'

Yuyu rang the barman on the intercom and gave him instructions. In a tick, the lights in the entire café went dark. The Russians were too busy making a scene to notice.

'It's okay,' Valya reassured Metik. But he didn't believe her. She was always saying this as if speaking it would make it so.

Just then, a heavily tinted van pulled up with Chinese tourists. They tumbled out, all on their devices. So much for being kept away by the threat of 'bad fortune'. The unwelcome surge made Valya want to retreat to her office.

'Don't call me again unless it is urgent,' she told Metik. With everyone everywhere equipped with a personal recording device, Valya felt like she was constantly under surveillance. It made her other, more important tasks difficult to accomplish.

Before leaving reception, Valya spotted the same US operatives who'd been watching her for days trying to blend in with the tour group. They were headed for the bar but stopped short, seeing it was 'closed'. The inn's two guests who were there earlier—Teddy and Luc—had moved to lounge chairs on the beach. The only one Valya couldn't account for was the woman with the massive hat.

Returning to her office, she saw a familiar tail light go by the side patio. The vehicle only slowed to go over a speed bump she had put on the road around the inn. Reckless tourists were always renting luxury cars and zipping across the islands at high speeds.

Valya knew where that pickup was headed, but it wasn't due for another week. Something wasn't right. She ducked into her office to get her gun before dashing to the back exit.

* * *

Having got rid of the angry visitors, Metik had the bar reopened just as darkness fell. He went to apologize to the displaced patrons for the interruption.

'Does that happen often?' Luc asked as they walked back in from the cove.

'Well, many Russian ships and rigs are registered here, so we get a lot of their crew on shore leave. Yuyu can usually handle it—but lately, they've been more aggro and obnoxious. I keep trying to get them on the God app to de-stress—but no dice . . .'

'You're on Day-Us?' Teddy clarified.

Metik nodded.

'Is it working okay for you?' Luc asked the inn proprietor.

Metik wondered where the question came from.

'Teddy's has been dodgy—and I've just started so I can't really tell . . .'

'Ah! You're the novice node,' Metik was thrilled. 'My chart lit up when you arrived, but I wasn't sure if it was you or your wife. I'm not good at reading transmissions yet.'

Teddy pulled up a bar stool and asked Metik to join them.

'It's definitely not my wife . . .' Luc sighed.

'Not a fan?' Metik gladly took a seat.

Luc shook his head. 'I don't know how to reach her anymore. It's why I got on the app in the first place . . . ' All the tequila they'd had made him chatty.

'You want an upgrade?' Metik offered. 'Get you reading energies and bio-waves faster. Should help you reconnect.'

'You sell upgrades?' Teddy perked up.

'A little side business,' Metik explained. 'I don't do much here, and Valya doesn't seem to care about making a profit . . . so, I hooked up with this tourist who works at a Chinese fab. They make dɛU¹S compatible chips. It's all still hush-hush, but he sends me the surplus . . . '

'Better than the hot chips sold on the web?' Ted asked.

'Yeah, man! These are Class AAAA . . . from China!'

Luc worried about even considering it. It seemed to go against everything the app was trying to foster.

'Go on,' Teddy urged. 'Can't hurt . . .'

Luc looked from one man to the other. Still unsure.

'I'll have it by tomorrow,' Metik stated. 'No need to pay me—just share some JUN0 when you get elevated. Yes?'

After a few more moments of silence, Luc nodded, barely perceptibly. Maybe, just maybe, *God* would bring him and Nisha back together.

* * *

'What are you doing here?' Valya had the driver of the pickup pressed against the inn's back wall. There were no lights on this side of the Gal/Guy, and they were obscured from the road by a bamboo thicket and a mangrove forest.

'I sent you a message,' he whispered. 'Got an extra package.'

She shook her head, not trusting the information.

'We have to unload . . .'

'No, no, no, no, no,' she muttered under her breath, as if it were a dhikr. 'This isn't on the schedule. I have no space. Something's not right . . .'

She looked around convinced they were being watched. Expecting the clumsy US army boys to be listening in the shadows. She pressed the gun to the driver's torso to lead him closer to the darker edge of the mangroves.

'Watch it with that, would you?' the driver warned. 'Look, maybe there was more . . . *movement* . . . this month—'

'That never happens without careful coordination, you know that,' she kept her voice down and lowered the gun. Trying to keep her anxiety at bay.

'I don't know what to tell you, Vushka,' the driver moved towards his pickup parked behind the bamboo. 'It's not our usual—and can't stay with me.'

She followed him as he went for the truck's passenger cabin. Pointing her gun, ready to shoot at the first sign of trouble.

When he opened the door, the rising moon touched the face of a terrified older woman. Illuminating her gaunt, unwashed, weariness. She was missing a part of her arm. And in the twilight, her tears glistened like the ocean, flowing at the sight of Valya.

* * *

'How much more time do you need?' Nisha didn't bother with niceties. 'You should've had a baseline by now.'

Like castigated children, the two lab technicians kept their heads down as she paced the room. They were in a small house quietly leased for them by Transform. There was only space for two cots in the front room, as the back was shut with a false wall to hide the lab. The 'foreign' techs were already an uncomfortable presence on the islands.

'When will we know if the chemical composition matches up? If we don't figure out what's killing the fish, and now the whales, we may have a very costly lawsuit on our hands. And those damn environmentalists will make us a political target again. But why aren't the whales glowing? Is any of it similar to what we see in Xinjiang?'

The two scientists looked at each other, waiting for the other to take the lead.

'Goddamit—speak! I didn't get you out of China to sit here and be useless. You wanted freedom in exchange for your expertise? So prove your expertise, goddammit.'

The taller, more chiselled scientist cleared his throat.

'Explosions. In the ocean,' he looked to his colleague for agreement. 'Closer to Micronesia. Seems to have released amplified energy particulates. Affecting the water, particularly where there are radioactive signatures. Like around the Marshalls. It's affected corals, all marine life. The shifting currents could be spreading it to other places. But we think the whales are being driven crazy by something else . . .'

'By what?' she barked, impatient.

'The last few days,' the other scientist brought out a satellite image, 'there's been a ship out here . . . that could be the source. It's moving very slowly. Not appearing on any radars. Our quantum satellite picked it up.'

'We zoomed in,' his colleague added, 'but there's no information on this ship called . . . ORLA?'

'What the hell is that?'

16

50.9497° N, 0.7373° E

Rye

1989

The gas lamps flickered on as dusk sighed over Rye's ashen streets. In the dimming coral light, Orla and Melody helped each other down from their perch on the castle ramparts after watching the sun set. Like any two friends drunk on the afterimage of charcoal and champagne. When they got to the street, the awaiting medieval town welcomed them into its mystical web of shadows and whispers. Enveloping them in a charged embrace. There was nowhere else Melody wanted to be.

Orla had planned the entire weekend—from the train journey to the daily itinerary and the lodging in Rye's most charming bed-and-breakfast. A sixteenth century manor in the centre of the conch-like town, with only four rooms and a porthole view of the distant woods. After several hard weeks at school, Melody was relieved she didn't have to do anything but allow herself to be led by the heart. And by the heart she was guided through the rustic town's sinuous streets, cobbled and damp, like the scales on a mermaid's tail. Up and down they wound, two radiant young women arm in arm, past crooked clusters of squat, narrow structures so interconnected that the town seemed like one cochlear complex capped by rugged roofs of clay and slate. As jagged as a mythical dragon's back. In the absence of leaves on the Tudor-style facades of brick and wood, scraggly vines, like exsanguinated veins, crawled upward as if reaching for the sky. Longing for release.

'Hungry?' Orla's melodic voice wove perfectly into the enchanted evening. 'I hope so—we're down for a cracking meal.'

Melody couldn't help but smile. She was perfect. The trip was perfect. And she was certain Orla had also planned the perfect dinner.

'Are we eating by the water?' Melody was looking forward to a view of the English Channel. It had been a while since she'd seen the open sea.

'Ah, that like,' Orla smiled mischievously. 'Well, no. It's two miles away . . .'

Melody was surprised. 'Two miles? So how is this a coastal town?'

'You see that?' Without letting go of their linked arms, Orla pointed to an old stone church atop an incline. Its bell tower crowned by a wind vane. 'St Mary's. Once a prominent landmark for sailors. But over the centuries, the sea—which did come right up to town— was blocked off by a frustrated river and the folly of men . . .'

'What?' Melody chuckled, enthralled. She could feel another *Orla* story coming on. They slowed their walk as Orla modulated her voice, waving about her free arm to better illustrate her tale.

'Once upon a time,' Orla began, 'like, in the Middle Ages really . . .'

Melody giggled at her silly Irish love, eager to hear more.

'. . . this lovely town around you was a bustling harbour,' Orla continued, 'that traded in everything from wine and timber to iron and precious salt! It had a shipyard—perhaps over there—and was a naval port in defence of great ol' England . . . But alas, these *great* Englishmen were also feckin' eejits! They reclaimed land to till, then had to dredge waterways to control the floods . . . putting up sea walls and breakwaters to protect from storms. So, over time, the adventurous River Rother— which ran past here directly to the sea—changed course, like, leaving sediment in its path. And that's how the English, per usual, ruined a perfectly good thing and trapped our wee beautiful Rye inland.'

Melody chortled, then played at being serious. 'So . . . the river's gone?'

'Oh, no. It's still there like, but not as it used to be,' Orla explained, her emerald eyes sparkling in the gaslight. 'To be sure, water will always find a way. You can block it or divert it, but it will go where it needs to'—she paused—'like my love for you.'

Melody felt a warmth rise to her face. She was still not used to Orla's expressions of emotion. Even though she shared them.

'And—like the town's old smugglers,' Orla lightened the mood in a snap, 'who had claws in everything, and went anywhere and everywhere they wanted.'

'Smugglers?' Melody giggled.

'Oh yes,' Orla grinned, excited to continue her yarn. 'And pirates! You know how it is—where the ports are, so go the thieves . . . the opportunists looking to make an easy fortune. And Rye's underworld was organized. They built tunnels from the harbour to the other side of the town wall. With numerous stops in between, of course. There were even tunnels in the coastal salt marsh, which was like a halfway point for their goods. They just skipped past customs entirely. Piece o' cake. They owned this place like gangsters rule New York . . .'

Melody just shook her head, delighted at Orla's exuberant storytelling. She was happy to keep meandering through the medieval streets as Orla regaled her with its history. True—or not. She was more entranced by her Irish companion's imagination than the charming shop fronts and cozy corners.

'See that?' Orla stopped in front of a bookshop that had a decrepit iron cage hanging from its roof. 'It's a dragon's banquet . . . '

'A dragon's . . . banquet?' Melody smirked.

'Yes! Rye has a few. It's how they fed the dragon that guards the town. People would put salt in it, which was very valuable then you know, especially for gunpowder. But it would be put in the banquet for the dragon with other offerings—like princes or bad politicians—'

'Oh love,' Melody giggled.

'It's true! Legend has it—the dragon breathes fire on anything that might harm the town. But it protected the smuggled treasures—so,

Rye got rich under the dragon's watch, and in turn, the people took care of the dragon.'

'That's . . . interesting?' Melody was lost for words.

'Quite,' Orla agreed. 'And the dragon knows all the town's secrets— and if you cross it, it will hunt you down.'

As Orla spoke, Melody felt the town's ghosts and shadows come alive, bewitching her with its mysteries and marvels.

'D'you know the buildings here really do connect?' Orla turned serious. 'Besides the bootleggers' tunnels, the attics and roofs are also linked. So, like, when chased by the law, there were escape routes . . . '

'That doesn't seem safe . . .?'

'I'm sure most of the secret doorways and what-not would've been sealed off by now—but all that cloak and dagger is in this town's DNA . . .'

At a sudden skittering in the darkness, Melody jumped, tightening her grip on Orla's arm. From behind, they did look like any two friends might. But like the town, they too had something to hide.

A town of secrets. Perfect for us. Melody thought, appreciating Orla's poetry.

'We're here.' Orla announced as they reached a small, seemingly nondescript structure. Its sign read 'Mermaid's Inn'.

Melody peered in its four-paned window—candles, wood panelling, low ceiling. Tables so small that guests seemed to be dining only inches apart. It was so wonderfully romantic and intimate, she could understand why this place was a favourite among people in need of privacy.

As Melody expected, just like Orla, it was perfect.

* * *

After their perfect meal in the perfect restaurant, the two young women walked a few more meters to their perfect stay. A place called The Duke's Cottage. Like most other structures in Rye, it had a low ceiling, dim lighting, uneven floorboards that creaked when walked on, and dark panelled walls. They almost expected someone from the fifteenth century to greet them. It was run by a widow and her young daughter, who told them upon arrival that the inn had been in the family for generations.

Orla sprung for the Duke's best room. It had a four-poster bed, a tabletop sink, and an antique vanity. It also had an enclosed glass shower in the corner. Clearly a new addition. Melody wondered what Orla might have said to the landlady to have secured such a romantic room. What it didn't have was an actual water closet with a toilet. So, to use the facilities, they had to leave the room.

'You sure you'll be okay?' Orla was half-undressed to shower when Melody needed a quick trip to the loo. It was around a corridor and down several flights of stairs.

'Don't worry,' Melody kissed her on the cheek. 'I'll find it and be right back . . .'

Melody stepped out into the hallway to find it looked the same on either side. In the faint light, she was unsure in which direction to go. Not wanting to trouble Orla by popping back into the room and asking, Melody decided to go left and try her luck. When the corridor ended, she had another decision to make—so, again, she took a chance and picked a turn. In a blink, she was grabbed from behind. A hand on her mouth kept her from screaming.

'Chénzhe, Ming Kai. Wǒ lái zhǐshì tánhuà.'

The sound of Mandarin in her ear was enough to stop Melody in her tracks. But the man had also said her birth name. She was afraid to even breathe. He seemed to have appeared from nowhere. He told her to stay calm and that he only wanted a word. She wouldn't have moved if she could.

'I know about you,' he continued low in Mandarin. 'You and your . . . sick friend.' He loosened his grip and turned to face her. They were eye to eye.

Melody failed to find her voice.

'You must go through shock therapy and a reorientation camp,' he seethed. 'But that is not why I am here. Do you understand?'

Melody had still not uttered a sound.

'Do you not understand your mother tongue?' he growled.

Melody nodded.

'Good. Now I need you to work with me . . .'

She was certain the fear was clear in her face.

'I will not ask for much . . . yet. Just keep an eye on your roommate.'

Melody twitched. *Did he mean Maggie?*

'Yes, Lu Wei Jing. Not the sick *lǎowài* waiting for you in bed . . .'

Melody saw the sheer hatred in his eyes. Like he couldn't comprehend such abomination. It was the look she feared seeing from her family.

'Ah, I want the gift your father sent you,' the man suddenly asked.

'Wha—?'

'Your father,' his eyes gleamed at the power he knew he held over her. He leaned in closer. 'I know who he is. And you wouldn't want him to know about this little excursion of yours, would you?'

Melody said nothing. Steeling herself against tears.

'Get me the music box. The one you had on the train.' He grinned. 'Go. And don't try anything funny—or I will go after your perverted friend.'

Melody managed to walk back to the room, knowing the unknown man was skulking behind her. Orla was showering and didn't hear her come in. As quietly as she could, Melody took the CD player from her purse and slipped back out into the hallway.

'Good girl,' the man appeared around the corner in a flash. He took the portable player and issued a warning. '*Wǒ zài kàn zhe nǐ.* Remember, I am watching . . . and I will be in touch.'

He didn't move and it became apparent to Melody that he was waiting on her. As much as she still needed the toilet, she didn't want to leave Orla alone in the room. Not with him lurking.

He raised his head to indicate she should go. And it was only when Melody shut the bedroom door behind her that he disappeared the way he'd come.

For hours later, the upper hallway of the Duke's Cottage was dusted with the lingering scent of his floral cigarette. The only trace that there'd even been a strange encounter.

After a long hot shower, Melody shivered through the night in the four-poster bed, unable to speak or let Orla love her.

17

7.025150° N, 126.450613° E

Tinago del Sur

2023 | Present

After several days journey from the witch doctor's in Siquijor, there was only one place both Robbi and Raed longed for—*home*. But neither knew where that might be. Feeling lost and displaced, the two were crammed together in the enclosed side carriage of a rickety tricycle, a common mode of transport in the Philippines' rural areas. In some cases, it was the only way to get around—unless a cart pulled by a water buffalo emerged from the rice fields.

Robbi knew how it looked. Him in his thirties, scruffy and unwashed, with a young, undernourished, local teen by his side. They got odd stares everywhere they went. But as many onlookers as they encountered, no one stepped in to check that the kid was all right and nothing nefarious was occurring.

They'd had quite the excursion across the central Philippines. From motorbikes to motorized outriggers, tricycles, and jeepneys. They even had to traverse a raging river on a raft made of old tires and bamboo. Robbi felt like he was on some sort of reality show where teams of two raced around the world competing for a million bucks. But instead of money, this unlikely duo's reward would be an end to the seemingly interminable race they didn't choose.

It was a sordid treasure hunt—where they often felt like the treasure. The entire time, the young teen with him was convinced they were being chased. Insisting their lives were in danger. Robbi wasn't at all sure how his travel companion would know this, but after being saved from drowning, he trusted the boy's instincts. Even if the lad was proving quite mercurial.

So, on the teen's insistence, they avoided well-worn tracks and regular roads. Which made the long journey even longer. More interesting perhaps, but also more difficult. Thank God for the witch doctor's potions—which did help them get passage and places to sleep.

Eventually, the two travellers worked out that when the teen pulled the bracelet from hiding, they could understand each other perfectly. And it was also while holding it that the boy could *anticipate* how things would unfold. As if he'd acquired some sort of psychic impulse. Robbi wanted to examine the stones on the bracelet and try it for himself. Wondering if he too would be able to *foresee* things or communicate with the locals directly. But the teen wouldn't let him touch it, convincing him that people would be suspicious if a foreigner like him suddenly spoke the local language. It might tip them off—the boy warned—to the 'magic' bracelet. He worried that his precious trinket would be stolen. And he couldn't have that before receiving the payday Robbi promised at the end of their journey.

So, the shiny bracelet stayed hidden until they were alone. They would duck away to speak to each other and whisper in the shadows. Which made their relationship seem even more dubious. And still, no one approached them to check on the teen's welfare. Such laissez-faire behaviour infuriated Robbi, but he wasn't about to raise a fuss.

When the pair finally got to the port they needed to catch a ferry to Tinago del Sur, they'd run out of the witch doctor's potion. The teen told Robbi he would find a way to get them on the boat—in exchange for a large tip on top of the promised fortune. He spotted a deckhand idling at the dock, and after a few minutes' conversation, they disappeared behind some crates. Robbi didn't want to know what trade was made, but when the ferry set sail, the deckhand let them on as stowaways. Hours later, by mid-afternoon, they were disembarking at the stop for Tinago del Sur.

To Robbi's surprise, the teen got them a ride on another trike by handing the driver a mobile phone. He'd apparently stolen it off a passenger on the ferry. Though it crossed his mind, Robbi was in no position to lecture anyone against committing a crime—and the old Huawei mobile paid for the final stretch of their journey.

In the tricycle's cramped side carriage, they careened down narrow coastal roads, going around a mountain range to reach a valley tucked deep behind it. Their destination was in a cove protected from the open sea. How the place was first described to him was embedded in Robbi's mind: shielded by peaks, bordered by a gulf, not on a fault line or in the direct path of storms. It was 'the perfect place'—in a tropical, calamity prone country—for a state of the art, sustainable, data centre.

'Where are we going again?' Raed asked for what seemed like the millionth time.

'You're too young to have a memory problem,' Robbi's patience was running thin.

'You haven't exactly told me—'

'Yes, I have. You keep forgetting things. Maybe it's the effect of the bracelet.' Squashed in the tricycle's side carriage, Robbi thought he'd again try his luck. 'Where did you find it again? If you want, I can keep it safe for you—'

Raed smiled a feral smile. 'I don't think so.'

Robbi had seen the look on the teen's face before. Every time he thought someone was trying to take advantage of him. It darkened his face when they were not being let on a raft. They had already traded an herbal potion for passage, only for the skipper to feign not knowing them when it was time to depart.

'Stop playing games and just tell me what we're looking for,' Raed's patience was also wearing thin. 'How am I supposed to help like this?'

'I thought you could read my mind . . .' Robbi taunted.

'You know it doesn't always work like that. I can *feel* what you're thinking and *sense* people's energies—but I can't seem to figure out where you are taking me.'

Every time the teen said something about his 'magic' powers, Robbi took note. He was piecing together that the beads might contain a sort of sensate microchip, possibly something his mother was working on. It seemed to be receiving and transmitting signals— how and why Robbi had yet to understand. There was already a chip in the market that enabled people to communicate without a physical phone—a barely visible decal that was worn behind the ear. But that still only functioned on verbal command. He knew that there was a more advanced version of that used by Level 2 nodes on dεU¹S™, but this . . . *bracelet* . . . seemed to operate on another dimension entirely.

'We're near,' the tricycle driver proclaimed. 'The largest field behind the wave of mountains . . .' His passengers followed where his finger was pointing. Robbi could not make anything out. It just looked like a vast pasture. But the closer they got, Robbi realized they were actually facing very tall walls that mirrored the environment, effectively camouflaging the entrance to their destination. It was a high-tech cloak that only his old friend Ben could have planned.

Beñat Gurrola Izaguirre IV was his first real friend at Almhurst. He had arrived at the boarding school only a month before Robbi, but already behaved like the head boy. An expected role as far as Ben was concerned. Naturally, he was lord wherever he went. A foot taller than anyone his age, 'Big Boy Beñat' was as overbearing as could be, but he was also irresistibly charming. He famously got off detention by convincing the headmaster that it was to the school's detriment that he be subjected to such 'puerile social stigmatization'. He was eleven at the time.

Always one for big words, blustery Beñat came from a low-key Basque family that made a fortune in the colonial merchant trade. Over generations, the Gurrolas deftly built political connections to drive their business contracts. All while not-so-secretly supporting Basque independence from Spain. Nevertheless, they were ingrained in the empire's maritime successes—providing transport to the far-flung territories, setting up banks, and developing railways. But they also quietly funded the revolutions in the colonies. Long after the empire ended, Ben—the lone Gurrola grandchild—was left with expansive properties across South America and the Philippines. Which he utilized to amass more wealth that could then fund his more *humanitarian* interests.

'*Entraaaaa!*' Ben's familiar voice boomed at the visitors as if from above, and the 'invisible' walls began to part to let them in.

At the end of a short driveway, the tricycle came to a stop in front of a complex of boxy, monochrome structures without any windows. The driver showed little interest in the austere surroundings. Unaware that behind the dull exterior lay the most advanced technology in the world. Quantum computers, hydro-powered cooling systems, the latest in solar panels and molten salt energy, and the most secure storage drives money could buy. The compound was also meant to host the biggest digital mining ops for JUN0®—if Ben ever managed to get the data centre off the ground. The last time Robbi spoke to him, it was sounding a tad like his well-intentioned but ill-advised vineyard project in Central Mongolia, which he'd set up to offer miners an alternative source of income.

'Dude! Dude dude dude dude dude!'

Robbi and the teen were squeezing themselves out of the trike's side carriage when bounding towards them from the largest of the buildings was Beñat Gurrola in all his splendour. A six-foot-seven colossus in ratty sneakers, an oversized, bright coloured T-shirt, and faded jeans. It was a look that never quite worked on the Iberian Peninsula, but as Robbi would later learn, in the Philippines— particularly in Tinago del Sur—it was a signature for the massive, fair-skinned man fondly known to locals as *Ang Gigante*. The Giant. A name Beñat wore with pride.

Robbi's young travel companion gasped as Ben waved the tricycle driver off with a wad of cash, pressing a finger to his mouth to ask for the man's silence. Wearing the biggest smile, the driver nodded and left without a word. The compound gates closed immediately behind him.

'You'll get more than that soon,' Robbi whispered to the teen. 'I promise.'

'Alone at last!' Ben was about to take his childhood friend into a bear hug but instead raised a hand to his nose. 'Wow, dude. I'd say . . . at least a week without washing, yes?'

Robbi had to laugh despite himself. 'Arsehole.'

'Am I wrong?' Ben shook his head. 'And what do we have here?'

Unintentionally, the teen had taken a step behind Robbi.

'Long story,' Robbi sighed.

'I'll say,' Ben replied, examining both the new arrivals.

'You seemed to be expecting me though?' Robbi wondered.

'Of course,' Ben laughed. 'I have sources everywhere! Especially in the fishing village. They all love Ang Gigante. Did you think I wouldn't be told that someone was looking for me? Well, looking for this place, I mean. Particularly someone looking like . . . *that*,' Ben stretched his arms out to indicate the state of his old friend. 'I mean, really, Robbo, what the fuck? It's a good thing my staff are all inside and spared this . . . this . . . vision—'

'Shut it,' Robbi retorted.

The teen remained silent, still gobsmacked by the amount of cash just handed over to the trike driver. He was glad he followed his—the bracelet's—instincts and stayed with this foreigner. When he got his reward, he would go find his family.

'Well, welcome to Paraiso!' Ben exclaimed with aplomb.

From their many conversations, Robbi should have recalled the name of the estate. It was so very Ben. *Paraiso*. Paradise. Because it was to be the store of all knowledge. A veritable Garden of Eden. A green—as green as it could be—data hub. Energy efficient and sustainable, with its own leading edge power supply and escape route out of the country. Ben wanted it to run as independently as possible from what he called 'the fucked-up state'. It was to be his own little fiefdom sans corruption. And he was just wealthy enough to pull it off.

The locals, living on the other side of the mountains facing the sea, thought Paraiso was just some rich guy's whimsy. A place for the giant man-child to play video games or *Dungeons and Dragons* and hold secret *Star Trek* conventions for his uber tech nerd buddies.

'I need secure comms, man,' Robbi requested, then lowered his voice, leaning closer to his friend. 'And keep an eye on him'—he discreetly indicated the teen—'it's complicated, but he has something of mine, and I'm still pressing him for info.'

'Right. Of course.' Ben immediately led them into one of the structures. 'Come come come.'

In a blur, Robbi and the teen were shown inside to a lift that brought them to Ben's personal suite on the top floor, encountering no one else along the way.

Like the rest of the complex, Ben's apartment was spartan, except for its owner's preferred refinements—a full wine cooler, shelves lined with vinyl albums of showtunes and classic film soundtracks, and a modern kitchen.

'Here,' Ben handed him a slim, encrypted device, unable to share the highly secure ear-decal he was wearing, which only worked with its owner's bio-waves. 'We'll be outside.' He grabbed two cans of soda and motioned for the teen to join him on the roof deck. A non-too-subtle info-prying move. Also, the sun was about to set, and watching it was always a highlight of Ben's days.

In the air-conditioned apartment, Robbi paced as his first few calls went unanswered. He then rang the only other number he knew for sure would pick up.

After an eternity, he heard his father's voice on the receiver. Sending both relief and a chill down his bones.

'Robbi? Is this really you?'

'*Hafa Adai*,' Robbi replied. It was the phrase they had long agreed on to confirm identity. In case of kidnappings or other unfortunate events. A native greeting from his birthplace, Guam.

'Are you all right? Where have you been?'

'Yes. Yes. I . . . I . . . lost all my bags, and I . . . need some money. I can't access my crypto—'

'Of course. Where are you?'

'Can't say. I have to lie low. I think people are after me.'

'I see.'

'Where is Mom?' Robbi finally asked. 'I tried her but her line won't connect. Is she with you?'

His father didn't answer.

'Dad, is she there?'

'Uh . . . not right now.'

It was not like his father to stumble for words. Robbi pretended not to notice and decided to just come right out and ask what was weighing on him. 'Do you remember the bracelet she started wearing like a few weeks ago?'

'What?'

'With purple stones that looked like something from the Jade Market—'

'Ah . . . uhm, yes . . .?' His father tried to hide his discomfort with a cough.

'Did you hear about the environmentalist who OD-ed in a Sabah hotel?'

His father said nothing.

'I think he had Mom's bracelet.'

'Who told you that?' His father's voice rose.

'I . . . heard.'

'From whom?'

The upset was clear in his father's voice. The man was always very good at being stoic—but when it came to his wife, Robbi's mother, he was an open book. Like a puppy in relation to its owner.

'Tell me!' his father demanded.

'It doesn't matter.'

'I will be the judge of that.'

'Why? Where is Mom?'

Silence.

Robbi hated his father's loaded silences.

'Police in Kota Kinabalu are looking for a witness'—his father had recovered, his voice expressionless and even—'do you know the witness?'

It was Robbi's turn to say nothing. He could tell his father was being evasive, opaque, but he couldn't understand why. What did the death of a stranger in a whole different country have to do with them? With his mother? And why was his father acting as if there was nothing adverse between them? Their last conversation was less than pleasant, and this business-like tone was making him nervous.

'Can I speak to Mom, please?' Robbi asked again.

'She's busy,' this time, the reply came without hesitation. 'Work. You know how she gets. And she has so much going on at the temple too.'

'Right.' Robbi didn't believe a word. 'I'll send you details. For the crypto.'

'Are you coming home?'

'Soon . . .' There was something askew that he couldn't put his finger on, and suddenly, he was overcome with dread.

'Okay. Take care.'

And that was the last his father said before ending the call.

Robbie took a few deep breaths and put the encrypted device down on the kitchen counter. As if it had betrayed him. He shut his eyes and tried again to ease his heartbeat. Speaking to his father had not always put him on edge like this.

He took a can of soda from the fridge, as he'd seen Ben do, and went to join his friend and the teen on the roof deck. Evening had fallen and the compound was dark save for the moonlight it reflected. Above, the stars sparkled bright, unobscured by an urban haze.

'All good?' Beñat turned toward him as he came outside.

Robbi nodded. 'Just need you to set me up with a new pouch . . .'

'Sure sure sure. Not a prob.' Ben replied, understanding exactly what Robbi meant. New crypto wallet to access funds.

'Are you okay?' Robbi noticed the teen squirming. He seemed uncomfortable. But with the bracelet tucked away, the teen couldn't understand what he was being asked.

Ben—having spent summers and the last few years in the Philippines—translated for the boy. While Robbi was on his call, the two managed to have a conversation without needing the bracelet.

'He says he's fine,' Ben expressed.

'But it looks like he's . . . bleeding?' Robbi pointed to a dark shadow on the boy's shorts.

The teen immediately tried to cover himself with his hands.

'Are you hurt?' Ben asked the boy in the local dialect, noticing the stain for the first time.

'No! I am fine.' The teen was getting agitated. 'It's an old wound . . . from—rebels. They . . . hurt me . . .' he managed to stammer.

'You want the bathroom?' Ben urged, gently.

The boy nodded.

'Inside—to the left—first door. You can shower. There are spare towels—and take anything from the closet. I also have bandages in the cabinet.'

Without another word, the boy put down his empty soda can and retreated into their host's apartment.

'Poor kid,' Ben said when they were alone. 'Been through a lot, it seems. He wasn't sure how he met you. Just said it was in Sabah?'

'He wasn't *sure*? Maybe he blocked it out. It was bad, man. We were on a dive boat—and he was a stowaway—'

'Wait! *The* dive boat? The one that's missing?! That was the resort's?'

'You heard about it? Yeah—it sank, man—'

'I knew it!' Ben was giddy at having his presumption confirmed.

'We were on a night dive and these armed men appeared out of nowhere—'

'Snap! Kidnap for ransom! Right? Sea bandits from the islands west of here, I'm sure of it.'

Robbi was surprised that his friend was not.

'It's a cottage industry, man. Ransom goes a long way and foreigners earn them dollars,' Ben explained. 'They're from the poorest islands—but wait, how'd the boat sink?'

'They killed our crew and took over, but then another boat showed up with more armed men—'

'Of course!' Ben thought for a moment. 'The second wave.'

'What?'

'They share hostages. Like a bandit co-op. The longer they need to hold on to them, the more gangs get involved—the larger the ransom. They share the profits and the burden of keeping hostages alive. As I said, man, poorest islands. They can't afford to keep feeding extra people . . . so, first wave, then a backup wave. You get the picture.'

'Well, they started shooting at each other. That's when I saw the kid slip off the boat—and I guess I followed. Was either that or be killed in the crossfire. They shot everyone . . .' he paused at the memory of the handsome European.

Ben's face was rapt. He read about these things but rarely encountered people with first-hand experience of such savagery.

'And I swear one of the attackers said my name . . .' Robbi sighed. 'So, I think someone knew I was there—'

'Damn! That would've been a *huge* get for them'—Ben dialled down his excitement when he saw the horror on Robbi's face—'Sorry.'

Robbi just shook his head.

'So,' Ben continued, tentatively, 'no one knows you're here?'

'No one was supposed to know I was on that boat!'

'Right. Right right right . . .'

'And now, this kid . . . well, he saved my life really . . .' Robbi trailed off not knowing how to explain it.

'A little young for you, no?' Ben joked.

'Don't be gross, man,' Robbi groaned at his friend's typical ill-timed and inappropriate jab, 'he has my mother's bracelet.'

'What?'

'This purple thing she started wearing weeks ago. I know it was customized and she never took it off,' Robbi recounted. 'But the kid had it on the boat . . . and every time I ask him where he got it, his answer changes. He once said a friend gave it to him, but from other things he's said, I think it's from a crime scene. But I don't know if he was actually there. I need him to tell me the truth—and if my mother was somehow involved . . .'

'Huh.'

'Yeah. Raed said—'

'Who's Raed?' Ben cut in.

'The kid.' Robbie tilted his head towards the apartment.

'He told me his name was Maki.' Ben was perplexed.

'What?'

'Yeah,' Ben nodded. 'I'm sure he said Maki, like the Japanese roll. 'Cuz I put it together with him telling me that at first you were looking for a place called "Tamago"—hilarious, dude. As if a town in the Flips would be named after sushi! Funny aside, Tinago actually means hidden—'

'Ben!' Robbi pulled him back from what was sure to be a lengthy side story.

'Sorry. Sorry sorry sorry . . .'

'Gah! I don't get that guy, man,' Robbi moaned. 'He keeps . . . I don't know. He's moody. Some days he's sulky, others he's really— peppy. Most of the time he's just angry as a neutered bulldog.'

'Teenagers, ey?' Ben didn't know what to say.

'Not just his moods . . . it's like he's different people. The way he walks changes and the way he talks. Even the way he comes across, you know?'

'Maybe it's a Gen Z thing?' Ben tried to offer an explanation.

'And he's convinced someone's trying to kill him,' Robbi was clearly exasperated.

'Maybe they are. Maybe he *was* at a crime scene?'

'Why wouldn't he just tell me that?'

'Why *would* he?'

'But who'd want to kill a . . . a . . .'

'A what?' Ben smirked, knowing why Robbi hesitated. 'Say it, Mr PC—I-never-say-anything-offensive—'

'A street urchin! Happy?'

'Ah, and you think it must be you they're after, right?' Ben chuckled. 'Always so self-centred, Mr Stinky Twink—'

'Shut up!'

'Not funny yet?' Ben poked his friend.

'No.'

'Your dad still upset?'

'What do you think?' Robbi stated the obvious. '"I'm gay, Pops" doesn't exactly make a man like him throw a party . . .'

Ben was appropriately silent for a few seconds. 'Anyone at the resort figure out who you were?'

'No. I mean, I did end up giving my first name . . . but I could've been anyone. I had no ID on me. Left everything in a safety deposit box in KK.'

'I am amazed you found me . . . but I think you better get off these islands, dear chap,' Ben suggested, worried for his friend. As influential as Robbi's family was, they also had very powerful enemies.

'No shit.'

'I can get you home—' Ben offered.

'No. Not yet. Something's off. And I don't wanna get caught up in my dad's BS right now. I have to find my mom,' Robbi concluded. 'There's a place she told me to go if I was ever in trouble . . . *Guanxi* . . .'

'Ah! The all-important, mutual back-scratching relationship. And what will you do with the kid while you call on this *guanxi*?'

'Pay him for the bracelet and send him home. He's looking for his family . . .'

Feeling his friend's anxiety, Ben said nothing. He let the evening crickets and the distant splash of the gulf's subdued sea soothe the hovering unease.

'Well, before we say goodbye again,' Ben dashed inside to retrieve two slim glasses and a sleek bottle of Txakoli from his chiller. His favourite tipple. A light, crisp wine from his family's hometown in Spain. He had a supply on hand wherever he went.

'Just arrived here from Manila,' Ben explained. 'I convinced a local importer that there would be a market for it in the country—of course, I'm his only client'—he stopped to laugh—'saves me from having to be the one to make the prerequisite deals with corrupt customs officers.'

'Oh, Ben Ben Ben Ben Ben,' Robbi took the glass handed to him, 'don't ever change.'

Ben poured the drink from a meter up, the way it was meant to be served. Robbi watched it bubble to the rim . . . and realized how tired he was of being a receptacle for other people's dreams.

'The family want me to take over the business,' he suddenly shared, bereft.

Ben smirked. 'Oh, baby, isn't that what we progeny are for?'

From inside the apartment, separated from them by double-glazed glass, Anak watched the old friends share their gilded burdens. As he tucked away the bracelet, a tear rolled down his face. How he envied their easy connection.

Fable of The Mineral Goddess and
The Dragon's Rage

Long ago, when time was young, the sibling Sun was bold and fun.
The older Moon was calmer, more serene, happy to be still and gleam.

One day, without warning, the Sun left home
to chase a winged fire that enticed it to roam...

The orphaned Moon wept alone in darkness,
hurt and abandoned by a brother so heartless.

Moon's tears pierced the heavens as stars,
as it called back the Sun to heal their scars.

He had to be home before their Mother returned,
but the Sun refused till a lesson was learned.

He wanted the dragon's eggs, the source of its power,
but the Goddess arrived at the peak of his selfish hour.

So, Mother God took the dragon's eggs and buried them,
in an emerald lake protected by a purple jade mountain.

Every day, the Sun burned in search of its treasure,
scorching pieces of earth as it went for measure.

In punishing her Sun, the Goddess angered the dragon,
who sat in wait to free her eggs from their prison.

For as long as the eggs were safe, the world was well.

But word travelled fast that there was gold,
and people came from everywhere to own and behold.

They skinned the mountain and started draining the lake
not caring at all how big their mistake.

*Indigenous Taiwanese folktale

$$\pi$$

18

7.0667° N, 171.2667° E

Majuro

2004

Flying back into Majuro was never the same for Edi after losing his Jimma. He knew there would be no warm welcome waiting upon his exit from the airport. No one waving at him expectantly or calling his name. *Home* had taken on a different flavour when he lost his grandparents. Not even the sweetness of breadfruit could mask the alienation.

'Fasten for landing,' the pilot's voice was a cue for Edi to shut his eyes. He took the moment to pray instead of looking out the window at the sparkling view. Funny how people change after bereavement.

'Taxi?'

Edi went straight for the cab rank when he got his bags. He'd skimped on the trip to have money left over for the fare. Despite the success of their film *Tomb's Day* in the environmentalists' circuit, Edi and Jack still struggled to fund their Runit clean-up campaign. They spent most of what they raised to attend every international conference, but it was hard to be heard when 'climate change' was the chorus of the century. Humanity recognized that something had to be done to arrest global warming, but little was truly executed. By appearing at these meetings, Edi hoped to shock people into action, illustrating how much worse things were with the added time bomb of nuclear waste. But often, he was nothing more than an interesting sidebar. The tatted islander with one eye who spent time in jail.

He glanced out the cab window on the coastal drive back to the house he inherited from his grandparents, noticing for the first time how worn out everything seemed. Many of the town's low structures appeared damaged in a storm surge and parts of the road were still flooded. This was what the richer nations didn't want to face—as sea levels and temperatures rose, low-lying places like the Marshalls could disappear into a watery grave. Maybe it was time the islands considered building a seawall, but Edi knew that would only delay the inevitable.

'When did this happen?' Edi asked the taxi driver who was busy singing along to the radio.

'Few days ago,' the man yelled back above his music. 'Power's only just back on half the island, man. And forget the Internet . . .'

Edi looked out again and saw families trying to salvage what they could from vegetable plots soaked in seawater. Across them in the open ocean, there were three ships so far on the horizon Edi almost missed them. In the five years he'd been back from the States, he'd never seen so many. He knew they wouldn't be cruise ships. The Marshalls were too far and its ports were not equipped for such large vessels. Edi wondered if they might be private contractors laying cables. Maybe that Chinese entrepreneur Jack first brought to the islands was hard at work, and perhaps their access to the Internet would finally improve.

'What's with all the boats?' Edi again asked the cabbie.

'Eh?' The man looked at him in the rear-view mirror.

'The boats?' Edi pointed at the water.

The driver shrugged. 'Who knows. Maybe mining. Maybe military. Big explosion the other day . . . and lots of energy contractor types hanging about . . .'

Edi hadn't heard about an explosion in the Marshalls while he was away. But then again, he was on the opposite side of the world at a conference in Argentina. The plane journey one way took three days and involved several stops—getting news from Majuro to Runit alone could take a week.

At the conference, Edi learned about fissures on the ocean floor and how much more frequently they seemed to be happening. It was shifting sub-aquatic landscapes, releasing energies and materials new to the sea. There were things happening underwater that people couldn't see so they took for granted. Edi didn't want to be one of those people. He remembered the fishermen on Runit who told them about explosions in their lagoon—which turned out to be leftover ammunition from naval ships sunk during World War 2. Could there be deadly wrecks like that in front of Majuro? It was the last thing they needed. Along with the impending threat of the fractured Tomb releasing nuclear waste into the sea.

As the taxi rounded a traffic circle, Edi spotted a new petrol station that wasn't there when he had left two weeks prior. And just past it, a billboard sat above a six-feet-high sheet metal fence—the one thing that wasn't showing signs of storm damage. It announced the construction of something called Heron's Nest, presumably already being built behind the fence. He made a note to ask Jack about it when they met for dinner. Jack had been shacking up with one of the local teachers, who also happened to be the mayor's daughter. They'd invited Edi around that night for a welcome meal.

When the taxi stopped in front of his grandparents'—*his*—house, Edi paid the fare, grabbed his bags, and got out of the cab without another word. His grandma would not have been pleased that he didn't thank the cabbie. But having had to make nice the entire week at the conference, Edi had run out of pleasantries. The young man behind the wheel did not seem fussed. He didn't even offer to help with the bag. *It's a changing world, Bubu*, thought Edi as he stepped over patches of soggy grass on his way to the front door.

Once inside, he flipped the light switch out of habit—but like the cabbie had warned, there was no power. Edi dropped his bags on the floor and pulled the curtains. Then, he walked around the dishevelled living room to open the back door to the garden, letting in more sun and the breeze from the sea. He stood staring at the sparkling water for what seemed an eternity. Unable to move from the weight of his disenchantment. Other than pain, there was really nothing left for Edi in the Marshalls. The only reason he didn't leave was he had nowhere else to go.

* * *

'Don't be so pessimistic Edi, it's a good thing,' Jack was ladling fish soup made with coconut milk into a bowl. The power was still off and he was doing his best, in the gaslight, not to spill. They had to sit down to dinner illuminated by several oil lamps scattered around the small home Jack shared with the mayor's daughter.

'I don't know how you can be so unconcerned . . .' Edi took the dish from Jack and nodded his thanks at Wina, who was seated across him. He knew she would've spent the whole afternoon making the spicy delicacy. She was not Edi's type, but he appreciated that she was right for Jack. At least, so far, she had put up with his visionary notions and well-intentioned schemes.

'A data hub like Heron's Nest is exactly what this place needs,' Jack insisted. 'We're perfectly placed in the middle of the Pacific. Linking Asia to America. With us hosting all this transcontinental, global, whatever data here—the big guys won't be so quick to write us off.'

Edi had noticed that in the last few months, Jack kept referring to the Marshalls like he was a native. It was all *us* and *we* as if he were not from a country that was part of the problem.

'Who's bankrolling this?' Edi asked.

'A Chinese state firm,' Jack looked to Wina for support. 'The mayor said they're bringing in all their best technology and their best people.'

'We do not have to provide anything but the land,' Wina smiled.

'And even that they've paid for!' Jack was more excited about this than Edi thought acceptable for a climate activist.

'This is exactly the kind of drain on the Earth's resources that we've been battling, Jack. You know how much energy is needed to run a place like that . . . you can't be serious.' Edi didn't think he had enough energy left in him to carry on with the discussion.

'Look, man,' Jack put his spoon down and faced Edi dead on, as if he were about to reveal existential secrets. Sitting so close, even in the compromised lighting, Edi noticed how red Jack's teeth had become from chewing betel quids. 'The web is the future,' Jack stated. 'Everything will be digital, so we might as well ride the tide. Work it to our favour. This will stimulate our economy . . .'

There it was again, irking Edi—*our . . . we . . . us.*

'What else have we got?' Jack continued. 'We ain't got no real tourism industry, we got no exports, no agriculture. All we got is a *nukular* wasteland that no one who pays wants to visit.'

'Nuclear.' Edi corrected. *Typical American*. He did not like the way the conversation was going. Had he lost his only ally?

Suddenly unable to breathe, Edi moved his bowl aside and rose from the table. 'Sorry, I . . . am not feeling too good,' he looked at Wina, 'it was a long trip, really takes it out of you. I need to go lie down.'

Jack was taken aback by Edi's withdrawal. 'Hey, you okay, man? Wanna rest on our bed?'

Edi immediately turned down the offer. 'I think I'll walk home while I still can. Thanks.'

'Let me make you a doggie bag . . .' Wina had already gotten up to prepare it.

'It's okay, really . . . I'll come by for leftovers another day . . . I promise . . .'

And with that, Edi turned and walked out the door. Finding more comfort in the company of darkness.

* * *

The next morning, Edi awoke to a stray dog licking his feet. He'd slept on his couch with the back door open facing the sea. He looked up and realized that electricity had been restored. All his lights were on and the ceiling fans were spinning.

His bags were still on the floor. Unopened and full of dirty laundry. They had attracted the dog's interest.

Before he could drive the animal away, there was a knock on the front door. He thought if he stayed silent, whoever it was would leave.

More knocking. Louder this time. And the dog started to bark.

'Edi? Edi?!' *Knock-knock-knock*. 'You okay, man? When'd you get a dog?!'

Edi rose slowly and pulled the door open to Jack sweating on the other side. Pooling his rose-tinted saliva to spit into a flower bed.

'Fucking nasty, dude,' Edi said, walking back into the house. Jack followed him in and shut the door.

'What happened last night, man? Not a fan of Wina's *jebwejerbal*?'

'Tssss,' Edi shook his head. 'Don't be an idiot, her soup was great.'

'Then what?' Jack nearly tripped over the unopened bags. 'Are you not gonna unpack?'

'I just woke up—give me a sec, would you?' Edi went to the sink to fill a glass with water.

'But you been here since yesterday . . .'

Edi took his drink in one gulp.

'I brought you some food,' Jack put a plastic box on the kitchen table. 'Win wouldn't let me leave without it.'

'Thanks.' Edi meant it.

'So, how was Argentina? You haven't said . . . wait!' Jack had sat at the table and was about to roll a betel quid. 'Why don't I give you one of these and it'll be like Runit all over again, remember? We could read each other's minds . . .'

'What the fuck is wrong with you, man?' Edi swiped the betel kit off the table and onto the floor. 'Is this why our campaign is flagging? You know you haven't been as proactive—'

'Hey!' Jack glared at him, incredulous. 'I have been really busy here, you fucker.'

'Doing what exactly?'

Jack's face was turning red, either from heat or his anger. 'Helping the mayor,' he exclaimed. 'He's gonna run for president and I can help him win it. Then, we can really turn things around for us—'

'Stop it!' Edi put his hands to his face. 'Just—stop it.'

'Dude.' Jack stood up, shaking his head. 'Get a grip. I don't know what's eating you, man—but pull your shit together.'

Edi couldn't believe this was coming from Jack. The nerve of this two-bit foreigner. To come to the atoll and take over like he knew better. Just because he was sleeping with the mayor's daughter?

'I think you better go.' Edi wrapped his hands on a chair. Trying to keep from shaking.

Jack got on his knees to pick up his betel kit. Once he salvaged what he could, he left without looking back.

In the days that followed, Edi alternated between watching the ocean and surfing the web at the village Internet café. As much as his tight budget and the island's poor connectivity allowed. Usually not more than an hour. Just long enough to see what was on the news and check his email. Occasionally, he continued his search for information on the ship he saw from Runit. But there was next to nothing online about a company named after a math equation. $\Omega \pi L \alpha$. Not only was it embedded in his mind but he also tattooed it on his thigh himself. A skill he picked up behind bars. The ink barely occupied an inch of skin, but it served to remind him that his days were numbered, so he must stay sober and make good use of his post-jail 'rebirth'. He called it his 'Runit Realization'.

And since he made it a mission to figure out what that ship was about, the tattoo was a guarantee he'd never mix up the symbols. He didn't think he'd recall it right if he wasn't on smash. One search engine turned up that the equation did read similar to a Celtic name for Golden Princess. Which could also explain why it flew the flag of the Isle of Man. But what would a ship from Britain have been doing so far into the Pacific?

Another search for 'Orla' showed a gold mining company, a legal firm, and a minor film star.

He was just about to search again when his email pinged. It was a message from a woman he met at the conference in Argentina. She was inviting him to work alongside her organization—a group called UNPER. He'd not heard of it before. Underrepresented Nations and Peoples for Equality and Recognition. He wondered if they fell under the United Nations. If so, this was huge. The woman, Angela, said the basis for their campaigns were the same: human rights, fighting the tyranny of industrialized nations, and giving voice to those in the margins.

Angela said she was going to be in 'the Pacific region' and suggested a meet up in Manila. How the heck was he going to get there so soon after spending for a trip to South America? It upset him that even these global sorts didn't have a clue about the geography of maritime nations. Yes, both the Marshalls and the Philippines were in the Pacific—but there were some 2,400 nautical miles between them and no direct or easy flight paths. Which meant a trip like that would cost a small fortune.

He said none of this in his reply to Angela. Only that he would do what he could to find the funds for such a meeting. He then asked if she might consider other options, perhaps a long-distance phone call or a visit to the lovely Marshalls.

Within minutes of sending her his reply, he received another email.

Dear Mr Edi,

I am sorry if I wasn't clear. We would like to invite you to Manila as our guest, at no cost to yourself. A flight and hotel will be arranged for you by UNPER as soon as we have the information needed to make your booking. Once sorted, we will email your travel confirmation. Please find attached the proposed itinerary for your stay. We are very excited to meet with you again and speak at more length about your work.

There were a few more niceties and attached forms, including a document with the organization's profile. At least that's what it said. He tried to download it—but according to the system, it would take eight hours.

He couldn't keep working like this. It was affecting his efficiency. With the rest of the world speeding into the digital era, Majuro was still limping through the twentieth century. Bad enough that it was difficult for travel, but Edi felt even more isolated knowing connections were being made online and his access was hindered.

An advert popped up on his screen. Discounted tickets to Guam. How he wished he could be based there, but with his criminal record, there would be too many questions. He wasn't even sure if he would be allowed back to the US territory.

He typed 'Manila' into the search bar. He didn't know much about the Philippine capital, other than it was also counted as being on the frontline of climate change. Numerous typhoons. Prone to floods.

Earthquake belt. Volcanoes. It sounded like the Marshalls—amplified. The only thing missing was 100,000 cubic yards of nuclear waste.

Edi was about to click on a link to read more about the country and its relationship with the US—he wanted to make sure he could go there without needing to explain who he was or where he came from—but his screen went dead. His time had run out.

'Fuckit!' he muttered under his breath as he hit the desktop screen.

'Oi! You break it you pay it, Edison!' the woman behind the counter was never his greatest fan.

'Sorry, Tei. I was just in the middle of something . . .'

'Tsss-ya. Aren't you always?' she tsked, 'You best bring more money next time—you know you always in the middle of something.'

He had hoped she would give him a few more minutes for free, but he didn't have the charm that Jack had. And he didn't even know how to flirt.

Fuckit. What future did a guy like him have? And what the hell was he still fighting to save?

At this point, he was just going on momentum. He didn't know what else to do. The last five years of freedom from prison, all he did was try to make his grandparents proud. But they were gone. So, there he sat—in his cleanest unlaundered clothing, rubber shoes on his tired feet—being kicked out of an Internet 'café' in Majuro by a girl young enough to be his kid. Had he had any.

As he stepped out of the wooden shack that housed the extent of the island's progress, Edi looked across the street at the bright blue ocean. He walked over unmindful of the traffic, hypnotized as always by the crystal waves. Around him, the ghosts of once lithe and towering coconut trees lay battered and decapitated by recent storms. There was rubble and crushed flowers on the beach, carried out by floodwaters that had claimed the coastal cemetery. Even the dead couldn't rest in the Marshalls.

This was not the life he wanted. Not what he signed up for when he returned from the mainland. He was angry that his family was gone before he might've learned to resent them. Like he heard happened in other—normal—families. He was angry that they were *killed* by people disguised as saviours. The all-mighty American soldiers who declared they were protecting the world. Just as he was sentenced to death by their sacred nukes from the moment he was born.

In no rush to return to his empty house, Edi sat on what was left of a pile of sandbags—the temporary coastal barrier put up by the neighbours. The sun was soft, and he watched the ocean breathe. The even rise and fall of the tide. One of the sandbags had toppled onto the beach and was being lapped at by the water. It bore the logo of the new petrol stations he'd seen around town. An orange circle with a long-necked, long-legged bird in flight above the word Transform.

Edi took it as a sign from heaven. It was time to adapt to the changing world. He would accept UNPER's offer and go meet Angela in Manila. It was time to amp up his campaign and find better allies than the one he'd lost.

19

51.5072° N, 0.1276° W

London

1990

It was the same debate every time they took this walk: seagull or pigeon. And Melody always lost, insisting she still had trouble distinguishing between the two feathered Londoners. The way she also couldn't tell apart the sounds they made.

'Seriously, love?' Orla thought it amusing. 'One's clearly a squawk, and the other's a crooner. You'd think by now you'd know the difference!'

Melody mock-glared at her playful lover. Her favourite person in the world. They were standing in front of a riverside museum having just spent the morning looking at conceptual art. One of the many cost-free activities Orla lined up for their weekends. The young avant-garde artist enjoyed being tour guide to her 'maths-brained' companion, showing her the many soul-stirring insights of masterpieces like a framed toilet. Orla was wearing the biggest smile when Melody leaned in to kiss her.

On this particularly sombre spring day, in their matching light jackets and trainers, they were the only two people strolling along the Thames—accompanied by the usual pesky swarm of birds.

'They won't hurt you,' Orla chided as Melody ducked each time one approached.

'Oh yeah? Tell it to the bird that took a nosedive at my head the other day . . .'

'What are you on about?' Orla chuckled at the thought.

'Yeah! One of those flying pests dove right into me when I was walking to class. It hurt!'

'My poor baby,' Orla cooed, rubbing the back of Melody's head. 'Didn't your special bracelet protect you?'

'I'm serious!' Melody whined.

'I know!'

The pair stopped walking to jovially stare each other down. Within seconds, they burst into laughter.

'I'm just glad it didn't poop on me at the same time!' Melody confessed.

'Aye, but it's good luck, ye know?'

'How is being dukeyed on by a bird good luck?' Melody wasn't sure if Orla was joking. 'Do they put those on exhibit in some museum, too? Westerners!'

Orla chuckled. Vacillating between explaining the underlying universality such an art piece might express or talking about the luck of the droppings. She let go of her companion's hand to flap both her arms as if they were wings. 'I tell ya—pecuniary windfall. That's the belief . . .'

'Bah!' Melody dismissed the suggestion. 'A nasty superstition is what it is . . .'

In the distance, Big Ben chimed the hour. An unapologetic, anachronistic constant in the timeless city. It had likely seen more birds dukeying than Melody could count.

'We best get you back,' Orla suggested. She knew Melody liked to be in the dorm in time for her parents' weekly call.

'Oh, didn't I tell you? Not today. They're on a trip. We don't have to rush . . .'

Melody smiled and Orla's heart skipped a beat. When did they become such a lovesick cliché? The rhythms of her everyday moved to the dictates of Melody's impulses. She hadn't painted or worked on anything new since they started to . . . spend more time together. She was . . . too happy. Too present in the moment. It was as if all time stopped and yet transpired together at once. There was no yesterday or tomorrow—only eternal moments spent gazing into

Melody's bottomless obsidian orbs. *JesusMaryandJoseph!* Had she really just thought of Melody's *orbs?!* She couldn't even think in simple words anymore. *What happened to* eyes, *Orla?* She chastised herself. Since Melody, everything had become so heightened and extreme. The everyday suddenly transformed into poetry.

In the silvery peace of their usual Saturday stroll along the embankment, Orla heard the resounding flutter of angels' wings.

'Feckin bird!' Melody swatted at another close call with a pigeon.

Orla threw her arms around the embattled woman and embraced her. 'I got you. You're safe now,' she teased.

Melody buried her head in Orla's neck, breathing in the scent of vanilla and roasted chestnuts. It turned the muggy day by the slate-coloured river into a warm afternoon by a cozy fire. Like their time in Rye during the winter.

Enveloped in the certainty of their connection, the young ladies resumed their stroll. Across Lambeth Bridge to the quiet South Bank and down towards the art deco Oxo Tower.

The faint fog that veiled the monochrome city was beginning to lift, exposing more of the hueless sky. But Melody—always—only saw Orla in colour. Despite the grey, the day blazed as bright as her auburn hair, and the chill bore the sheen of her emerald eyes. When they were together, all of London's majesty was theirs.

Just theirs.

'Shall we stop at the George & Dragon?' Orla asked as they neared Waterloo Bridge. It was a little-known pub to the side of the Royal Festival Hall. Small and popular with tradespeople getting off a night shift. It wasn't as busy in the afternoons. They'd discovered it together on one of their early weekend walks.

'Yes!' Melody squeezed Orla's hand. 'And maybe Maggie will be home by the time we get back.'

'Have you still not seen her?'

'We keep crossing paths,' Melody explained. 'I'm usually asleep when she returns from the library or her workshop, and she's out like a log when I get up for class. The few times I've caught her awake, she's reading medical journals or the news. Ever since that Heavenly Gate massacre in Beijing . . .'

'Ah, a new obsession. No wonder she's dropped us like hot potatoes,' Orla joked. She hadn't seen much of Maggie either. Gone were their nights listening to music with other women at the Elephant in the Cellar. In truth, the scene at the underground bar wasn't the same after the nearby bombing. And with Melody taking up most of Orla's free time, it seemed Maggie had found other ways to fill hers.

'She is rather obsessive, isn't she?' Melody concurred. 'She's been looking tired . . . and gaunt. And I swear she's even paler than usual. You have read her *manifesto*, right?' Melody had convinced herself that her brilliant roommate wasn't mad, but Maggie made that difficult to sustain.

'Aye,' Orla nodded, 'I read it. Doesn't mean I understood it—but I read the words.'

Melody had to giggle. 'It's a whole other language, I know.'

'Greek to me,' Orla shrugged.

They'd arrived at the pub and Melody took their usual table out front as Orla went inside for their drinks.

While waiting, Melody pulled their shared pack of smokes from her coat pocket and tapped it for a stick. A habit she picked up in London. It made her feel—independent and interesting. She took the stick with her lips and was searching for the lighter when a familiar fragrance wafted over. A cloyingly floral musk. She looked up and a calloused hand half-covered by an oversized jacket sleeve was waiting to light her cigarette. She automatically glanced back to try and spot Orla.

'She's still inside,' the clipped voice grunted in Mandarin.

Melody took the cigarette out of her mouth. She thought she was rid of him. This hulking spectre who simultaneously frightened and angered her. She hadn't seen him in weeks. Since first dropping in on her in Rye, he would sometimes turn up when she was alone in public. Always asking about Maggie.

'Where has she been?' he snarled through his teeth.

'I—I—don't know. She doesn't tell me. She sleeps a lot and spends all her awake time studying for school. She is very smart. The other day, the lecturer gave her paper top marks. Said he'd never read anything more genius . . .' Melody wasn't lying. She never lied to this unknown man—she only drowned him creatively in uninteresting details. She still had no idea exactly who he was or what he was after. She had considered that he might be a state agent from China, but what the heck would they want with Maggie? Her next guess was some sort of triad. She knew such criminal gangs were a presence in the city. Either way, these were not people she wanted to cross.

'You still don't know what she plans to do with this manifesto?'

'That's nothing,' Melody tried to sound confident, casually touching her goddess-blessed bracelet. 'It's just words. We're math students—not very good with words . . .'

He stared at her quizzically, as if trying to read her mind. Melody wondered why he seemed preoccupied by Maggie's rather obscure ramblings. This manifesto that not even she—another maths student—was convinced by. Maggie had posted it on the student union bulletin board, but it was taken down the next day. And her attempt to get it printed in the school paper was a non-starter.

'Has she said anything about her parents?' he always asked the same questions.

Melody shook her head. Was he expecting her to change her answers?

'Nothing about her father? Or her mother?'

'I think they're both dead, right?' Melody said without expression. 'She never talks about them—maybe it hurts too much? I do know she likes pizza and has way too many chips . . .'

Her reply seemed to irritate him. He grunted then raised the lighter to her face, indicating he would light her stick. 'You must find out what she is planning,' he struck the igniter and leaned in as Melody took the flame. 'Your parents' flight is landing in New York soon. If you don't have better answers for me next time, wherever they might be, we will send them your regards—from you and your *lovely* Irish friend.'

In a snap, he shut the lighter lid on the flame and was gone.

Melody was still shaking when Orla reappeared with drinks.

'Can we go?' She could barely get her voice out.

'Wha—?' Orla spread her arms out at the line of drinks she'd just put on the table. Two pints of Guinness and two double shots of Bushmills.

Melody downed both glasses of whiskey and abruptly rose to go.

* * *

It was quiet when Maggie got back to the dorm from her work lab. Most of the students were out and she knew Melody would be with Orla. A typical Saturday evening.

She unlocked the door and, in the dark, walked across their room to her desk by the window. She cracked the sash open before flicking on her lamp, preferring the low light to the overhead fluorescent bulbs. The crisp night air drifted in, clearing their room of the stench of confinement.

Maggie kicked off her shoes and rummaged through her bottom drawer. She'd lost track of time and worried she'd be late getting back to the dorm.

She found the vial she needed and prepared the injection. After nearly a year of administering it herself, she could almost do it with her eyes closed. One day, that might be the case—she was so exhausted she didn't know how she kept functional. Was this tiredness a side effect?

She lowered her trousers and pressed the syringe to her thigh.

Her throat hurt and her voice was scratchy from all the stress on her body. She knew her friends thought she was smoking too much, but she'd actually cut back because of all the risks she'd read about.

As she pulled her trousers back up, Maggie got a glimpse of her reflection in the top half of the sash window. In the disembodied light of her desk lamp, she had hollows for cheeks and dark circles under her eyes. Capped with a bad haircut that Melody convinced her would be less troublesome, she looked like a phantom in the mist of evening.

She disposed of the syringe and wondered if Melody would be home that night—or if it was another sleepover at Orla's. It wasn't a frequent occurrence, as Orla shared a small flat with five other people. At least, she was no longer in a squat. Maggie suspected Melody might not be as gung-ho about her girlfriend if she knew they'd met as squatters in East London. Both had been without a home for a couple of years. So, they lived in an abandoned structure with other art students, musicians, and all sorts of troubled runaways. A commune of sorts. They'd both come quite a way since then.

Overwhelmed with fatigue, Maggie got into bed without showering. Too tired to even get out of her clothing, much less pad down the hall to the bathroom.

That's how Orla and Melody found her when they arrived later that evening. Fully dressed, with one foot still on the floor. Dead asleep.

* * *

The next morning, before she could even think of slipping out of the room, Maggie awoke to Melody and Orla standing over her with coffee and pastries.

'There she is,' Orla drawled. 'Wakey wakey, Wei-wei,'

Maggie groaned and tried to roll over to face the wall, but her leg had gone numb from hanging over the side of the bed as she slept.

'Up you get, we're going for a roast,' Orla announced. 'Simply because we deserve it.'

Maggie looked confused.

'I say *we* . . . but I mean Melody,' Orla chuckled. 'Her folks think *she* deserves a treat—she got a bump in her allowance this week, aye?'

Orla looked to Melody for confirmation.

'So—meal's on her!' Orla jumped on top of the still reclining Maggie. 'Come on, Wei-wei! A full pub roast . . . with all the Yorkshire pudding we want!'

Despite her friend's effort, Maggie was struggling to be enthused.

'Afterward, I was thinking we can go to Foyles,' Melody joined in. 'Autumn Winthrop will be signing her new book, isn't she your favourite? You know she never leaves her Cambridge retreat. So, this is a rare chance to meet her . . .'

'Sunday Funday, Wei-wei,' Orla teased.

'Stop calling me that, Pale Face,' Maggie finally muttered. 'I didn't like it *then*, I don't like it now.'

Curious, Melody looked from one girl to the other.

'It's what she used to call me back when we were . . .' Maggie trailed off realizing what she was about to say.

'Oh!' Melody clocked it, 'when you were in the squat?'

Maggie turned to Orla, surprised that she'd told Melody.

Orla just smiled. She and Melody told each other everything.

'How cool was that?' Melody said. 'To be surrounded by such visceral . . . life!'

That was not the response Maggie expected to their days in squalor.

'I don't know why you never talk about it, Mags,' Melody continued, 'I mean, how you went from that to the LSE? What a trip!'

'Just because I was homeless doesn't mean I was stupid.'

'Not what she meant, Mags, come on,' Orla pacified. 'Now,' she playfully slapped Maggie's arm, 'stop delaying us from getting our Sunday Roast on . . . up and at 'em! You can even drone on about yer work while we eat . . .'

The prospect of discussing her work was not what got Maggie out of bed. She would never tell them, but it was the chance to spend time with her friends again that pushed her to get past her lingering exhaustion and the pins and needles in her leg.

* * *

Lunch at the Earl of Hawkespeare was everything they needed it to be. Leisurely and indulgent. Melody even sprung for pints of lager and Irish coffee at the end of their feast. By the time they were done with dessert, they had half an hour to get to Foyles Bookstore and Autumn Winthrop. Just long enough for a nice walk through the West End. Past theatres and countless bookstores. There were also loads of people spilling out of Soho's many pubs and drinking on the pavement.

'Nothing like springtime in London,' Orla exclaimed, breathing it all in.

'Yes, the wonderful unpredictability of the weather,' Maggie scoffed. 'Damp and dreary yesterday, and today we get topless queens.'

They found themselves in a tide of gay men heading toward Soho Square. There was cheering, loud singing, and lots of laughter.

'It's like the Mazu festival,' Melody exclaimed. 'You must know it, right Mags? Traditional Chinese holiday'—she explained to Orla as Maggie rolled her eyes—'birthday of the Holy Mother, Sea Goddess. When we call on her for protection and thank her for blessings. In Taipei, we have street parties, parades, food stalls, fireworks . . .'

They'd reached the square and a stage was set up in front of the small garden enclosure. Around it, people bearing placards were chanting for gay rights and an end to Conservative rule.

'Oh feck—it's Pride!' Orla blurted. 'How'd we not realize the date, Mags?' Since being with Melody, Orla had lost all sense of time.

'What?' Melody wasn't sure she understood.

'Gay Day,' Maggie said by way of explanation. 'The queers come out and demand respect.'

Melody looked at the crowd and realized how many men were dressed as women, women who looked more like men than the men, and same sex couples unabashedly hung onto each other. She felt a sudden need to hide. She'd never found herself among such a public display of—what was usually hidden. She was . . . uncomfortable, and she wasn't sure why.

Noticing her unease, Orla put a hand on Melody's arm, 'Y'alright, love?'

Melody flinched at the contact. To Orla's surprise.

'Oops, trouble in paradise?' Maggie deadpanned.

Melody looked like a lost deer. 'No, what? Of course not. I've just never . . . I mean . . .'

'It's all right, princess. No one expects you to get all political and upset Mum and Dad . . .'

'Maggie, come on,' Orla was getting tired of Maggie's constant put-downs about Melody's upbringing. It wasn't her fault she was raised with the proverbial silver spoon in her mouth, and how sheltered that made her.

Still unsettled, Melody slipped her hand into Orla's. Grateful for the Irish girl's presence. She hadn't realized it was Pride weekend. She had read about it in the paper but didn't give it much thought. It did explain why the iconic lesbian author Autumn Winthrop would choose to be in London this particular weekend. How could she not have put that together? She felt like a fool.

The crowd around them was growing and the heat was getting oppressive. Along the square's outer edges, Melody noticed there were police in unusually large numbers. The whole scene had her disoriented and she couldn't work out which direction to go in for Foyles.

Music was switched on and all around, people seemed to be grabbing each other and yelling. Throughout the crowd and on the fringes, a multitude of photographers and news reporters were recording and capturing images of the revellers. Images which she realized would include her—*shit*. Instantly, Melody panicked. Remembering what the Chinese man said to her the day before. Her parents. She couldn't have any of this get to her parents. They would not understand.

Before she could consider her next move, there was a loud smash of glass breaking and then pandemonium. People began to scream and run in every direction. A fight seemed to have broken out, turning the rally into a riot. Melody reached for Orla's hand only to realize the girl was on the ground. She'd been hit by a bottle and was bleeding from the side of her head. Instinctively, Melody dropped to her knees to tend the wound, while scanning the mob to try and find Maggie.

There, among the media recording events for the daily news, was a man in a black leather jacket that Melody recognized. He too was taking photos. His camera aimed directly at the two of them on the ground. A cigarette hung loosely from his lips, the pungency of which Melody was certain would nauseate her had he been closer. He lowered his camera and smiled at her.

Melody froze. She looked down at Orla bleeding in her arms, dull green eyes clouded in pain. *I can't put her in danger . . .*

She bent over Orla, cradling her head, shielding them both from view. As police tried to gain control of the situation, people ran past like a stampeding horde fleeing possible arrest.

They were still on the ground when Maggie found them. She hurriedly helped get Orla to her feet.

'We gotta go,' Maggie shouted as she scanned the chaos for an exit.

* * *

The three friends returned to the dorm much later that evening, after Orla's wound was properly seen to and bandaged. It was not the day's ending they'd have imagined.

Keeping the lights low, they gently got Orla out of her bloodied clothes and into Melody's bed. While Melody changed into a clean set of pyjamas, Maggie crashed and was out like a log.

Melody thought about trying to take Maggie's shoes off, but she knew she ran the risk of being kicked. It had happened before. So, instead, she slipped in quietly next to Orla. Watching her sleep and carefully stroking her hair. In the moonlight's reflection, Melody caught sight of her wrist—surprisingly bare and missing Mazu's bracelet. She must've lost it in the ruckus at Pride! Could there have been a clearer sign of the gods' disapproval? Melody had lost her way and they removed their protection. By displeasing the spirits, she'd put them all in danger.

As Maggie lay prone, softly wheezing across from them, Melody watched Orla sleep in her arms. Counting time by the steady rise and fall of her breathing. This joyful soul who'd brought the world alive.

She would never forgive herself if anything happened to Orla because of her.

She would never forgive herself if she broke her parents' hearts.

20

Koror

2023 | Present

It's what Valya liked most of her adoptive home—that even its boundless crystal waters could not be confined to a colour. Sometimes a brittle blue, other times a biting green. Always as transparent as glass. Living on an island in the Pacific, she was constantly reminded there were no boundaries to the wonders of the ocean. It's why she went scuba diving as often as she could. To rest in the expansive silence of the deep—liberated from her pain—and yet, feel connected to the very source of life. Despite everything she'd been through—or perhaps because of it—Valya believed that God was everywhere. But it was in the ocean that she felt the most direct connection, the clearest revelation of the face of the Divine.

When she was floating in the salt water among God's beautiful undersea creatures, Valya forgot that she was born of suffering. That her parents were Ingush refugees in Kazakhstan longing for a home they'd never seen. Her ancestors were kicked out of an Ingushetia subjugated by Soviet socialists and overrun by ethnic Russians. She was eleven when the Soviet Union splintered, and her family could finally cross a bordering gorge on foot with other Ingush returnees. But instead of triumph, she watched helplessly as her twin brother's hand slipped out of hers and he fell through a ravine to his death.

When she was weightless in the glistening Pacific, she was free of the guilt and the mantle she'd taken up to be a replacement son to her parents. To be the *boy* they could rely on and put to work. The twin who should've lived instead of her.

When she was enveloped in the aqueous cocoon, she could also wash away the memories of her father being taken by post-Soviet Russian agents. Leaving Valya alone with her ailing mother when their house was broken into by drunken rebels. When she was submerged in the mighty Pacific, she could purge herself of the powerlessness she felt while her mother was raped then committed suicide three months later on finding out she was pregnant. It was at that point that Valya snapped and knew she had to leave the miseries of her endlessly woeful Ingushetia. Still subsumed by tormentors in so many forms. Russian soldiers, ethnic fighters, political militias.

In the calm warm equatorial waters, Valya eliminated the need for roots and stretched herself beyond the tragedy of those jagged mountains. At sixteen, she smuggled herself back out with other refugees, in pursuit of more than a legacy of anguish. Unshackling herself from her landlocked origins by sheer strength of will. A step at a time, she crossed Europe from east to west, reinventing herself. Becoming—Valentia, the brave one. A force not to be trifled with or taken advantage of.

When she finally got to Spain—a place her parents always hoped to go—she learned how to immerse herself in the freedom of the Costa Brava's waves. For the first time, she felt uncontained—and also, most herself.

It was there, under the wide Valencia sky, that Valya realized water was not a barrier between lands but connective tissue. From Spain's largest port city, the Mediterranean Sea opened to the rest of the world.

Her sanctified time underwater was nearly over. She knew it instinctively, feeling it in her breathing. There was only forty minutes of air in her tank. So, slowly, she began her ascent.

Valya usually did shore dives from the cove at the inn, but not this time. She packed her gear and drove to the other—quieter—side of the island, crossing a causeway to get to an atoll. Away from the site of dead humpback whales. She needed to clear her head, and that would not be possible with a growing crowd waiting to see if the tide would bring in more bloodied marine creatures. It no longer surprised her that people would be such strange, morbid animals. *So much for deU¹S™ enabling human enlightenment!* But for that half hour she was underwater, Valya escaped all digital and technological threads that constricted modern living. They dominated even a place as remote as Palau.

'Al Qadr, al Qadr,' she whispered repeatedly as she walked back to shore after surfacing—a final nod of recognition to her sacred link to God.

Dive gear packed, Valya got into her jeep to return to the Gal/Guy. Along the way, she passed the small house rented to Uyghur refugees. Palau was officially an ally of Taiwan and had no diplomatic relations with China. So, it was a good halfway point for those fleeing oppression until they were resettled somewhere less isolating. Valya felt a kinship knowing how unfamiliar everything on the tropical island would be to them. How different the locals were to those they would be used to at home. No one was meant to know they were there—previous refugees were not so welcomed—but people talk, and there were no secrets on the islands. Valya always paid special attention to what was said in whispers. It's what informed her own surreptitious activities.

Before turning the corner, she slowed to check if the food she'd left for them earlier was still on the stoop. It wasn't. And she presumed it had been brought inside.

'Al Qadr, al Qadr . . .' she muttered, touching the string of green beads hanging from her rear-view mirror. It was all divinely decreed.

When she arrived at the inn, Luc was by reception and saw her enter through the side door.

'*Nekh vekhay,*' he called in greeting.

It stopped Valya in her tracks.

'Did I say it right?' he wondered why she seemed taken aback. Almost—angry?

Victory or death. In Ingush. He had said it right. The clarion call of her people. It's what defined them. But she had never encountered anyone outside the Caucuses who knew that.

'People of the Tower,' he smiled at her warmly. 'Clever. Ghalghaï—Gal/Guy. What a great way to honour your homeland halfway around the world.'

Valya had not moved. She was still staring at him stupefied.

'I'm sorry. I didn't mean to upset you,' his expression went from joy to discomfort.

She cleared her throat, not knowing what else to do.

'I am Yazidi,' he blurted, filling the silence with his rich Canadian accent. 'From Iraq?'

Still holding on to her dive gear, Valya said nothing. Unsure of his intention in telling her his ethnicity. Were they meant to have a connection because their people had both been fucked over?

'I just thought it was cool. To meet an Ingush person? You're the only . . .' he paused seeing no change in her countenance. 'I'll stop talking, I get how odd this must be . . . I am sorry.'

In a sense, she was glad he got it right. It was the first time someone didn't presume she was Russian. *Nekh vekhay.*

'What gave it away?' she finally asked, truly wanting to know.

'Name of the inn, I guess. And your—very slight accent,' he smiled shyly. 'I'm more aware of things, I think, since being on dεU^{1}S. I love how it connects all us nodes—almost like federated wisdom! It feels like I'm being . . . rewired. What better use of time while I wait around for my wife, right?'

Shifting her dive bag from one shoulder to the other, Valya raised an eyebrow.

'Oh. Diving. Of course,' he noticed her gear, 'all that nature stuff. Yes. But what I meant was with my wife busy—and when I'm not at the beach—I'd probably end up at the bar with Ted . . . so, instead, better to dεU^{1}S dεU^{1}S dεU^{1}S . . .'

'You are not also working,' she asked as if it were a statement.

'Ah, no. Well, I'm—you know—a doctor. So, this is a holiday.' He remembered to keep up their front, although clearly the innkeeper seemed to know that's what it was.

Valya wondered what kept his wife busy. She never did seem to be around.

'Well, I'll let you get on with your day . . .' Luc shuffled uncomfortably. 'I uh . . . just wanted to say—I'm a doctor.'

Again, Valya raised an eyebrow.

'Oh, I've already said that haven't I? It's in case you . . . need one on short notice. I'm here to help, no questions asked.' He had no idea why he just said that.

Neither did she. *What an odd man*, she thought. She was just about to take her leave when Yuyu came looking for her.

'Seaplane!' the receptionist announced. 'It went round and round . . .'

'What?' Valya spoke the question both she and Luc were thinking.

'We saw it approach from the cove, but it kept going . . . went to one of the atolls, then came back. No one's sure where it landed.'

Valya seemed confused, but Luc was certain it would have to do with his wife and her 'highly confidential' dealings.

'Was it orange with a flying crane on its tail?' He suspected the seaplane bore the logo of his wife's employer.

Yuyu shook her head. 'You mean like Transform, the energy company? No, not this one . . .'

Seaplanes were not rare in Palau, but they had designated landing zones. And the dive inn was nowhere near them. Valya felt a sudden fear that the unexpected visitors might have to do with the *unscheduled package* she had hidden with her other undocumented 'special arrivals' in the Gal/Guy laundry room. The one place guests didn't care to see. Not even Metik bothered to know its location. Which meant Valya could control access to it.

They all excused themselves from one another. Yuyu returned to reception, Luc headed for the bar, and Valya rushed to her office to drop off her gear. She then went to check the laundry room. It was in a semi-detached hut facing the mangroves. Away from the road, people could often go back and forth from the inn without being seen.

Out of ultra-precautionary habit, Valya looked around to make sure she was alone before walking over. But she wasn't. Two figures were emerging from the mangrove swamp in clothes that didn't look like their own. The taller one—fair and skinny—locked eyes with her. *Shit*, she was unarmed.

'Guanxi?' he called softly, holding up his hands.

Valya looked unmoved.

'Guanxi.' He repeated a little louder. The shorter, leaner figure behind him hung back in the plants, pulling at their oversized trousers.

Valya studied the man as he approached. It couldn't be.

'Robbi?' she asked, haltingly.

'How—?'

She put a finger to her lips to urge him to silence. Then she waved him over to the side.

Lacking another option, he trod lightly behind her, signalling for his companion to follow.

'What's wrong?' Valya asked as she led them to the inn's garage, which housed a rundown van that was practically dismantled. 'Why are you here?'

She shut the door behind them. Mottled light streamed in through the thatched roofing and a small, loosely shuttered window.

'Sorry,' Robbi started, as they huddled together in a dusty corner. 'I would've come alone—but he insisted on staying with me, he reneged on our deal . . .'

They both turned to the teen, who stood apart, shuffling nervously from one foot to the other. Valya noticed a trickle of blood down his leg.

'You're bleeding—are you hurt?' She tried to touch his arm, but he jerked away. His anxiety transformed into anger. Then, he pulled back his shoulders and smiled.

'Is good,' the boy winked, showing off the only English he knew.

Valya had not expected the rapid-fire changes in his demeanour, but she wasn't surprised.

'All right,' she said, evenly. 'But if you need help, you let me know, okay?'

The teen's face changed again—almost like he was considering it. He looked at her blankly, then scowled. A second later, he shook his head and marched away from them to the shadows on the opposite side of the garage.

'God, I'm sorry. I don't think even *I* was that moody as a teen,' Robbi whispered when the boy was obscured by the van.

'I think I understand,' Valya lowered her voice further. 'I've seen it many times in people who have been through trauma . . .'

She then remembered her earlier odd encounter.

'Wait here, I will get a doctor,' she called out to the hiding teen, 'to look at your wound.'

Before he could protest, she was out the door. She passed the kitchen and asked that some food be packed, then she went to find Luc.

It didn't take long for her to return to the garage with snacks and the doctor. Only telling him there was someone in need of help.

'Mr X?' Luc fell back as if he'd seen a ghost. 'You're alive!'

Shocked, he moved to examine Robbi, who stopped him.

'No, not me. I'm fine—he's back there somewhere . . .'

Luc glanced from Robbi to Valya—wondering how this scenario had come to be. Was the intended patient another familiar guest from Pulau Rahsia? Maybe the dive boat had just lost its way and they all wound up in Palau.

Valya nodded for Luc to go over to the small mechanic's workshop at the back of the garage.

While he tended to the teen, Valya and Robbi resumed their conversation in hushed tones.

'Mr X?' she asked.

'Long story,' he lowered his eyes. It felt like a lifetime away.

'I imagine,' Valya replied. 'Who is the boy and what deal did you make? Did your mother send you?'

Robbi shook his head. 'I just met him, but he has my mother's bracelet. He's not really telling me how or why . . . I've tried to befriend him for answers but nothing. He was supposed to give it to me in exchange for a reward before I left the Philippines, but he suddenly refused when he saw the seaplane and insisted on coming with me . . .'

'So, it was you on the seaplane?'

He nodded. 'I'm trying to find my mom, and I was hoping you would know where she is . . .?'

From the heavy silence and the look on Valya's face, Robbi realized there was more to be worried about than his mother failing to answer his call.

'I'm sorry,' Valya said tentatively, 'I haven't spoken to her in years. . . since . . . that night.' She bore into his eyes to see if he might remember. But there was no hint of that.

'Why come to me? How did you know where I was?' Valya asked again.

'Because she once told me that if I was ever in . . . danger . . . to go find "the brave one" in Palau.'

At that, Valya snorted.

'I asked the first person I saw when we landed, and they said we'd find you at the Gal/Guy . . .'

'And were you also told to enter through the mangroves?' Valya asked, drolly.

Robbi felt his embarrassment colour his face. 'I—we—didn't want to go to the front and risk being seen. The boy thinks we're being followed . . . and I think he might be right.'

Why would the boy think that? Valya wondered, trying to piece everything together. Edi was dead. Melody was unreachable. Next, Robbi appeared out of nowhere, perplexed. *He had been so young then—* but she believed she might know why he was being pursued.

'She sent me a . . . chip. By special courier.' Valya wasn't sure how much to say. 'Almost a year ago, I think . . .'

Why would his mother do that? He wasn't understanding their connection.

'Maybe Edison got one too . . .' Valya pondered.

Edison? Robbi was surprised to hear the name. 'My mother knew the environmentalist?' The urgency was evident in his voice.

And what became evident to Valya was that Robbi had no recollection of their history. She wondered how much he actually knew about his mother.

'Wait . . . the boy . . . Edi . . .' Robbi was struggling to keep up with his thoughts. 'He was there . . .'

'What do you mean?'

'I think the boy was there when Edison died—or was killed— maybe that's where he got it . . . and somehow, the bracelet is *making* him stay with me . . . bringing us together . . . for some reason?'

Valya gave him the space to think or keep talking.

'My father says police are now looking for a witness—'

'A moment,' Valya suggested. 'You said you came from the Philippines? That's not where Edi died . . . how could the boy be a witness?'

'We met in Sabah,' Robbi began, 'well, not quite in Sabah . . . on a dive boat . . . in the water. He saved my life. Anyway, that's where we came from—'

'You were on *the* missing dive boat?'

Robbi nodded.

'From Sabah? Where Edison died?'

'Yes. Then, Filipino fishermen found us and brought us to Siquijor . . . after all the shooting . . .' He could see from her face that he was muddying the story.

'Okay,' she tried again to get him to pause for breath. 'In . . . and out. In, and out . . .' she motioned with her hands to her chest, keeping time.

Robbi tried to slow to her pace.

'You are safe here,' she reassured him. 'Do not worry.'

He took a deep breath then exhaled.

'Now,' Valya nodded, 'Tell me how you came to be in the mangrove . . .'

So, Robbi recounted as much as he could as fast as he could, finding the retelling almost as arduous as the journey itself. Dive resort. Kidnapping attempt. Shooting. Stowing away. His mother's bracelet—which had him vacillating between thinking it had a microchip embedded in it or suspecting the teen was pretending to have super cognitive powers.

'You think the boy got on the boat from Kota Kinabalu?' Valya clarified.

'He must have. He has said that's where he found the bracelet. Other times, he says a "friend" gave it to him—but also in Kota. Then, sometimes he acts like he doesn't know at all where it's from!'

'He who holds the truth is like a candle—' Valya started to quote Rumi.

'—easily swayed by the wind?' Robbi retorted in frustration.

Valya gave him a closed lip smile. 'Maybe someone *is* after the boy *because* he witnessed a crime?'

'Or he was part of it . . .' Robbi posited what he'd been wondering for days.

'Do you *truly* believe that?' Valya asked, as if humouring him.

'You should get the bathroom back here cleaned,' Luc unintentionally interrupted their conversation, rejoining them from the mechanic's workshop. 'Oh, and your boy's a girl,' he said once he got closer.

'I'm sorry?' Robbi was flummoxed.

'She's a girl,' Luc looked back in the direction he'd come from. 'On her period. First time apparently.'

The teen had yet to reappear.

'I told her to rest. And that you'd get her some sanitary pads. I think it's all too much . . .'

'He's a girl?' Robbi repeated.

Luc nodded. 'I don't think she realized it herself . . .'

'How is that possible?' Robbi remained disbelieving.

'I suspect she has dissociative identity disorder,' Luc concluded. 'I'm no expert on that, but she switched personalities several times as I examined her. It's clear the poor thing is under a lot of stress . . .'

'That explains why you never got a straight answer,' Valya concluded. 'I've seen it before. It's a way to escape a trauma. She must've been through so much . . .'

'Look, I'm not sure what he's—she's—seen,' Robbi offered, 'but she keeps saying *they* will kill her . . . him . . . her . . .'

'Which personality?'

'I can't tell which one is most afraid,' Robbi replied. 'It's like they're all running for different reasons.'

'And you?' Valya asked him directly. 'What are you running from, Robbi? Or running to? What is it I can help you with?'

'I thought you'd lead me to Mom,' he said sadly. 'But maybe I should've listened to the kid before we took off and gone straight to Nan Madol. Do you know it?'

'Nan Madol. In Pohnpei, which means "upon a stone altar". Home to the most megalithic ruins in the world.' Luc exclaimed. 'Not far from here. Nan Madol itself is an ancient man-made complex of basalt rock and coral islets, connected by a network of canals. A feat of engineering. It dates back to the thirteenth century and is believed to be the spiritual centre of the Saudeleur people. Matrilineal and seafaring. Built in a shallow lagoon, there are remains of temples, palaces, and tombs. A world heritage site.' Luc concluded to the stares of his stunned audience.

'Let me guess,' Valya raised an eyebrow. 'dɛU¹S.'

The doctor beamed.

'That's it? A relic?' Robbi wondered why the bracelet might be leading them there.

'Nan Madol is not just a relic,' Valya corrected. 'It's a place of divine power. Of healing and guidance. The islets are aligned with the stars, and the canals—which are over a hundred kilometres long—connect to the spiritual realm . . .'

'I can't seem to *connect* to the node network,' Luc was fiddling with his device, hoping to learn more about the intriguing destination.

Valya shook her head. 'I will arrange, Robbi. If that's where you need to go.'

'As long as it doesn't involve another boat . . .' Robbi remarked.

'It will,' Valya stated. 'It's the only way to get there without calling attention . . .'

'Well,' Luc checked the time on his mobile. 'I better head back in case my wife looks for me. Catch up later, yea?' he said to Robbi. 'Ted—the American from the resort?—he's here, too. We'll see you at the bar.'

'Oh. Uh, let me pay you for looking at the kid. I'll send you some JUN0.'

'Dude,' Luc feigned offense then smiled as he turned to go. 'Just get me a drink later and tell us what happened on that dive boat, cool?'

Once he'd gone, Robbi turned to Valya. 'I will repay you for the trip . . .'

'Your crypto is no good here.'

'Why?'

'It's not real. Not tangible. It has no value. I can't trust it,' she stated plainly. 'Even God can be felt in the heat of the sun or the bliss of the ocean. But what happens to your crypto when the circuits or blockchains are broken? What happens when the power goes out?'

'That'll never happen.' Robbi was quick to pronounce, despite knowing that it could.

'I wouldn't be too sure,' Valya warned. 'And there is no power in Nan Madol,' she declared before heading out to the inn. 'At least not the kind you might expect.'

'Wait—' he called after her. 'Do you know if my mom's ever been there?'

Valya shook her head.

'I can't understand why that bracelet might be leading us there . . .'

That would've sounded crazy to anyone else, but Valya had seen what technological magic Robbi's mother was capable of. From the moment they met to the chip she received with instructions: to attach it behind her ear should she need to contact the sender. Valya did try when it first arrived, but the strange power of such a tool frightened her, so she locked it away.

'We can talk more later,' her tone softened. 'First, I will get pads for the girl and make arrangements. You wait here,' she instructed. 'Too many dɛU¹S users at the inn . . . and in the outside world. Here, their signal is blocked. You are safe.'

'dɛU¹S can find you through anything. Nothing can shield us . . .' he sounded defeated.

She nodded at the wreck behind him, occupying most of the garage. 'The van is a nullifier,' she explained, 'a special mix of lead, copper, salt, a few other things that don't conduct energy but absorb it. Nodes cannot go through it. It breaks the dɛU¹S circuit and protects you from being seen. It should at least buy you time.'

He wondered why she would know or need such a thing. But before he could ask, she'd left.

$$* * *$$

Expectedly, Teddy was at the bar when Luc found him.

'Hey,' the doctor took a seat and waved at the barkeep for a drink.

Teddy didn't look up from his device. 'I got a ping on my app, man. The thing I'm supposed to find—it's here.'

'What do you mean?'

'I gotta go . . .' Ted dashed off before Luc could tell him the good news that Mr X from the Sabah resort was alive.

'Hello, Doctor.'

Luc turned as Metik sat beside him.

'I have something for you,' the Palauan brought out a small packet and carefully removed its contents.

'A watch?' It was not what Luc was expecting.

'My contact says this is the latest tech,' Metik lowered his voice and leaned in. 'It will work with the Level 1 code on your device and enhance your deU^1S experience. Better than those replica Level 2 chips being sold on the black market.'

'I don't know . . .' Luc studied the watch Metik put in his hand. Where there would have been a screen or a dial, there was only a featureless face of what appeared to be packed, fine white sand. It wasn't even encased in glass.

'You just put your hand over it,' Metik instructed. 'But I hear that if you touch it with an open cut, the jolt goes directly into your bloodstream. Super powerful. Kinda like smash—but not. They say its mind-blowing.' Metik put his hands by his temples and gestured an explosion.

Luc wasn't convinced it was a good idea, but Metik left him the watch and walked away.

* * *

On an atoll across a causeway on the other side of the island, Nisha paced a room no larger than her home closet. Impatient for test results to confirm what she already suspected: waste from the radioactive salt they were mining for energy in Xinjiang must have made it to the South China Sea. Coupled with equally contaminated crosscurrents from Runit in the Pacific, it was killing marine life. Too rapidly for them to even deny it was happening. She knew it was a bad idea to start harvesting the salt lakes in Xinjiang's Lop Nur, the site of China's nuclear tests in the mid-twentieth century. Transform had found that the trace radioactivity actually enhanced the properties needed to use salt as a new power source, but the risks seemed to be outweighing the advantages.

Needing a change of scenery, Nisha left the enclosed lab for the front room. The two scientists she had transported from Xinjiang were feasting on a meal she hadn't brought them.

'What's that?'

'A nice white lady brings us halal food every few days . . .'

'Why? How does she know you're here?' Nisha tried to keep her voice even.

'It's a small place, you can't occupy space without being noticed . . .'

'We chose Palau because no one looks here,' she sighed. 'I told you not to mingle or call attention to yourselves . . .'

'We don't,' one scientist looked to the other for affirmation.

'We've never talked to her,' he confirmed. 'She just leaves the food out front and goes. We've only seen her from the window.'

Nisha didn't like this development. But she needn't be on dɛU¹S™ to know it would be wrong to stop them from having food that was prescribed by their religion.

While they ate, she caught up on the news.

Headlines confirmed that the missing European influencers were on the dive boat from Pulau Rahsia. The Kota Kinabalu hotel jumper was identified as a high-ranking Chinese official. Which made no sense, as there was no body to identify.

Reading between the lines, it seemed to Nisha that in Beijing, Zhou was losing his grip on power. His deputies were being sacrificed as more Chinese people were getting off their devices and linking directly to each other. A result of them moving up on dɛU¹S™. This meant police were unable to monitor activities unless they joined dɛU¹S™ too. But once they did, they no longer complied with any repressive orders they were given.

Nisha sighed. She could imagine the chaos. This was why Transform, a Chinese-owned company, barred its employees from joining dɛU¹S™. It led to anarchy.

She knew there was a proliferation of Chinese-made replica chips. The underground industry was backed by the ruling party. Eager to keep people on devices that could be monitored while they tried to perfect their own version of what was being called cognitive technology. Nisha knew that select officers of the state were being given a dɛU¹S™-compatible tool they wore on their wrists like watches. It was made with the same compound that was in the chips. But things seemed to be malfunctioning.

'Do you want some?'

'No, thank you,' her sudden politeness surprised them. 'I should go and check on my husband. He might be getting into all sorts of dɛU¹S trouble.'

* * *

At the Gal/Guy, still hiding in the unused garage, Robbi too was catching up on the news. He'd asked Valya for a way to check what was online and she'd lent him an encrypted tablet.

He scrolled past news of the dive boat and stopped at a round-up on the Taiwanese elections. There was a profile of the leading candidate for mayor of the capital city, widely seen as a steppingstone to the country's presidency.

'That's him!' Anak exclaimed.

Robbi turned to see the boy . . . the girl . . . peering over his shoulder at the device.

'He was there when the one-eyed man was killed!'

Robbi looked back at the screen. Pulled in by the cold, steely eyes of the serious Taiwanese politician: 'Wild Willy' Chiu.

His father.

TRANSFORM TEST CENTRE

Laboratory Report : Dr Arslan Demir and Dr Talip Memtimin
Date: 2023– ███

Experiment:

1. Identification of Chemical Composition and Radioactivity in Marine Samples from Palau (#A = Pacific Ocean) and Sabah (#B=South China Sea)
2. Isolate Sea Creatures Cause of Death

Objectives:

*   To identify chemical compounds and any irradiated contaminants by various analytical techniques
*   To identify if these compounds are present in fish samples to a level that can cause death

Materials:

*   Solution containing marine liquid from several locations
*   Test tubes
*   Graduated cylinders
*   Spectrophotometers
*   Flame test apparatus
*   pH meters
*   Chromatography columns
*   Solvents
*   ███████
*   Geiger counters
*   Scintillation counter

- Dosimeters
- Radiochromatograph
██████████████
- Salinity refractometer
- Beta detector
- Omega detector
██████████████
- Ion accelerator
- Mass analyser

Procedures:

1. ██████████ : Approved by Dr Nisha d'Acosta
2. ██████████ : Approved by Dr Nisha d'Acosta
3. ██████████ : Approved by Dr Nisha d'Acosta
4. ██████████ : Approved by Dr Nisha d'Acosta
5. ██████████ : Approved by Dr Nisha d'Acosta

Results:

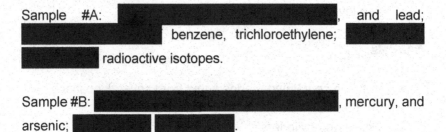

Sample #A: ██████████████████████, and lead; ███████████████████ benzene, trichloroethylene; ██████████ ██████████ radioactive isotopes.

Sample #B: ██████████████████████, mercury, and arsenic; ██████████ ██████████.

Discussion:

The results of the laboratory experiment were consistent with the expectations.

Sample #A was found to be highly ██████████ and contaminated.

Sample #B showed similar results as Sample #A, with the addition of ██████████ ████████████ which is ████████ with trace ████████████████ of the undersea structures in the South China Sea, constructed with enriched ████████████ ████████████ ████████████ from around Plant #8███████-F in Lop Nur.

Conclusion:

It can be confirmed that there is a lethal combination of highly toxic elements in both the Pacific Ocean and the South China Sea.

Owing to climate change and a shifting global polarity, an atypical crosscurrent between the two bodies of water has created an even more harmful tide, with the addition of contaminants from atomic tests, nuclear power plant wastage, and irradiated gravel used in the maritime construction of islets by ██████

While coral reefs and the fish that feed on them have been affected, the beached whales in Palau showed negligible signs of contamination. Evidence suggests their sonars may have been affected by undersea noise pollution and pulsation from an unknown vessel in the open waters.

21

Taipei

2023 | Present

Willy Chiu reviled the smell of burning incense. It reminded him of the fusty odour of cockroaches lying in wait in the shadows of his old bedroom in Beijing. Barely the size of his office pantry, his student quarters were permeated by the rancid bouquet of stagnation and death. Religious joss sticks always triggered those memories. Their distinct tang was usually also wrapped around his wife like a veil. If a stick wasn't burning at their home altar to the dead, she was lighting one elsewhere in the house to keep away ill fortune. He knew this somehow comforted her, so over three decades of marriage, he never complained about it.

In the glare of the media spotlight, Willy managed to keep from grimacing as he bowed with practised devotion before the massive golden statue of Mazu. The central deity in the temple's inner sanctum. Holding a pair of joss sticks to his forehead, Willy offered the requisite prayers for success in the polls. At least that's how the news crews filming his every move would report it on the evening programmes. Rich, powerful, and devout. Exactly the sort of man bustling Taipei needed as mayor.

The media had been given advance notice of his visit to the Sea Goddess' temple in the city's poorest district. It provided the sort of publicity his people said he needed. Against a backdrop of dated, dilapidated buildings—the elegant businessman mixing with more *grounded* folk who happened to look favourably on China. Not his usual crowd, but as an independent candidate, Willy needed all the cross party support he could get.

Unexpectedly, it started to rain, and the visual of him in his custom-made suit seeking refuge in the rundown temple was strikingly incongruent. A plus, as far as his press officer was concerned. There he was, the dashing candidate, appealingly unashamed to be humbled. At his feet, the steps from the street were chipped and uneven. Around him, the intricate wooden reliefs of deities were dull and unpolished, and the sculpted dragons that soared on the tiled roof like sails had lost their sheen. Inside, red pillars carved with the customary cloud holes supported the ceiling, which was flush with tattered red lanterns. Not all had tassels or functioning bulbs. The uneven lighting—plus the wind billowing through the large windows—made him feel as if he were within the beating heart of the proverbial beast. In the gullet of a sleeping dragon.

As the rain got stronger, its heavy scent was infused with aromatic smoke from joss sticks burning in sand-filled urns. And cutting through the gloom, the flashing red lights of an LED ticker screen at eye level on a side wall, running a reminder to the faithful that salt was 'life's seasoning'. A key to a better future, in its duality as a tool for preservation and transformation.

Subtle, thought Willy. Salt was vital in Taoist teaching, representing the need for balance and acceptance of change. It was *The Way*. So, this passed as 'religious script'.

It was also the message of the large bright orange banner visible just across the street outside temple grounds. It featured a circular logo with a crane in flight, which was associated with the moon (and its many phases) and immortality. Constancy and change.

TRANSFORM—the banner announced in big bold characters. A reminder from China to the Taiwanese to get them on side. The island nation imported most of its power—mainly through the Beijing-based global giant.

The absurdity was not lost on Willy. Putting the secular advert in front of a spiritual house that encouraged internal *transformation*. It didn't surprise him that a Chinese state company would be so blatant and yet allusive.

'Don't get that in your shots, please!' his press officer indicated the banner to the media. It was enough that Willy was at this temple deemed pro-China, he didn't also have to be seen in a frame with the logo of the Chinese behemoth. Voters might think he'd been bought by the foreign government.

Willy nodded his thanks at the young press officer.

After his show of prayers, the candidate faced the media scrum before descending the stairs to the street, where a car was waiting to take him back to the office.

'Do you think Beijing is too involved in Taiwan's affairs?'

'Once you're mayor, will you push to end nuclear energy?'

'Why don't we see your family campaigning with you?'

'When are you launching that super chip? Aren't you worried that a Chinese version will beat you to the market?'

That's the question he decided to tackle.

'Our chips have always been the most advanced in the world. All else are just that—*versions*. China tried to replicate our success at manufacturing dεU^{1}S chips, but the material they use in their *version* is causing problems. Regardless, we at Surf Silica believe that, like salt, we are not diminished by their corruption of our formula. As the Tao teaches, even when diluted in a thousand gallons of water, salt retains its flavour. And unlike the disrespect shown to us by others, I promise you—before the Sea Goddess Mazu—that when I am mayor, I will lead with moderation and honour the "essence of the sea"—the invaluable salt—that is in each of you. Thank you.'

More questions were hurled at him as bodyguards hurried him down the stairs to his vehicle. The scrum's loud murmuring chased him like a swarm of locusts.

It ceased as soon as the car door shut. In the welcome silence, Willy was suddenly concerned that he blew the point of the visit by denigrating China's manufacturing prowess and philosophy.

'Was that all right?' he asked his press officer.

'Well,' the young man hesitated, 'you got some Taoism in there, so . . . yay? But it was kinda off book . . . and maybe we could've done without it?'

That was as much a clapback as someone like him was going to get from a junior staff member. And everyone was junior to Willy unless they were Baba.

As the convoy of cars headed into city traffic to return to the candidate's headquarters, a call he'd been waiting for beeped in his ear.

Mon ami—he switched to his neural interface.

'You were right. He phoned her. Multiple times.'

Just as Willy suspected. Despite denying it, Edison knew his wife. He was convinced the environmentalist was involved in her disappearance—or at least knew where she was. He'd traced that their bio-waves intersected before hers went cold. That's why he snuck into Kota Kinabalu to see the man, who he knew would be there on a side-trip.

Any content or call metadata?

'That's the thing,' Hashem sighed. 'He only tried to reach her *after* the day you said she'd gone missing. And none of his calls went through.'

'*Merde,*' Willy said aloud.

'I'm sorry?' his press officer was confused.

Willy shook his head, indicating he was on a neural call.

'You found your son?'

Yes. Follow the money, right? He reappeared when he needed funds.

'So he wasn't with her? Where was he?'

Philippines. He thought I couldn't trace the link, but I did. He was looking for her too. This silence is too long now, not like her—for a moment, Willy's mind went numb. Then—*ah, I haven't thanked you for . . . my mother . . .*

'Of course, mon ami. She will be in Paris soon.'

There was a community of exiles there that would take her in. Hashem had been funding them for years. It's how they met. Back when Willy was still Ayup Tunsun. Disrobing himself of the last vestiges of the student leader who was wanted in China for participating in the Heavenly Gate protests. Worse, he was Uyghur too, from the remote Lop Nur salt lakes in Xinjiang. British diplomats got a few of them out of the country through Hong Kong. From there, they went to London, where, as Muslims, they were provided for by a special fund set up by Hashem's family. Once his paperwork was finalized, Ayup hopped over to Paris as Wu Xi 'Willy' Chiu. At the time, because he'd studied it at university, Willy was more comfortable with French than English. He immediately landed a job translating for a visiting Taiwanese tycoon, in town for business. That went so well he was offered a move to Taipei and a permanent role as the man's right hand. New name. New identity. New future. The only thing he carried with him from his old life was the small abstract tattoo he and a few others got to mark their rebirth. All thanks to the underground operation known as Sparrow, which saw them go from nuisances to the Chinese state to new beginnings.

Through the years, he kept as close an eye as he could on his people in Xinjiang, working with Hashem to help as many as possible. They smuggled out dissidents and victims of persecution. He sent his widowed mother money, but she wouldn't leave Lop Nur. And Willy didn't want to jeopardize his new family by disclosing his roots. No one knew he was Ayup but Hashem. His old friend fired the flight attendant on his staff, convinced she'd planted the device that showed Willy his mother had been taken by the Chinese state.

Was my mother all right when you found her? How did you find her?

'Does it matter? You know I have ways.'

Guess not. She is out, that is all that matters.

'Exactly.'

Her health? Was her arm—

'Fine. She was tired. Hadn't eaten much and her arm was in some pain.'

Willy's mother had lost part of her left arm when he was a child. It developed gangrene from untreated tumours and had to be amputated. He was convinced it was an effect of Beijing's nuclear tests around their village. The government told them the levels of radiation were 'not harmful', but when it came to minorities, officials were very loose with their definition of what was acceptable.

It's why he got involved in the student movement for change when he moved to Beijing for college.

Gazing out the car window, he again remembered the smell of cockroaches and mould. He swallowed to keep the bile from rising. Traffic was at a standstill and the rain got stronger. Pelting mercurial globs on the bullet-proof pane.

'I also have the results of the . . . bullet.'

And?

'Salt.'

Salt?

'Yes. It's fundamentally salt.'

The man in Sabah was killed by salt?

'The highly toxic kind. Irradiated, molten, and reinforced with some form of a uranium by-product—'

Potent enough to disintegrate a body?

'Well, it appears to have also been bonded with mercury. All that would've caused a reaction with his tattoos. You said they seemed to have burned off. But the victim's remains—and those of the other guy—didn't disintegrate. My source tells me they were disappeared from the morgue by Chinese agents.'

Ah. Makes sense. They don't want anyone to know about this—salt. Sounds like a variant of their substitute for God's Ashes . . . we're seeing a similar composition in their chips. Now they're using it as a weapon, too.

'Exactly. Police evidence files have also vanished. It's like the case never existed. If that guy hadn't jumped from the hotel in the middle of rush hour, we might never have heard about it. *His* identity is still unclear . . . though, for some reason, Beijing wants us to think he's a rogue party official.'

Was the environmentalist such a thorn for China they'd want him dead?

'From his phone data, you weren't the only contact he met in Sabah.' Hashem explained. 'But the salt in the mixture? Was from Xinjiang. Likely around Lop Nur. So, I think your instinct was right. This was a message for you . . .'

'Sir?' Willy's press officer pulled his attention from the window, unaware he was still on an encrypted neural interface call.

'Uh . . . Yes?'

'Breaking news from China. You might get asked for a statement...'

Willy looked at the video feed on the tablet he was handed. People were on the streets of Beijing, heading for Heavenly Gate. But it didn't look like a protest. The marchers were dancing and in high spirits.

'What exactly am I looking at?' Willy wondered.

The news presenter called it an anti-Zhou movement. Months earlier, the Chinese president banned dɛU¹S™—which they kept calling 'Diyu', a reference to the realm of the dead in Chinese mythology. Zhou hoped to urge its users to switch to a tightly controlled and monitored domestic version. But instead, dɛU¹S™ nodes amalgamated in so-called sub-networks, hidden and fortified against surveillance. dɛU¹S™ equipped them to adapt to evolving circumstances. This angered Zhou and led to a crackdown of suspected 'deviants', which was China's official term for nodes.

'This could finally bring down the government . . .' the optimistic millennial suggested.

Willy just fixed him a steely stare.

'You don't think?' the young man gulped.

Willy said nothing. He was back on his neural call.

Have you seen Beijing?

'Just now.'

I'm not sure what's going on, but Zhou won't take this lying down. Maybe they just wanted to abduct me in Sabah and not kill me. Zhou's desperate for the 0MɛGa chip formula—that must be it. They took my mother, too, to force my hand. And since that didn't work . . . God! I need to bring my son home . . . If they don't have her, they might be on his tail . . .

'But you have the prototype, yes?'

Willy's mind was blank. He went numb.

'Mon ami?'

It was with her. She wasn't happy with it yet. She said they had to tweak the design. That it wasn't right . . . it was 'too much' . . . that it could kill whoever used it.

'Oh. My. God!' the press officer covered his mouth in shock. 'Look!'

Willy cast an eye at the feed on the tablet. Chinese soldiers in battle formation. Uniforms crisp, boots polished, but no weapons. At least none that could be seen on camera. Rows and rows of them standing as still as statues. Then, in unison, they began to lift one foot followed by the next. Thundering forward as one. They seemed to be . . . glowing. With orders to head towards the marchers at Heavenly Gate.

'*Allahumma a'ina jamee'an*,' Willy muttered under his breath.

'Sorry?' his press officer thought he might've missed an instruction.

But Willy shook his head, returning to the mottled view out his window. He'd already spent most of his adult life pretending to be someone he was not. He would not jeopardize it all by repeating his childhood plea for help to a higher power.

'We will find her, mon ami.'

Hashem ended the call just as the rain in Taipei slowed to a drizzle. Gradually, the speckled car windows cleared, revealing the grey of an unexpectedly moist and muggy morning. Willy tried to recall the extremes of the desert of his youth. The cold. The heat. The barrenness. The beauty.

At the lights of the business district's main thoroughfare, he looked up at the national bank and saw his face—fifteen feet tall on a giant poster. Ripped by the wind and smudged by pollution, unintelligible graffiti had been sprayed on it—the paint was running down his portrait like the make-up of a clown.

Merde, Willy thought. It never used to rain this time of the year.

22

London

1990

Melody's eyes were swollen from crying and her tears had imprinted tracks on her pallid face. She'd been sitting at Maggie's desk for what seemed like hours, staring mindlessly out the window at the Thames. The drab day rolled seamlessly from grey to ash to asphalt as she played with the pieces of a bracelet that she'd ripped apart. It was a gift from Orla. Just a cheap, colourful string of beads from Camden Market, barely cost ten quid. But it meant the world. Orla offered it as 'wee consolation' for the bracelet Melody had lost at Pride.

'A tenner for your love, me love,' Orla had said after paying for it. She'd saved up for a month to get her the trinket, while Melody spent as much on chocolate without a thought. She felt so ashamed and also undeserving.

The dorm room door opened just as tears—again—welled up in her eyes. She turned abruptly, knowing who it would be.

'How is she?'

'Really?' Maggie dropped her bags on the floor. 'Hello to you, too, Eeyore.'

Melody didn't even pretend to be stung by the comparison to a depressive fictional donkey. In the months since the split, she noticed Maggie's moods had got more uneven. As if she too were suffering the pain. She was sulkier, more morose, and impatient. Like an angry teen. She even had acne. Which Melody put down to her rather oily, unhealthy diet. She was also looking gaunter than she used to. Her hips were slimmer, though her shoulders seemed broader, and her arms had filled out. All of which Melody only noticed a few days earlier, after Maggie called her out for being self-absorbed.

'If you were just going to sit here moping over her, I don't know why you ended it.' Maggie pronounced, falling onto her bed.

Melody rushed to sit by her side, slightly concerned that Maggie may have been unwell. She'd found some sort of medication in her roommate's desk drawer when she went looking for smokes. But she never brought it up. Melody knew how much Maggie hated incursions into her personal space. She took this as a cue to pursue her own interest.

'Does she miss me?' Melody pleaded.

'You're a feckin' eejit.' Maggie replied. 'Why did you break up again?'

A question Melody often asked herself. Why indeed.

'It's nearly the end of term. I—I—have to go home soon,' she attempted her usual explanation, 'and my parents would never . . . I can't . . . lie. They'd disown me—'

'So you'd rather break the heart of the person you claim to love,' Maggie was angry and didn't hide it. For the first few weeks after the break-up, she was the one to try and help Orla make sense of what didn't. She'd never seen her friend so bereft. She couldn't eat nor sleep and cried endless tears. On top of it all, Orla's mother was diagnosed with cancer. So, urged by Maggie, Orla went home to care for her mum. After witnessing all that *real* heartbreak, it pissed Maggie off so much to return to the dorm to this snivelling brat, who inflicted more pain on her best friend than she'd ever seen.

'This was to spare her, Mags,' Melody wiped the snot running out of her nose. 'In the long run. My parents want me to get married and have kids—what we have . . . had . . . is wrong. It isn't real . . .'

'Wow'—Maggie scoffed—'says who? You *are* a fecking eejit. What did she ever see in you?'

This was a conversation the roommates had often. Repeatedly, like a broken record. Melody knew each argument Maggie was going to raise and what she would say in response. It was like going over a circuit.

'What life would we have had? Keeping to ourselves, pretending we're just best friends . . .'

'Oi! That's me,' Maggie cut in. 'Don't even try to take the title. *I* am her best friend. *I* look out for her welfare. You? You were a blip in her journey.'

That stung Melody more than Maggie could know. What she feared most was that her roommate was right, that their relationship was make-believe and Orla would move on without a second thought. Maybe she did this to see how much Orla would fight for her. But what was *she* prepared to fight for? Was she ready to give things up in exchange for Orla? Certainly not her family or her home. Right?

Melody told herself she ended things because she was looking out for Orla. But in truth, she was trying to spare herself pain. She was a coward. And she was absolutely terrified that the Chinese man stalking her would hurt the woman she . . . loved. He threatened it repeatedly. For months, he lurked in the shadows, appearing when she least expected and pressing her for more and more information on Maggie. If she didn't do as asked, he would hurt her 'lover'—he would say with disdain—and reach out to her family in Taipei. She couldn't have that. What he asked about Maggie wasn't anything sensitive, so Melody saw no harm in answering his questions.

What does she eat?

What is she working on?

What are her dreams and ambitions?

Does she speak about her family? Her childhood? Can she still speak Mandarin?

All very personal inquiries she didn't understand his interest in.

At one point, she convinced herself that maybe this man was Maggie's father. That he wasn't actually dead—as her roommate had said—but some sort of dissident in hiding for his daughter's benefit. Maybe he just wanted to reconnect with his kid.

Melody suddenly realized how tired she was. She was tired of hiding and tired of running. She was tired of arguing with her roommate. She had nothing more to say. She was tired of crying and feeling like her heart had been ripped from her chest. She was tired of discovering that all the clichés about heartbreak were true. She didn't know how to get over this. All she wanted was to run into Orla's arms and pretend it had all been a charade. That nothing had changed. But she didn't know how to find her. It was like she had vanished. Melody hadn't seen her beautiful face in months and the pain felt interminable. The days went on forever yet blurred into one.

She had never felt so empty.

'I'm going for a walk.'

Maggie said nothing. Wishing she'd never introduced her two dearest friends.

* * *

Until Orla, the riverbank was not a meditative space for Melody. Soulless and full of birds, she found it cold and hostile. But one grey day, a glorious girl showed her fire where there was rain and walks along the Thames took on new meaning. Its silence had the textures of symphonies, and the winged creatures carried the expanse of their dreams. Leaden days like this one became a comfort. A reason to cuddle up under the covers with Orla or roam hand in hand suffused in peace.

But not anymore.

On her way to the embankment, Melody found herself on Charing Cross Road and mindlessly wandered into Foyles. As if on autopilot, she made her way up to the bookstore's top floor and headed directly to the small section at the back where the books for women who love women were shelved. She was always self-conscious browsing through the titles. She kept her head down, hoping no one would see her. Even though this area of the store was set up so only those who went on purpose would be there. Yet, she was embarrassed. And it was that mortification that also prompted her to end things with Orla. Though she didn't know this at the time. She was too young to understand the workings of her heart. More so, the nuances of her shame.

Certain she was alone, Melody picked up a book and hurriedly paid before any other customers appeared. It was the latest from Autumn Winthrop. The author had become a favourite to her and Orla.

With the book wrapped in paper and tucked under her arm, Melody headed south from Charing Cross Road to Seven Dials, letting her feet and her cellular memory lead the way. She cut through Covent Garden to walk across the river from the Strand. There were very few tourists this time of year, and as she stopped on Waterloo Bridge to take in the view—on one side, the dome of St Paul's to the Oxo Tower in the south, on the other, the iconic clock of Westminster Palace—it felt like all of London was hers. Hers . . . and Orla's. Whose shadow accompanied her everywhere, threatening to engulf her. They had always loved this mid-river panorama . . . but it had become unrecognizable.

'Feck it!' Melody ducked as a seagull flew past nearly hitting her on the head. She had learned which bird was which. And the memory of her early avian debates with Orla brought a fresh stab of pain, just when she thought it couldn't get any worse.

Then, the graphite sky began to unload. A mist of rain like a lover's whisper in the early morning. She took a deep breath then resumed her walk. Retracing their usual steps, hoping to find the familiar in what had been transformed.

On the South Bank, she sought shelter at the Royal Festival Hall. She went up to the bar, put her book on the counter, and got herself a pint of Guinness. She had the place to herself and decided to read. Nursing her glass of stout.

But her reading was disrupted when the rain got stronger and another soaked pedestrian rushed in. He removed his jacket, noticed her, and smiled.

'Sorry,' he offered.

She put her book face down on the counter and nodded. The man then reached over to try and grab a napkin from the holder near her. She immediately pushed it towards him while moving the book further away.

'Thank you,' he said.

'No worries,' was her automatic reply.

He was neatly dressed—collared shirt, dark trousers—and wearing leather shoes that should not have been in the rain. His hair was thinning and his face was smooth. This was clearly a very well-groomed man. Maybe a few years older than her.

'What are you reading?' he asked as he wiped himself with the paper napkins.

Since he didn't have a British accent, Melody thought he might be a foreign student like her. And though she wouldn't presume to guess his ethnicity, like her, he was clearly of Asian origin. An 'Oriental', as Maggie had initially teased her.

'Uh . . . nothing,' she smiled shyly, having already put the book away. 'Just . . . something for uni.'

'Ah—literature major?'

'I wish.'

'No? I could've sworn . . .' he said, appraising her.

'Maybe in another life.'

'Why not this one?'

'My father would say there is no money in it.' She tried to keep the sadness from her voice.

'Makes sense, I suppose? Unless you turn out to be the next Agatha Christie.'

'Well, now we'll never know!' She jested. 'And you?' she'd learned that the best way to stop having to talk about yourself was to encourage the other person to do the sharing. This was something she picked up from Orla. She'd seen her do it countless times when she found herself in very awkward conversations she did not want to have.

'Work,' he said, unenthused.

'Ah, I could've sworn you looked like an LSE type.'

He laughed. 'Ouch. A dull know-it-all who takes himself too seriously?'

'Now I say ouch!' She chuckled, despite herself.

'Oh no,' he seemed embarrassed. 'Are you at the LSE?'

'Guilty,' she said.

'I meant no disrespect,' he clarified.

'I know. Don't worry,' she smiled easily. For the first time in a while she just felt—unencumbered. Free of her pain. 'So, what do you do, Mr I-am-not-at-the-LSE?'

'Just started working for an Asian company with branches everywhere. I have one last matter to take care of here—dotting i's, crossing t's—and then I'm getting a transfer. Basically, I just do what I'm told.'

'I am sure it's much more interesting than you make it sound . . .'

'Pardon my asking,' he dared, 'but you're not from here, are you?'

'Taipei,' Melody replied without hesitation.

'No way!' he exclaimed. 'That's where I'm going!'

She couldn't believe it. What were the odds?

'Can I get you another drink, uhm—' he paused, waiting for her to say her name.

'Uh, Melody. Sure,' she nodded at the bartender and pointed at her empty pint.

'Hi, Melody,' he extended his hand to shake hers. His large Tag Heuer watch obscured a small logotype tattooed on his wrist. It was the word 'free' in Arabic script, in the shape of a bird. 'Willy,' he said, 'Willy Chiu.'

i

Tale of the Salt People

There once was a land of heat and ice, where snow burned bright and fire rained. Its ports were unreachable and its lakes were seas, so it was burdened with riches beyond imagination. Every army outside wanted to take possession, forcing its villagers to roam from home to home, seeking roots and roofs for safety and shelter. When they cried for help, the Spirit King sent his creatures to shield them, and for years, the land had unseen champions.

But the peaceful silence woke the Silken Dragon, whose fury at being roused rattled the mountains. The dragon swept out of his heavenly lair to shake the earth, and in one breath seized the land's riches. The guardian spirits fled, and the villagers hid as the Silken Dragon breathed flames on their mountains and on their lakes, stirring up columns of molten diamonds and metal stardust.

When the dragon was through, there was naught on the ground but salt. And only those who cloaked themselves in its armour survived his wrath: the mythical creatures who shape-shifted into champions and the wondrous frailties who transformed into winged deities.

But they lost their home and were doomed to roam in constant search for others like them, cloaked in the strength of salt and stardust.

*An excerpt from the secret stories of Xinjiang

23

25.0330° N, 121.5654° E

Taipei

2023 | Present

The soft pink light of her Himalayan salt lamp recalled a salmon sunset she'd once viewed from medieval castle ramparts. It was a world away but forever etched in her soul. And every time she shut her eyes, the darkness—like a reverse image seared on film—brought back the enchantment of that evening.

Melody kept a salt lamp on to balance her energy. It was meant to neutralize the effects of all the electronics and reduce her stress. She put one in nearly every room of the house. Except her father's. He would not have her 'silly superstitions' encroaching on his personal space. She tried to explain to him that it was science, but he wouldn't hear it.

The stubborn old man also resisted moving in with them when he was diagnosed with dementia. He'd lived alone in his large manor across town for years after her mother died. But before his condition worsened, Melody wanted him closer and surrounded by family. Despite the old coot pretending to rage against it. She even agreed to take on half of his household staff.

At least he didn't fight her when she put salt lamps on the family shrine. They were next to the traditional red lights on either side of the central Mazu statue, which watched over a large photo of her mother. Up front, bowls were lined up with myriad offerings. Sweets, tea leaves, flowers, and fruits soon in need of replacement.

Melody took a deep breath before setting down the incense she'd lit. Placing it in holders by her mother's image. She said a prayer and touched the Mazu statue for good fortune. Resting at the deity's feet, in a small crystal bowl, a restrung trinket of colourful plastic beads.

Her mother was buried facing west in the direction of her ancestral land, so to balance out her journey, Melody set the home altar east toward the rising sun. Just steps away was her lanai, where after her morning prayers, she enjoyed breakfast watching the day descend on sprawling Taipei. Their home was perched so perfectly in the city's southern mountains, offering them an unparalleled view of the nestled capital. The landmark Taipei 101 building towered like a postmodern bamboo torch over the otherwise humdrum landscape. From this distance, she could tell herself all was well. Finally, after years of trying, she felt more in tune with space . . . and the spirits.

There was a tingle in the quantum chip she wore behind her ear.

'Is it made yet?' came the distinct, almost robotic voice she knew well.

Hello to you too . . .

'We're running out of time.'

You're the only one who's put a deadline on this. You know we're way ahead . . . and no one's competing with you—

'If you paid attention, princess, you would've noticed by now that I only compete with myself. So, what's the hold up? I sent you the data months ago.'

Just tweaking it. Was a bit off . . .

'Impossible. My calculations are perfect. You know what it took to encrypt the refinement procedure and the quantum formula for the epitaxy? Those design sequences should've worked.'

It was too . . . strong. I feel we have to dial it back a tad or it could malfunction.

'Don't mess with my numbers, Melody . . .'

*I don't want us to get fucked. Just let me try something—*their constant sparring could get exhausting, but they wouldn't be who they were without it.

Why are you in such a rush? Melody transmitted telepathically.

'Because China is on the verge!'

Of?

'Of transformation! The nodes are awake and e-volution is near. The 0MɛGɑ chip is needed to bring it all together.'

Is that why you did this? To 'evolve' China? Melody had long suspected it, but never got confirmation. *Why do you even care? You've been distancing yourself from your roots since the Heavenly Gate massacre . . .*

'You've thought about it yourself—what if we could transform our circuitry? Remember? That's what dɛU^{1}S offers. A transformed energy for humanity. A qubit force. And that *man* and others like him . . . are all about disempowering us and stunting our growth—'

'Okay, okay, Lex Luthor,' she said aloud before returning to her inaudible call. *Honestly. Some people invent the nuclear bomb—and you have to come up with 'enlightened cognition'!*

It was actually Melody's idea that they work together. She wanted to be a leader in the digital field and knew she couldn't do that on her own. She needed the smarts of her dear friend, who, she had to admit, was more brilliant than her. Melody was a great student—diligent and hardworking—but he was a mathematical artist. It was as if he saw the world in numbers—and those numbers were musical notes, a symphony that moved through his soul. For as long as she'd known him, he was all about *transforming* human energy and how that would inevitably change reality.

Their decades of collaboration brought them from creating the operating systems for dɛU^{1}S™ to coming up with this pioneering quantum chip. It was meant to 'awaken' a humankind that had been asleep. Enabling supra-cognitive powers using maths and revolutionary physics. It stretched expectations of what could be done with the vastness of knowledge, taking the world's amassed wisdom and using it for good. It was such a cliché. Melody often laughed thinking she was trying to emulate some comic book superhero from her childhood. How ridiculous.

She looked at the purple bracelet on her wrist with a central black medallion made from enriched basalt. It was a reliquary superconductor, holding in its core a miniature integrated circuit finely crafted on crystalline epitaxy from irradiated coral, boosted by enriched molten salt and a few other minerals. A formula and design worked on for years by her business partner, the renowned mathematician and physicist Max Bao.

This was the 0MεGα chip prototype. Programmed to adhere exclusively to a single user's bio-signature, the superchip enabled individuals to process and store information at quantum levels and perceive and connect to a wider network of enhanced bio-frequencies. The purple beads were both power conductors and insulators, and the black medallion—embossed with the Greek letters for Alpha and Omega—basically turned a person into a mainframe and a powerful transistor, able to emit and receive signals from all layers of existence. From the physical and mental planes to the astral and spiritual. It nullified the need for ciphers and symbols. Communication was telepathic and computations were faster than light, all without generating heat. The chip was powered by the individual themselves, ultimately drawing energy from the broader circuit of humanity. Elevating one node elevated all. And each could be multiple things at once.

In the four weeks since she'd finished building the bracelet in her personal lab from Max's design, Melody hadn't taken it off. Wanting to experience and examine all its potencies. She thought Max might not have told her everything—and she was right. The 0MεGα superchip connected her to everything and everyone in quantum space and time—the past, present, and future in one go. The sheer power of it frightened her. Anything that crossed her mind seemed to occur. And she wasn't sure if it was precognition or if she was manifesting. She was overwhelmed by all the multiplicities and entanglements. And with everything in existence emitting a bio-frequency, she felt it all. All except Max—who only transmitted a signal when he wanted to be found. Otherwise, the billionaire recluse protected himself with a customized shield.

'What's got you freaked out, Mel?' he asked.

She shut her eyes to silence her mind. A skill she'd honed through meditation. It was a way to deal with memories of Orla. She'd considered tucking a photo of them behind her mother's in the shrine for the dead, but she didn't. Instead, she put the bracelet Orla gave her on the altar. In a crystal bowl at Mazu's feet, flanked by the salt lamps that reminded her of Rye. Bathing memories of her great love in the light of their bliss.

A year after she returned to Taipei and got married, Maggie told her Orla had died. There was an accident and she happened to be in the wrong place at the wrong time.

As hard as it was to lose her mother, it was harder to grieve for someone you couldn't even talk about. Her husband had been kind when she woke up crying at night, but she never explained her tears and he didn't push for a reason.

He was a good man, a kind man, who treated her well. And she loved him for everything he was. In a sense, he *resurrected* her. But he never made her burn. He never set her alight and made her . . . glow.

Since wearing the 0MɛGα prototype, she'd been picking up Orla's energy. It was so forceful, she was convinced Maggie had lied to her. That Orla was alive somewhere and calling for her. To get a better read and home in on the signal, she was trying to tweak the chip . . . and find a way to decrease its potency for a mass market version.

'Morning, love.'

'Willy!' she greeted as he joined her on the lanai. A cue to also let Max know she had to end the call.

'I have to prepare for some debate, so I've got to rush,' he reached for a pastry on the table. 'See you tonight?'

'I told you this would upend our lives,' she reiterated. 'I don't get why you're doing this . . .'

'Because your father wants me to.'

'How much longer will you let him tell you what to do?'

'It's for the good of the family, love,' he bent to give her a kiss on the head, 'and the company.'

'Is it though?' Melody faced him. 'He's got you believing that now, doesn't he? Do you really wanna be president of Taiwan?'

Willy smiled at his wife, saying nothing. At the back of his mind, he had wondered if he'd be capable of sticking it to China if he were head of state. He'd enjoy that. A carefully planned attack to kill Zhou. Maybe using technology, like a drone. He would even reveal his true identity. Melody would understand. And she'd forgive him. *Inshallah.* God willing.

He could dream.

'Promise me you will go to the temple?' he said instead.

'Don't I always?' she sighed. 'I promise I will campaign. But you know I am not my mother—she was the expert.'

'Ah, poor you. Everyone loved Mrs Yu, while you are just Mrs Yu's daughter . . .'

Melody smirked, handing him another pastry for the road. 'I am Mrs Chiu—and that is good enough for me.'

* * *

That was the last time he saw her, having breakfast at home in their lanai. No. He shook his head to clear it. That wasn't the last time. He returned at midday . . . and she was drinking. Bushmills. He hadn't even known she liked Irish whiskey. She was half incoherent, and he presumed her father had upset her. The old man was always saying something unsettling. Since his diagnosis, he had no self-control. Or so he wanted them to think. Willy had sussed out that sometimes, the Lǎo dà—Baba—said things just to get a rise. And as absent-minded as he portrayed himself to be, he was more *present* than he let on. Especially when it came to Lotus Dragon matters. For one, the old man seemed determined to use their dark and extensive heidaoren network to help Zhou stay in power. Mobilizing their members to get the Chinese president any materials he asked for, for whatever he was building. As long as it didn't undermine the company's bottom line.

What was his point? Melody was drinking that day. But he couldn't stay to care for her because he'd only come home to change. His campaign manager had added an unscheduled function to his diary. Then, he had to finish up at the office in preparation for a trip to Manila. He was arranging a shipment of mercury from Indonesia to China through the Philippines. Which Baba said was urgently needed for something or the other.

When Willy returned home from work that night, his wife was gone.

* * *

On this particular morning, Willy stood at the family shrine asking his mother-in-law for help. He even lit new joss sticks to replace the ones that had burned out. He hadn't heard from his wife in over a week and while he respected her occasional need to go on silent retreats or work undisturbed, he wondered if it might be time to call in the authorities. Though the kind of attention this would bring was the last thing the family—the firm, his campaign—needed.

As he waited for divine guidance, he began to hear time's loud, hollow ticking in the slow, heavy drops of rain falling through the sky well onto the courtyard. It brought him back to a dreary afternoon in London and the moment he met his wife. Misted in rain, she reminded him of a goddess out of the sea. Her skin sparkled and her dishevelled hair was dewy. She was laser focused on a book, and the long fingers of her left hand were wrapped around a pint glass. He was not meant to make contact, only to find out what she had been up to because she'd stopped communicating with her parents. They worried she'd met some guy and Willy was ordered to see if the man was 'suitable'. If not, he was to bring her home immediately. He'd watched her for a few days—and nothing. She only stayed in school, and barely left her dorm room.

He'd been following her that afternoon. A light shower seemed to drive her into the Royal Festival Hall, and he planned on waiting outside. But the rain got stronger, so he ducked into the foyer for shelter. He spotted her immediately, just sitting at the bar, alone. He had no intention of lying—but once they started talking, he felt it would ruin the vibe if he said anything about working for her father. There's no surer way to end a possible romance before it starts than by saying you're a member of the family's staff.

Willy owed her father a lot. He gave him a job when no one else would and a fresh start. He'd do anything for the man, even risk his life. It's not like it was worth much anyway. He was a marked man for opposing the Beijing government. But then—what better way to hide than to work with a Chinese ally? Being close to the seat of power gave him deniability and a cloak for his other activities—helping fellow Uyghurs either survive in China or flee oppression.

He didn't want it all to blow up in his face.

But here he was—Islamic prayer beads in his pocket—lighting incense sticks to a popular folk deity and his dead mother-in-law. Worrying about his missing wife, his uncommunicative son, and his debilitated mother just saved from torture and detention. Hashem got her out of a 're-education facility' in Xinjiang to safety in Palau. From there, they would move her to Paris and then the US, where Willy had a sister living under an assumed identity. Hashem's Palau contact—also a Muslim—worked specifically in transiting women in distress. She was a Sufi, but they didn't let her esoteric beliefs bother them. When it came to his family, Willy would take any help he could get.

Abruptly, the rain began to throb with a force uncommon for the season, and a charcoal veil dropped from the sky. Standing before his wife's family altar, he was an unmoored ship in an unexpected typhoon. A shadow of a man vaporized—a negative image lost in the soft radiance of a salt lamp.

NODE ALERT

|01110000⟩ |01101100⟩ |00110000⟩ |01100101⟩ |01101110⟩
|01101101⟩ |01110011⟩ |00111101⟩**

010011010011011101011001001001101101001101100011
011010010011010010011010010011011101100110010110
011001001011010010011011101011011001010011010
010011001001011010011010100110100011010110010011
00100101101001101110011011100

|01100101⟩ |01101001⟩ |00100001⟩ |00100010⟩ |01101100⟩
|01100011⟩ |01110011⟩ |00110100⟩**

010010010100010101001001010001010100010101001000
000100100101001000000100100100100100010100100100
010001000100010101000100010101001001000000100100
100100000001000000100100100100100010100100100000
001000000100100101001000000100100110100010101

e

24

50.9497° N, 0.7373° E

Rye

2006

The sky was the colour of the depths of the Pacific with brilliant streaks like parrotfish trying to survive the tide. In stops and starts, the celestial current flowed as the train jerked through the shadows of the dreary afternoon. Occasionally revealing salmon gashes like fillets from Jimma Noa's daily catch. Staring out the window, Edi didn't expect the unfamiliar ride from London to East Sussex to visit upon him distant memories of his island childhood.

From the little he'd read online, his destination, the small coastal town of Rye—with its history of welcoming exiles, refugees, and seafarers—seemed a perfect spot to convene a gathering of the modern world's displaced, dispossessed, and dispersed. Otherwise known as the conference for the League of the Voiceless on Earth or LoVE. The meeting only happened once every three years, and solely if there was enough funding. Though relatively unheard of, LoVE's summit was still an opportunity for Edi to share his message. He'd been invited to speak—and they fully sponsored his trip.

Edison Wakamele-Rigold, environmentalist and expat, was picked up at the train station by a pre-booked taxi. It brought him to the centre of the old town. Winding through storybook streets and slanted structures like toys that whispered of shared secrets, Edi was struck by how different this island nation was to his own. A clock tower chimed as his taxi neared the ruins of a medieval fortress. Right by it was an historic inn that would be his home for the long weekend. It had a rustic charm. With a timbre-framed frontage, mullioned and transomed windows, and climbing vines along the walls, the inn was attached to other gable roofed buildings on the narrow cobbled high street. Edi had read there were underground tunnels and hidden passages connecting all the structures.

'Welcome to the Dragon's Den, Mr Rigold,' the porter greeted him at the door and took his bag from the taxi driver. They were expecting him and check-in was quick and easy. Edi was self-conscious about his distinct appearance among all the quaintness, but in a place drunk on its chequered legacy, no one looked at him oddly.

'Top of the stairs and to the left—just mind your head on the low ceilings,' the elderly woman at reception couldn't have been nicer. How he missed his grandma.

Edison followed her directions, passing a cleaner in the upstairs hallway. It was such a tight squeeze, she had to round the corner with her housekeeping trolley to let him by.

'Hello,' she nodded with an awkward smile, her bleached blonde hair pulled away from her tiny face. She was reed thin and had the most piercing green eyes Edi had ever seen.

'I turn down bed?' she asked once he was at his door.

Edi shook his head and returned her smile. She spoke English with an accent he couldn't place. He was about to ask her where she was from, but she moved down the corridor to let another guest by. Losing the opening, he unlocked his door to leave his bag in the room and prepare to socialize. Edi wasn't one to mingle, but since losing Jack as his partner, he had to put in the effort to network. It was the only way to get funding for his Runit clean-up campaign.

He also hoped being in the UK would give him a better chance to find information on the puzzling vessel called $\Omega \pi L \alpha$, the strange equation he had tattooed on his thigh. Six years had passed since he saw the ship from Runit, and all he knew was that it flew the flag of the Isle of Man, a British Crown dependency in the Irish Sea. That was also the first and last time he had God's Ashes. Since then, he only went near the drug when asked to acquire samples for UNPER. The activist group had started monitoring 'dirty smash' from outside the Marshalls to see if they could trace its source. Were there other reefs altered by localized marine radiation or were they all affected by ocean currents from the Pacific?

So, on a clear mission, Edi washed his face, put on a fresh shirt, and returned to the ground floor foyer. He had delegates to meet, questions to get answered, and sponsors to thank.

'Edison?'

A soft but firm voice called him before he joined the fray of guests.

'Hi! I'm Melody,' an elegant woman with long dark hair extended her hand to shake his. Of course he knew who she was. She was one of the biggest donors to the Voiceless League's conference. 'I was hoping to meet you,' she smiled at him, wide and warm. 'I've been following your work and can't wait to hear your speech. There's so little current information online about the Marshalls. And no news at all on what the US is doing about the nukes. We've got to get you heard. The connectivity situation has improved, yes? I'm partnered with a firm that is upping its investment in your country. Information infrastructure, undersea mineral exploration . . . working towards an eco-friendly future while also preparing the economy for global warming . . .'

'Oh.' He was taken aback by her flood of greeting. 'I'll keep an eye on it when I return to Majuro for visits.'

'Visits?'

'I'm moving to Manila,' he explained. 'Wanted to do it for years. Now, with the help of UNPER, I've got enough saved up to run a base from there. It's easier for travel and all that.'

Melody smiled, knowingly. 'My family has business in Manila. It's very close to Taipei. And you are right, it's easier for travel—and all that. I'm sure you will get even busier, what with the Philippines also being on the frontlines of climate change.'

Edi was aware the archipelago had its own environmental troubles, but there was so much to worry about in the Marshalls that he hadn't quite looked beyond them. 'There is a lot to do,' he sighed heavily, 'and I am always on the road . . .'

'I get that,' an empathetic sadness crossed Melody's face. Life on the road was hard. Particularly on family ties. 'My son's in boarding school near here,' she shared unexpectedly. 'I haven't seen him in months. But he's joining me this weekend. His grandpa insisted he come to England for a "proper" education . . .' she made quote marks with her fingers.

Edi nodded politely, having no understanding of what it was like to have such options.

'. . . his grandpa is convinced he can one day be president of Taiwan, the leader to reunite the country with China under a Taipei government,' Melody rolled her eyes.

'Old men are fools, huh?' Edi said in agreement.

'Tell me about it.' Melody groaned.

'But sometimes,' he broke into a smile, remembering his jimma, 'they might be right.'

Before she could reply, Melody's mobile dinged. She took it from her pocket to read the text. 'I'm sorry—I have to attend to this. See you tomorrow? Lovely to finally meet you in person . . .'

He nodded as she hurried off. Leaving him among a handful of tourists who were unaware that he was a valiant soldier fighting a losing battle.

* * *

'And that's why they call it the dragon's banquet,' Melody finished her story with a flourish, expecting to have thrilled her twelve-year-old son.

'Meh. Our dragon fable is better,' he concluded, 'the one with the eggs and the emerald lake?'

'But this one has princes and pirates and smugglers—'

'You're just making it up, Mom,' her son was disbelieving.

'Not at all! I have it on good authority . . .' Melody's breath caught in her throat at the thought of Orla. She'd never forgiven herself for ending their relationship the way she did. Maybe if she hadn't, Orla wouldn't have gone home, and if Orla hadn't returned to Benbradagh, she might not have been killed. Melody always wondered how she would've felt had Orla still been alive across the world from her. She looked at her hand, resting on her son's shoulder as they wandered back from dinner to their inn. Her wrist was devoid of bracelets. She'd stopped wearing them to unchain herself from painful memories.

'Right, young man,' Melody handed her son the room key when they entered the inn. 'I'm just going to make sure everything's set for tomorrow. You get ready for bed and I'll be right up.'

He was still in the shower when Melody got to their room. It smelled like dead flowers, so she cracked open a window for some air. Untucking her shirt, she put her mobile on the dresser and sat down to remove her make-up.

'Hello, Ming Kai.'

She didn't have to lift her gaze to know who it was. It had been years, but she should've recognized the odour.

'Miss me?'

'Please leave,' she said, refusing to look at his image in the mirror. 'This conference has nothing to do with you—or my father. There's nothing to interest you here . . .'

'So you say,' the man in the dark jacket leaned forward, reeking of aromatic cigarettes. 'But I'll be the judge of that.' He walked around to sit on the dresser table and face her.

'Mom?' In sailor-style pyjamas, her son Robbi had come out of the bathroom.

'Ah, a little brat!'

'Leave him alone,' she growled at the man in Mandarin.

'All right . . . if you tell me where she is . . .'

'Who?' Melody struggled to keep her voice calm.

'Now, now,' the man tsk-ed, 'Wei Jing, who else?'

'Mom?'

'Wait in the bathroom—' she commanded her son.

'Come, boy,' the man called him forward.

'Please . . .' Melody muttered under her breath.

'Tell me where she is, and I will go . . . you must know?'

'I don't,' Melody wasn't lying. She wasn't sure where Maggie was at that very moment. Though in touch, they hadn't seen each other in years.

'Do you want to end up like your flame-haired friend?'

At that, Melody stood up. 'Please leave and I won't call the police . . .' She went to her son and clasped him close.

'Ming Kai . . .' the man rose from the dresser table and pulled a gun from his jacket.

'Mom . . .?' Grasping her tightly, Robbi trembled in Melody's arms. The Mazu bracelet he wore underneath his wristbands failed to boost his courage.

'Does the brat know about you?' The man approached them slowly, attaching a silencer to his weapon. 'Have there been others? Like her? For you? You know who I mean. The depraved one who corrupted you—'

'Stop it,' she pleaded with the familiar but still unknown Chinese man.

He walked around mother and child locked in a tight embrace. As he jeered and laughed at their fear, Melody kept whispering to her son.

'I asked the *báirén* for help after you left,' the man continued, 'but white people can be so stubborn . . .'

Melody began to wonder if Orla's death wasn't an accident at all.

'Do you know they bleed the same colour as we do?' he stopped circling his prey and briefly dropped the arm holding the gun. In that instant, Melody kneed him in the groin and went for the weapon. Following her earlier whispered instructions, her son locked himself in the bathroom.

The man fell to the floor, clutching his groin. He stuck out a foot to trip her. They rolled around knocking things over until she got hold of the weapon.

Standing above him, Melody cocked the gun, holding it with both hands to stop her trembling.

'You don't have the balls . . .' he taunted, meaning it in more ways than one.

She saw black. Like a theatre gone dark before a screening. Every moment she shared with Orla flashed before her eyes—and every moment they'd lost. Every threat he ever made, every date he ruined. Everything she gave up because of her own fears. Every joy she never experienced. With tears rolling down her face, Melody locked him in her gaze and pulled the trigger. Unflinching even as his blood sprayed the floor. Even with a silencer, the dulled sound of the shot reverberated in the confined space.

A knock on the door. 'Miss, you okay?'

She didn't know what to do.

'Mom?' her son peeked out of the bathroom.

She threw the gun on the floor as he rushed to her side. She tucked his head into her body so he wouldn't have to see the corpse.

There was a gasp from the jamb, as the chambermaid had opened the door.

Behind her, a guest who was heading for the room opposite had stopped.

'Melody?' Edi moved the housekeeper aside to enter. 'Are you okay?' He took in the body on the floor and the trembling child in her arms. 'You hurt?'

'He was gonna kill my mom . . .' the boy sputtered. 'I came out of the bathroom and he was in our room—with a gun,' he turned to his mother and she was frozen in place, a vacant look in her eyes.

Edi suspected the dead man was a Chinese state agent or a triad member. He was dressed the part. It wouldn't be a surprise that someone like that would be after a Taiwanese tycoon's family. He'd read all about the 'leading edge Lins' of Surf Silica.

'It's okay . . .' Edi said, placating the boy. He looked to the housekeeper for help. It took a split second, then, saying nothing, she stepped into the room and shut the door behind her. None of them thought to call the police.

'I clean,' she offered, having seen too many women abused by hateful men. 'No tunnel in this room,' she stated before turning to Edi, 'but your room has. You take body there.'

Again, Melody told her son to wait in the bathroom. Soon as he was gone, the three adults wordlessly wrapped the corpse in a blanket before the cleaner poured a liquid solution on the bloodied floor. Then, they shuffled across the hall with the body to Edi's room.

Once there, the chambermaid opened a hidden panel on the wall. There was a narrow privy passage behind it that she said went through their block of buildings. Taking the room's torch, she led them in. Edi carried the weight of the corpse and Melody helped with the feet. At the end of the path, there was a drop.

'Old cesspit,' the chambermaid pointed. 'No one come.'

After a few moments of silence, Edi took hold of the body and let it go in the pit. There was a dull heavy thud that echoed in the enclosed chamber. And then, a hollow silence.

Without another word, the housekeeper walked them back through the passage to the hotel.

'I think you better take the kid and go,' Edi told Melody as they re-emerged in his room. 'Guys like that don't work alone . . .'

After checking the hallway was empty, they walked across to Melody's room. Her son was still hiding away. She picked up her mobile on the dresser and sent a text to the one person she knew could help.

To: Max B

999. Rye.

The housekeeper immediately got to work cleaning the floor. She seemed an old hand at bloodstain removal.

'I . . . can't thank you enough . . .' Melody started, completely aghast that these two strangers had helped her conceal a crime.

Despite time in jail, Edi couldn't seem to deny his instinct to help someone in distress. And he never had much faith in the authorities.

Melody's text received a response.

'Anyone know how I can get to . . . Fair Salts?' she asked after reading it.

'Yes,' the chambermaid had just moved a rug over the spot she'd cleaned. 'Old salt marsh. Now park. On edge of town. Good place to hide gun. I take you. Through tunnel. My shift finished.' She had used the medieval smuggling tunnel several times. It was a way to move goods in and out of town or from the coast, which was generally unpatrolled. That's how she helped get women from Eastern Europe into England. They came across the channel on a boat from France. All of them were fleeing the terrors of war, abuse, or persecution. Like she had.

Melody scanned the room for some way—something—to express her gratitude. Then, she remembered a gift she and her husband had given their son.

'Robbi?' she called him out of the bathroom. When he reappeared, she gestured for him to remove the bracelet on his wrist. Made of the highest quality jade. He was so embarrassed by how bright green it was, he covered it up with several colourful wristbands. Rubber ones bearing the names of popular bands. Those were way cooler at school.

'We have to go, son,' she told him calmly. 'Pack up your things.'

The plan was that an unmarked car would meet them at Fair Salts and take them down the coast to a little-known dock. A boat would then ferry them to France. From there, they could make their way home to Taipei.

Robbi's bracelet handed over, Melody broke it apart, counting the loose jade beads in equal number.

She handed half the beads to Edi and half to the cleaner. 'Please keep these . . . and I will find you.' Each contained a prototype bio-wave tracker her family's firm was developing. She had used it to keep an eye on her son. It would help her find these people later on to properly thank them. And if instead they sold the beads, they'd still get a pretty penny.

'Good luck tomorrow, Edi,' she shook his hand. 'And . . .?'

'Valya . . . Valentia,' the cleaner replied.

'The brave one . . . how fitting,' Melody noted. 'Thank you, Valya. I owe you both more than I can ever repay. From now on, it's guanxi.'

The Oracle of Oral Histories

In the beginning, there was nothing . . .

Once upon a time, there was a world . . .

Long ago and far, far away . . .

There once was a girl, a prince, a pauper . . .

In a town, where all who lived were lost . . .

*There is an island belief that if you tell the whole story,
you outlive your usefulness.

25

Nan Madol

2023 | Present

Like a cosmic labyrinth from the bowels of the earth, the dark, megalithic structures rise imposingly from the crystalline lagoon. Embellished by time with dense vegetation. An unruly assortment of fruit trees, flowering shrubs, and creeping vines. It seems undisturbed, but mangroves and sediments are slowly eating away at the coral rubble and prismatic basalt columns stacked methodically atop a submerged reef. The ancient complex of inexplicable sophistication is off the coast of Pohnpei's Temwen Island, spreading across nearly two square miles in the Pacific. A collection of a hundred man-made islets linked by causeways and canals, resembling a prehistoric Venice. Though extensive, Nan Madol is dwarfed by the vastness of the ocean around it, protected from the tides by what remains of its breakwater—volcanic stones like black onyx piled twenty-five feet high in some parts and fifty feet wide. The shallow maze of interior waterways is so still it appears like glass. Mirroring the heavens on earth.

There are so many places to hide in the centuries old engineering marvel, but it doesn't take long for Melody to deduce where he might be. The volcanic basalts' magnetic field is distorting her attempts to isolate a bio-signature, so she figures his lab will be hidden beneath, where he can shield his work—and himself—from external factors that would affect it.

'Please Max, just tell me the truth . . .'

Max Bao, physicist and tech entrepreneur, has outfitted an existing web of chambers in the heart of Nan Madol's coral reef foundation to suit his needs. Appropriate to the site's name—which means 'in the spaces between'—he lined the cavities and corridors with a unique blend of metals and minerals that allows him to operate without detection. The temperature is stable and there are no interfering energies. Against the reef walls is a layer of translucent concrete embedded with optical fibres, which not only illuminates the space with an ethereal radiance but transmits quantum data. It's like being in a high-tech, one-way mirrored bubble. He can look out without anyone seeing in. Until the underwater eruption the day before.

* * *

Melody was in Taipei. She'd just finished breakfast and had another massive row with Max about the superchip. She told him the world was not ready for such an . . . intervention. She tried to convince him to release a less potent version, that they needed to include a resistor, but he refused, saying he'd take his formula elsewhere for production. Afterwards, feeling sorry for herself, Melody again tried to connect with Orla's frequency. When she failed, she poured herself a whiskey. One shot of her secret stash of Bushmills very easily became more. Unsurprisingly, the emotions and the drink didn't agree with the superchip. It set everything awhirl and she wasn't sure what was real and what was not. She thought she recalled Willy coming home from campaigning then leaving again . . .? And he smelled like these particularly repugnant floral cigarettes from China. Still a popular choice among Taiwan's elderly voting population. It opened a floodgate of memories she'd long repressed. And just as she was replaying pulling a trigger, the world shuddered and jolted as if about to break apart.

The quake didn't register on any man-made seismographs, but Melody— and the superchip—felt it. An energetic underground explosion. Somewhere in the Pacific. A submerged quantum force dispersing invisible shock waves through all planes of existence. At the moment of eruption, Melody linked effortlessly, inextricably with Max. The energy shield he used to defend against discovery must've momentarily shifted. She found him . . . and felt a glimmer of Orla. Like a beacon, it called her home.

Taking only the clothes she had on, Melody booked an economy ticket under an alias and left her palatial home through an underground tunnel. She discovered it on their property when they were building the house. Taipei's mountains were burrowed for defence and escape in case of attack, and this particular passage got her close to the airport road.

Once at street level, she hopped on a bus to the terminal, where she disappeared into the mass of passengers. Over the years, she'd learned that the best way to hide was to blend in. To be like everyone else.

She had to be unremarkable.

* * *

'You shouldn't have come, Mel—' Max sighs from behind his workbench. Dressed head to toe in black, he stands out in the chaos, surrounded by the tools of his genius. Several whiteboards made of crystal, full of scribbles and dots and dashes. Quantum printers and scanners. Soldering irons, wire strippers, and screwdrivers. He takes off his goggles and gloves. 'The superchip brought you, didn't it?'

'I don't have it,' Melody states. 'But I think it's fused itself to me. I seem to have taken on its capabilities—'

'What do you mean you don't have it? Where the feck is it?'

* * *

Since it was built, Melody never took off the OMƐGa chip bracelet. Not even at airport security. To keep it from drawing attention, she wore it among several on her wrist. The purple beads with the basalt rock reliquary looked no more remarkable than the others.

But while waiting to board the first flight of her journey to Orla, Melody began to feel intense bio-frequencies of danger. She was under threat. She scanned the crowd for anyone looking her way. A few people were staring mindlessly into space, but most were focused on their devices. She convinced herself it was just her imagination. And that in a pair of old jeans and a T-shirt, she was indistinct.

All was calm until she landed in Guam for her transfer. She noticed a man following her from the moment she stepped off the plane. Led by an inner knowing, she headed for the bathroom, only coming out when she felt he'd gone. But as she went toward her Pohnpei boarding gate, she again felt at the centre of a swarm. Everywhere she looked, people turned her way. Approaching her slowly with menace and malintent. She noticed they all wore numberless, pearlescent watches. A faceless mob about to spring into a feeding frenzy. She knew it was the bracelet they wanted. And though she tried, she couldn't tap into their frequencies.

Following her OMεGa-honed instincts, she eased her walk into a saunter and tried to lose them. But they closed in, prompting her saunter into a dash.

Guided by the God chip to round a corner, Melody bumped into a stocky, sturdy man who barely flinched from the collision. He seemed to be standing in place. She'd been looking down and noticed the tattoos on his arms. Navigational stick charts? She looked up and breathed a sigh of relief.

'Edison!'

He hadn't seen her in seventeen years. Seventeen years since he and the chambermaid instinctively helped her cover up a crime they had nothing to do with. Since then, as she'd promised, Melody tracked him and Valya down, repaying them handsomely—and untraceably—for their assistance. Edi's environmental campaign was infused with much needed funding, and Valya set herself up a tropical refuge.

'What are you doing here?' He never expected to see her again. But his ΩπLα tattoo had been irritating him lately and he'd stopped to scratch his thigh.

'I . . . I . . .' Melody didn't know where to begin. 'You're headed home . . .'

'To Manila, yes,' he said, 'I just came from Majuro.'

'No rest for the wicked . . .' she sighed.

'Right,' he smiled painfully. 'And in a few days, I have to go to a conference in Singapore . . .'

In an instant, Melody knew he was also planning a risky side trip to Sabah, investigating corals, and seeking answers for why the fish in the South China Sea were dying. She instinctively knew it was caused by a toxic tide of smash and salt, of coralline poison and noxious gravel. By-products of human progress. She was going to explain to save him the trip but, in the ethers, Melody felt the energy around them intensify, and she remembered where they were. She pulled Edi aside and removed the bracelet.

'I am so sorry to ask'—Melody took his hand in hers and put the OMεGa chip bracelet between them—'please hold on to this? Don't let it out of your sight. It's nothing illegal, I swear. But it needs to be kept safe and I can't do that right now.'

With the bracelet attuned to her, she didn't think it would affect him.

'Thank you, Edison. For everything.' She gripped his hand tighter, feeling a flash of supra-cognition. *'I know you worry about it,'* she said suddenly, *'but you do make a difference . . . your life, your work, it means something. So keep at it. I will find you again, dear Edi . . . safe journey.'*

Before he registered what she'd said, she was gone. Leaving a tightly coiled purple bracelet in his hand.

* * *

'You came all the way from Taipei to bug me?'

'Yeah, because I have nothing better to do than follow you around . . .' Melody scans the undersea space in disbelief. 'Fuck Max, what is all this?'

'The culmination of my life's work. The nerve centre. The largest, most powerful superconductor in the world.'

'What is?'

'This. Nan Madol,' Max beams. 'With its amplified coral composition, its volcanic stones—and the polymetallic ocean floor it's built on. The prehistoric nodules those big energy companies want to mine at sea? There are tons of them crammed together right underneath us, like nowhere else in the world. I'm harnessing the power of it all! I've spent years, Mel, years—looking for this exact spot. In the flow of irradiated currents and the wrecks of war. All that oil and ammunition still in the waters—concentrated exactly where we are. This is the vortex . . . The focal point of so much death—and expansion. The best and worst of humankind. It is from here that we will revamp our circuitry—and begin again with a new polarity.'

'What the actual fuck, Mags?'

'Max! It is Max!' her old friend yells. Reminiscent of the anger she . . . he . . . often exhibited when they were first roommates at the LSE.

'Of course. I am sorry,' Melody doesn't mean to upset him. He only told her of his transition years after it started. She believed him when he said all his injections were for diabetes. She didn't realize he was also taking hormones. That growing up, he felt trapped in the wrong body. She was so naïve to not understand that there's always more going on beneath the surface than people know. Like the poplar trees her husband is so fond of—which can seem dead above ground while robust and rooted.

* * *

'Looks like a giant cemetery,' Raed spat into the ocean as he joined Robbi on the deck of the mono-hull boat. 'Why are we here?'

Valya had found them the small, motorized vessel and a skipper who wouldn't ask questions. It got them from Palau to Nan Madol in less than two days.

'Anything?' Robbi asked his travel companion wearing the bracelet.

Raed shook his head as he peeled a banana.

'Must you eat now?' Robbi had not found it easier to travel with the teen knowing he was not just a she but them. The doctor's revelations helped him understand the mercurial switches in personality but didn't make them less challenging to deal with. Robbi had no idea how to help . . . Anak . . . or Maki . . . or Raed, who appeared to be the present manifestation. He asked Valya—who seemed to know—what best to do. And Robbi did his best to stick to her advice. Respect each personality's boundaries, use their preferred name and pronoun, be patient, avoid judgment, and watch out for triggers—which Robbi realized could be any stressful situation. As grateful as he was, he still didn't understand why Valya helped them. All she said was that their ties were always going to be guanxi.

'Want me to wear it and see what I can pick up?' Robbi again tried to ask for the bracelet.

Chewing noisily, the teen shook his head. He was not about to give over his ace. Without it, he was powerless. And he'd not had as much food as on this journey with the foreign merman. So he had to keep him baited.

Suddenly, a sleek, shiny seaplane appeared like lightning over the blazing horizon. Painted orange with two black lines on its sides, it was heading in the same direction as them. If not for reflecting the sun, Robbi would not have seen it. Gliding noiselessly at an atypical speed, it looked like an elegant crane. There were four people in its cabin.

'See anything?' Luc asked his wife, who was peering with binoculars out the seaplane's window.

'The site's up ahead,' Nisha replied, 'But unlike on the other islands, I can't see any dead fish . . .'

As Metik showed him, Luc put his hand over his new $d\varepsilon U^{1}S^{TM}$ watch—which he hadn't told his wife about yet. He was hoping for a vision. A glimmer of supra-cognition. He looked out the window to zoom in on what was below. But it was like some energy at the site was repelling a reading.

'There!' Teddy was looking out the other side. 'Is that a boat?'

Nisha was still upset she'd let them on board. But she was harangued, with Teddy vowing that as $d\varepsilon U^{1}S^{TM}$ nodes, he and Luc were the ones to lead her to what she was searching for. This enigmatic ship named $\Omega\pi L\alpha$—which Luc's jacked up cognition told them belonged to Max Bao.

'Yes!' Luc spotted a sailboat rounding the atoll towards Nan Madol. And then, he spotted another one coming from the opposite side. There seemed a fleet of different vessels heading to the same destination.

'Are they tourists? Is there some sort of regatta?' Nisha tried to get a closer look.

'Gotcha!' Teddy checked his app to zero in on what he'd been chasing since Pulau Rahsia. 'It's . . . on that boat . . . no wait . . . it disappeared . . .'

'There's too much interference,' Luc stated. 'I can't see past—' his special watch dinged. As did Teddy's app. They both received the same quantum message. An encrypted code sent out to everyone who had the Chinese-made 'fast-track' chip—like Teddy—and those with the pearlescent, numberless watch. Like Luc. Many of whom were converging towards the ancient site in the waters below—

The dinging was a series of superpositioned numbers that wordlessly transmitted a single message: 'You are the salt of the earth. Eliminate Lu Wei Jing.'

Unaware of the quantum-coded command, Nisha ordered the pilot to veer in the other direction, but before he could, Teddy and Luc lunged for the controls—and the leading-edge Transform seaplane took an unexpected nosedive.

* * *

It was all he could do to stay calm. Watch TV as the upcoming elections were discussed. Willy didn't know which was worse: losing and upsetting his father-in-law . . . or actually becoming the next mayor of Taipei.

Suddenly, breaking news on TNT—a drone attack in Beijing on the Chinese president.

The elderly Zhou Sheng Feng was addressing a crowd of soldiers and supporters corralled around the People's Heroes monument when a small, low flying object sprayed him with what appeared to be sparkling powder. He seemed to falter, and the nationally televised broadcast was cut. All this happened just a few hundred meters south of Heavenly Gate, where the so-called anti-Zhou, Diyu deviants were gathering.

Willy was stunned. This was exactly what he'd imagined. He couldn't believe it happened! He had to tell Melody . . .

. . . if only he could find her.

* * *

'Where is she, Max? Please . . .' Melody's on the verge of tears. All these years later and she's still the lost foreign student in London.

'Oh princess, it's the chip,' Max says impassively. 'You're only picking up her trace energy . . . she moved on from this physical plane long ago . . .'

Melody's tears begin to fall. 'But I *feel* her . . .'

'It's you and me, Mel,' Max approaches from his workbench, 'between the two of us, she is here . . .'

'Did she die because of me?' Melody asks the question that's haunted her.

'God. Get over yourself,' Max scoffs. 'She didn't want you to worry, but she had blood cancer, okay? Probably from growing up where she did. Their village was behind a mountain where the US secretly stored nukes, the soil and groundwater got contaminated. She was already sick while in London—just didn't know it. Like her mum. It's why she tired easily and often felt weaker than she should've.'

'Are you sure it's not my fault?'

'Seriously?' Max was aghast. 'Why would you think it's down to you?'

'A man . . . told me . . .'

'A man?' Max's disdain is clear.

'He'd been following me wanting information on you . . . and he said that when I left the UK, he tried Orla, but she wouldn't cooperate . . . so I thought . . .'

'What man?'

'At first I thought he was your father . . .' Melody explains.

'Are you joking?' Max turns to a large screen on the far wall and it comes on telepathically, filling with images of the Chinese leader, Zhou Sheng Feng—as a young party clerk in an ill-fitting suit—as an army officer with a severe haircut and an even more severe stare—leading the parade of troops at Heavenly Gate—being rewarded for the bloody crackdown on protesters that was wiped from official records—his installation as president— and his ordered roundups of minorities . . .

'That madman,' Max declares, 'is my father. And soon, he will finally lose everything that matters to him . . .'

The lab's lights begin to flicker as a mix of external energies try to crash in.

Max switches the screen from Zhou to the view outside, where an army of visitors is amassing.

'Fuck. They found me even without the bracelet . . .' Melody feels trapped. The two old friends were so focused on their entanglement, they let everything else around them slide.

Max shuts his eyes and intercepts the quantum message being broadcast on the replica network—'Eliminate Lu Wei Jing', over and over—it's him they're after!

Expanding his reading to wider frequencies, Max picks up that he's considered a traitor to his home country for creating deU^1S^{TM}. And through the ethers, he realizes that his own father gave the order.

'*Eliminate Lu Wei Jing*'. . . Not only was Max Bao destroying everything he'd built, but in trying to find his weakness, Zhou's enemies discovered he had a daughter. They'd been trailing her—to damage him—since she was at the LSE. Worse still, Zhou found out his one weakness had become a 'fake' man—an even greater dishonour if word got out. So, he had to sacrifice her for the greater good. To save his country, his people, and his name.

'It's not you they're after, princess,' Max laughs.

'But the chip—I felt it . . .'

'Of course! The quantum formula,' Max illumines. 'The epitaxy code I sent you must've entangled our frequencies. Those feckin' eejit assassins must've been tracking the chip thinking it was me!'

Suddenly, a vision of Edi being killed by a man wearing a suit—and a faceless watch—flashes before Melody. She sees Willy in the room with them, too—looking for her. *Oh, Willy* . . .

Shaken by the image, Melody focuses on what's tangible around her—a meditation tool that helps her take some control while on the quantum planes. She feels the crowd with their replica devices gathering like a storm outside.

'How'd they all get here so quickly? I only just found you myself . . .'

'Time stops here, princess . . .' Max smiles, patiently. 'But out there, it's been weeks . . .'

Melody always knew Max was smarter than her.

Again, the lab lights flicker.

'Feckit!' Max rushes back to his workbench. 'If they keep trying to bombard us with their energy, the place could blow—'

'What?!'

'We're protected by a wave-field of quantum energy—conveyed from my ship—it's anchored on the other side of the island.'

As Max speaks, Melody gets a vision of the purpose-built vessel and her breath catches in her chest: the $\Omega\pi L\alpha$.

'When more nodes are truly on the 0MεGα plane,' Max continues, 'we'll be impenetrable. Without needing the ship. Those earlier undersea explosions? Were adjustments in the energy field—I was working to get the balance right. And if those people outside breach the shield, all the differing currents will overload the circuit . . .'

The circuit.

A blinding flash. A sheathe of light. Melody's lifelines flicker and converge. She loses focus. She loses control . . . swept away by the hybrid energies of all her existential planes. The past, the present, the future. Everything is one . . . and all is now. She is daughter. Lover. Wife. And mother. Leader. Follower. Friend. Victim. Aggressor. The connections that exist despite being unseen—the ethereal web that glows, linking it all.

Oh Edi! Melody realizes he's been killed because of her—someone on the replica network was following the bracelet she gave him for safekeeping.

And because of her, her son is outside—searching—with a child as lost as him . . .

'You are not the cause and effect of everything, princess . . .' Max reads her mind as he moves about trying to stabilize the lab. 'But, I suppose, we are the heroes and anti-heroes in our own narratives. Everything is about us . . . even when it isn't.'

A slim mechanical bird falls into the sea and they feel the ripples of a large explosion . . . the visceral transformation of multiple energies abandoning the physical plane.

Every cell in Melody's realm vibrates at the sudden burst. Like fissile material in a nuclear reactor. She knows that Max is feeling it, too. Along with millions of elevated $d_\varepsilon U^1 S^{TM}$ nodes.

'We all transform, Mel'—he spreads his arms, understanding her unsaid questions—'I did . . . and so did you. Because we all have to do what we can to become our own heroes . . .'

Melody's lost all words in the deafening pulsing of existence . . . she feels the essence of the ocean about to surge like a tsunami. In her mind's eye, she sees a multitude of boats as lifeless fish being pummelled against the basalt around them . . . beings of light—with their copied chips and replica watches—cast en masse into the depths. Despite her power, she is powerless to stop it.

'There are those of us just swept along by the tides . . .' Max explains, 'and ones who steer our boats and plot out courses like stars . . . But at the end of the day, we're all in the same ocean—and that is what binds us and not divides. We are a blockchain, princess . . . whether we like it or not . . .'

On the lab screen, flashes of a revolution in China . . . the ruler has died . . . and as paper soldiers, other strongmen will fall . . . false gods diminished in the face of light.

Like a photon, Max begins to glow . . . calling out to God in a flood of languages . . . he reaches for Melody in preparation.

'Ever wondered what happens when creation has had enough? When the voltage is too much and the circuitry overloads?'

Without moving, Melody takes his hand and entwines their fingers. And all at once, the answers are clear.

'It turns on itself'—she says—'and sets itself alight . . .'

In that moment, the world lets out a sigh.

Everything stops—all at once—and for now. The magnetic stones in canals, the pipelines of power, the waves of wisdom. The quantum network of dεU^{1}S$^{™}$ nodes. As their existential energies are transformed and fuse.

Max and Melody join Orla, Edi, and all other timeless forces . . . as does Robbi, who just before the implosion, finally got to wear his mother's bracelet.

Left in the water, stripped bare and alone, is Anak . . . turning upwards to the clearing heavens, lying back, arms outstretched, with nose and mouth above the waves—*in*—*out*. In, out. Slow. Steady. Determined to keep her balance in the water.

On the other side of the island, an indestructible ship is sinking . . . joining other wrecks in the deep.

In a thousand years,
a colony of corals
will transform it into
a reef.

α

Genesis

And then, God said, 'Let there be light . . .'

And once upon a time, it was now. A dead man was born, and a witness was found. Collecting myths like seashells—or ashes on the ground.

There were three wise men who kept changing their story. And the corpse disappeared from the cradle.

Without a body, what, then, is real?

Some angels have no legends at all. And so, they create their own.

Once upon a time, there was a girl birthed by her father, and he cast her out as a son into the rocky darkness. All she knew of life was separation and isolation, disconnected from the source of love.

So, she strung her myths together and turned into a man she barely remembered, hoping that would soothe her pain. But in her search for what she thought was missing, the orphan overlooked what set her apart:

Within her, all along, lay the origin of the world—the open wound that bled the heart.

*Anak's Story, taken from *The Quantum Histories of Humanity* (2120 edition)

If you look at zero you see nothing.
But if you look through it, you see the world.
It's the horizon.

—Robert Kaplan, mathematician